A

Nathan Dylan Goodwin v
Schooled in the town, he .

Radio, Film and Television Studies, followed by a Master of Arts degree in Creative Writing at Canterbury Christ Church University. A member of the Society of Authors, he has completed a number of successful local history books about Hastings, as well as several works of fiction, including the acclaimed Forensic Genealogist series. His other interests include theatre, reading, photography, running, skiing, travelling and, of course, genealogy. He is a qualified teacher, member of the Guild of One-Name Studies and the Society of Genealogists, as well as being a member of the Sussex Family History Group, the Norfolk Family History Society, the Kent Family History Society and the Hastings and Rother Family History Society. He lives in Kent with his husband, son and dog.

BY THE SAME AUTHOR

nonfiction:
Hastings at War 1939-1945
Hastings Wartime Memories and Photographs
Hastings & St Leonards Through Time
Around Battle Through Time
Finding Henry

fiction:
(The Forensic Genealogist series)
The Asylum - A Morton Farrier short story
Hiding the Past
The Lost Ancestor
The Orange Lilies – A Morton Farrier novella
The America Ground
The Spyglass File
The Missing Man – A Morton Farrier novella
The Suffragette's Secret – A Morton Farrier short story
The Wicked Trade

(The Mrs McDougall Investigation series)
Ghost Swifts, Blue Poppies and the Red Star

Ghost Swifts, Blue Poppies and the Red Star
by
Nathan Dylan Goodwin

Dedicated to the memory of the McDougall family

Prologue

A broad smile rose on Harriet Agnes McDougall's face. A raspberry, and so late in the season. She crouched down and held it gently between her thumb and forefinger. Although it was beginning to bear the brunt of the coming winter, hardening and shrivelling somewhat, it would certainly still be sweet enough to eat, and yet, something inside prevented her from freeing it from the plant. It would be almost cruel to remove it now. Her smile gradually faded, and she realised that she was bestowing upon the fruit some rather human resilience in its having survived the first hints of winter.

Although she was sixty-five years of age and her once-dark hair was now grey-white, an active life had granted her the full and healthy body of a woman many years younger. Her bright turquoise eyes continued to garner admiring comments and observations, which, her parents had often informed her growing up, had begun at birth.

Harriet rolled the fruit tenderly between her fingertips, with strange admiration, then stopped abruptly.

The church bells were ringing.

She released the raspberry and, coming to, stood up, straining her ear towards the church, not a quarter of a mile away. They were ringing in such a way as she hadn't heard for a very long time; years, perhaps. They were sounding the Grandsire Doubles, an unmistakeable, complicated and significant arrangement.

The damp November air suddenly caught in her throat, as a realisation dawned upon her.

She walked briskly—almost running—through the vegetable patch and along the garden path to the house. At the kitchen doorway she didn't bother to kick off her garden shoes but rushed straight in, looking first into the dining room and then into the sitting room. John was sitting in his armchair in his usual position with his arms folded over his stomach and his head tilted back. He had aged significantly over the last few months and, with his tired and lined face, appeared much older than his sixty-five years. But then, she fancied that she had

1

aged, too. Perhaps it was not such a surprise, given all that had happened.

'John,' she said urgently, crouching beside his chair. 'Can you hear it?'

He sat up and pushed his glasses back onto the bridge of his nose. 'What?'

'Listen.'

His face furrowed in mild annoyance at whatever it was for which he was supposed to be listening. 'What?' he said again, shrugging.

'The bells of St John's. Can't you hear them? Something's happened... I think it could be the news we've been waiting for.'

John raised his eyebrows, pushed his head back and closed his eyes.

Harriet inwardly sighed, as she left the room, hurried down the hallway and flung open the front door. The bells were appreciably louder now, and there was other noise with it, too. Her sleepy little Sussex village had suddenly woken up with a start.

She rushed down the path and paused momentarily, placing her hands down on the black iron of the front gate. Before her, the village green—an almost perfect triangle of grass—was alive with activity, as her neighbours were moving about with a peculiar mixture of excitement and giddy indecision: Mrs Selmes and Mrs Plummer—sworn enemies since the dawning of time—were embracing; Mr Playford, wearing his Sunday best, was standing in the centre of the green, sobbing through a wide grin, his bowler hat clutched to his chest; the four Everndon girls were holding hands and dancing in a circle; the *elder* Mrs Ditch was running up the street; and, all around the village, doors were being flung open, revealing faces characterised by disbelief and joy.

It could mean only one thing.

Harriet took a short, sharp breath, trying to maintain an air of stoicism, as she marched directly across the green to the Post Office opposite. As she walked, she noticed the red, white and blue bunting suspended from the front windows of Asselton House in front of her. She glanced to the other houses nearby; to Forge Cottage, to Holmes House and to the Pump House, all displaying patriotic flags and streamers.

'Have you heard the news?'

Harriet glanced sideways, as she reached the Post Office. It was Mrs Morris. Her cheeks were the colour of a ripe tomato, and her eyes

2

were puffy and wet. She pointed at the Post Office window beside them.

And there it was: the confirmation of the cessation of hostilities.

The war had ended.

Harriet looked back at Mrs Morris, their faces mirroring each other with dual lines of tears. Harriet extended her arm, taking Mrs Morris's hand in hers and squeezing it gently. The most recent telegram—surely, God willing, the last—had been handed to her husband, Mr Morris, a little over a month ago.

'It's over,' Mrs Morris wept. 'It's over.'

Harriet nodded and pressed their hands together more tightly. It was over in a political sense. It was over in a militaristic sense. It was over in a global sense. But for Harriet and millions like her, it was not over and maybe never could be.

She released Mrs Morris's hand, smiled feebly and walked in a ghost-like trance back to Linton House. Inside, she could hear from the rise and hollows of John's breathing that he was asleep. She hesitated at the sitting room door, wondering whether to wake him and tell him the news. No, she reasoned, it could wait. He would only grumble at being disturbed and mutter something about its being an inevitability. She climbed the stairs and went to the front bedroom—the one shared by her two sons, Malcolm and Edward—and closed the door behind her.

The room was ready for their arrival; exactly as they had left it. Harriet passed between the two single beds and walked over to the mirror. As she rested her hands on the cold porcelain washstand below it, she remembered the comedy of watching the boys proudly running a safety razor over the first glimpses of facial hair; Malcolm first, soon (and unnecessarily) followed by Edward. How quickly the transition from boys to men had come and gone, she thought. She turned immediately, when her own pitiable reflection snapped into focus.

On the wall above Malcolm's bed were the display cases, containing an array of moths and butterflies, which he had collected and pinned himself. 'I'm a lepidopterist,' he had once informed her, when, at the age of ten, he had failed to return home before dark, following an expedition on the trail of the rare Silver-studded Blue butterfly. 'It means I study butterflies and moths,' he had proudly added. As the fleeting memory faded, Harriet's eyes shifted to one of his very detailed and precise sketches, which he had taped to the wall. A Ghost Swift moth with various parts of its anatomy annotated in his neatest handwriting. She scrutinised the picture for the umpteenth time, trying to revive something more, or something new from her memories of his childhood. She found now that her reminiscences of the boys' younger years existed in her mind like a collection of familiar short stories, ones which never changed, grew, nor were augmented. Nothing in the house, none of their possessions awakened fresh memories any longer. She imagined that, with time and age, they would further diminish, merge and finally fade into one warm but inaccessible sentiment of their youth. Perhaps, given the pain which came alongside the memories, that was the kindest thing.

She sat down on Malcolm's bed and carefully picked up his green and brown-striped pyjamas from his pillow, holding them in her lap for a moment, before raising them to her face and drawing in a long breath through her nose. The smell of him, of Malcolm, had gone. Now they smelt of nothing at all, but for several months after he had left, the smell of him had remained. With effort, Harriet could just about bring it to mind. It was a musky masculine scent, which seemed common to all young men, yet the subtle differences between the boys were sufficient for her to be able to tell to which of her sons a worn item of clothing had belonged.

With a myriad of emotions flooding her senses, the comforting embrace of Malcolm's bed suddenly appeared enticing. Although she was reluctant to crumple the fresh sheets, she kicked off her shoes, pulled up her legs and gently placed her head down onto his pillow. Her habit of sleeping on the boys' beds since they had gone had reduced in recent months, becoming furtive and clandestine, reserved for those scarce occasions when John and his stern disapproval were out of the house.

Harriet drew in a breath and held it for as long as she could, before exploding the air out in a noisy exhale. She closed her eyes, trying to change the track of her thoughts, determined not to cry. She pulled herself into the darkness of her mind, switching off her senses one at a time until all that was left was an empty blackness.

She woke suddenly and sat bolt upright. Her forehead was damp, and her thoughts were a muddled amalgam of dream and reality, neither of which offered her a satisfactory explanation of where she was. She had fallen asleep on Malcolm's bed, she remembered. But that was just moments ago, in broad daylight. Now, the room had been plunged into pitch darkness, yet there was a strange bright light streaming in through the window.

Harriet's dream quickly faded into oblivion, as she used the brightness to confirm that, yes, she was in Malcolm and Edward's bedroom. She had obviously fallen into a deep sleep, and it was now after dark. But what about the light? There was something unnatural in its quivering dance on the ceiling, which told her that it could not be moonlight alone.

Cautiously, she walked over to the window and saw a sight so unfamiliar to her as to induce a gasp: a giant bonfire in the centre of the village green and, more striking than that, from almost every house in view was to be seen the soft amber glow of light.

Harriet stared, mesmerised by a sight, which she had not witnessed for more than four years. Slowly, as she began to make sense of what she was seeing, her eyes picked further detail from what was before her. Crowds of people—their faces not quite recognisable from the low light—had gathered around the fire. A small group of village lads—spared from enlistment by a matter of months, or just weeks in some cases—hoisted up a life-sized effigy of the Kaiser. How it had been fashioned in such a short time, she had no idea, but that it was destined for the top of the fire, she was convinced.

She watched as the group of villagers behind the effigy formed into a procession of thirty or forty people and began to walk the length of the green. Across the way, the Queen's Head was lit up in all its glory, and silhouetted before it, stood an ensemble of silent village men.

She knew that she had to go out there, to be amongst them, her neighbours, friends and family.

Harriet descended the stairs and entered the sitting room, finding John in his armchair with his pipe pressed between his lips. The only light in the room came from the hot fire, which etched ugly shadows onto his face. She marched into the room, pulled wide the curtains and smiled.

'There!' she declared. 'Isn't that simply wonderous?'

John looked at her, baffled. 'Isn't what?'

'Why, the light of course. Just look at it! The village is all lit up—every house is glowing with the news.'

John raised an eyebrow, slowly elevated his right hand and removed his pipe. 'And the Lighting Order?' he asked, a trace of his father's Scottish accent just audible in his deep voice. 'I presume you've

5

spoken with PC Knight and he's passed on permission from the Home Office?'

'It's *over*, John,' Harriet sighed, turning from the room peevishly. In the hallway, she picked up her coat, then opened the front door, passing her arms into the sleeves, as she hurried down the front path.

She reached the village green just as the procession, singing the looped chorus of 'Rule Britannia…', turned at the apex and began to make its way back in her direction. She clapped spontaneously, as the grinning lads, now carrying the Kaiser effigy by his four splayed limbs, passed by. Harriet maintained a half-smile, as she caught the glinting eyes of those passing her gate. Almost all of them had lost a man to the war. Her smile widened when her gaze fell upon the mournful eyes of her sister, Naomi, whose son, Jim had been killed last September on the north-west frontier of India. Her other son, fourteen-year-old Frank, narrowly spared by his age, was one of the boys dragging the Kaiser through the village.

Naomi reached out and grasped Harriet, pulling her into the throng, which had now doubled in size. They walked together without speaking until the parade drew to an abrupt halt.

Moments later, the effigy was hoisted up and launched into the flames to a rapturous round of applause. As the fire quickly consumed the figure, the crowd began to fracture into smaller groups, but with a general movement further up into the village.

'Now what?' Harriet asked.

'There's a service up at St John's,' Naomi replied.

Harriet stopped walking. 'No, I don't think so,' she said quietly. The unwavering faith of her younger self was now broken, fragmented and complex: some days she thought that she felt His presence in her life; other days she doubted His very existence. What she was coming to realise of late, however, was the irrelevance of that question. Instead, she found herself asking how so many millions of men could be taken from this earth at such a young age. Whether the answer was of a divine or political nature, it was cruel and barbaric.

'Harriet?' Naomi pressed.

'Sorry… No, I don't think I'll come,' she answered.

Naomi took Harriet's hands in hers. 'I understand, but I've requested a song specifically for our boys.'

'Which song?'

'*Now the Labourer's Task is Over.*'

Harriet nodded mechanically and allowed herself to be led to the church.

The service, conducted by the Reverend Percival, was a sombre, yet celebratory affair. Harriet and Naomi had a central spot in a pew adjacent to the aisle. As the congregation sang *O God our Help in Ages Past*, Harriet glanced around her, not recalling a previous time when the church had been so well attended. She offered a weak smile to her brothers, Herbert and John, both of them escaping the threat of the telegram by the fortuitousness of only having sired daughters. Every seat had been taken, and many were left standing at the rear. The song finished and the congregation was seated.

'I should now like to read to you from the first book of Chronicles, chapter twenty-nine, verse eleven,' the Reverend Percival intoned from the pulpit. *'Thine, O Lord, is the greatness, and the power, and the glory, and victory, and the majesty: for all that is in the heaven and in the earth is thine; thine is the kingdom, O Lord, and thou art exalted as head above all.'* He paused, seeming to take stock of the congregation before him. 'It *is* a time for victory and celebration, and thanksgiving to our Lord, but, it is also a time for reverence and of solemnity, as we remember the price of that, our victory. The price paid by young men across our Empire and, it pains me to say, yes, from our little Sussex village. I look out amongst you all, and I see that cost etched on every face gathered here. And it is with all of these things in mind that I read the Sedlescombe Roll of Honour.' Another longer pause. *'Henry Robert Adeane, Edward Sidney Barwick, Bertram Henry Bateup, Harry Boxall, Charles Bryant, Frederick Bryant, Boyce Coombe, Leonard Cramp, Frank Crittenden, Reginald Dawson, James Dengate, Walter William Goodman, Edward Harris, William Hobbs, Christopher Hodgson, Charles Henry Johnson, Edward Cecil McDougall, Malcolm McDougall...'*

The vicar continued to read aloud the names of the dead men of the village, but upon hearing the names of her two boys, Harriet sagged down into the pew, as if receiving the news afresh.

Her sister, Naomi placed her arm over Harriet's shoulder and pulled her in close. Together, they sobbed until all twenty-nine names had been delivered.

'Our brave men, who have paid the ultimate sacrifice to their country, shall not be forgotten, and their death shall not have been in vain,' the Reverend Percival said quietly. 'Mrs Naomi Dengate has

7

requested that we sing, in memory of our fallen sons, *Now the Labourer's Task is Over.* Please be standing.'

As the congregation rose to their feet, the organ struck up its mournful drone, then they began to sing:

> *Now the Labourer's task is o'er;*
> *Now the battle day is past;*
> *Now upon the farther shore*
> *Lands the voyager at last.*
> *Father, in Thy gracious keeping*
> *Leave we now Thy servant sleeping.*

Harriet could not sing beyond the first verse. Her throat closed and her eyes filled with tears, as she thought of her two sons, killed within six months of each other, lying alone on a battlefield.

She stared blankly at the vicar, a long-familiar numbness sheathing her whole body.

Chapter One

Despite the organ's having fallen silent almost an hour ago, Harriet could still clearly hear the haunting tones of Handel's *Dead March* in her mind. Sitting in her kitchen, those monolithic sounds were all that she could hear over the unbearable silence that filled the house.

She was at the kitchen table, her quivering hands clasped around her china cup of tea, wondering if perhaps she had been too hasty in dismissing the kind offers of family, friends and neighbours, who had not wanted her to be alone today.

Taking a sip of the tea, she winced at its tepidness and went to put the cup down, but the shaking of her hands—worsened by the wretched music in her head, no doubt—meant that she caught the edge of the saucer and sent the cup tumbling to the floor.

Harriet leapt up and looked at the hopelessness of what she was seeing: the dark spray of tea on her black ankle-length dress, which she had purchased only yesterday from the boutique shop on Battle High Street; and the china cup—her finest—lying broken into eight pieces on the flagstone floor.

She began to sob, watching abstractedly, as her falling tears became absorbed into the small tea-puddle at her feet. She realised, of course, that she was not crying for the new dress, nor for the precious china cup, yet she couldn't stop herself.

A knot of complicated and deep internal emotion began to unfurl, as her crying increased. In a breathless wail, she sagged down onto her knees. Feelings and emotions, which she had tried to keep stoically restrained for the past two years, tumbled forth.

She clamped her hands to her ears to shut out the music playing in her head but, in filtering out the background sounds, the noise only intensified, resounding thickly, as though her mind were some enormous cavern. The horrid title alone, *Dead March*, made her shudder, picturing as she did a regiment of uniformed ghosts, trudging in death's footsteps. They had played the piece at both Malcolm's and Edward's funerals. Well, they couldn't be called funerals, of course, since there had been no coffin to put in the ground: 'A Service of Remembrance', Reverend Percival had piously designated them. Harriet had been against the idea, but John had got his way, insisting in

9

his pompous manner that it had been '...the right way to honour them'. She had failed to see past the emptiness of the gesture: a funeral—albeit under a different name—without a coffin or a body over which to mourn.

She hadn't mourned, though, she could see that now. Not properly, at least. After the remembrance services had taken place, John had drawn a line—both publicly and privately—under the boys' deaths, compelling her own grief to recoil inside of her, where it had taken on the form of a deeper, darker entity of its own, and which she could only ever acknowledge in the most cloistered of moments.

With her vision distorted by the tears and the biting pain behind her eyes, Harriet stood up, steadying herself with the table edge for a moment, before moving down the hallway to the parlour. The room, with its north-facing windows, had a slight chill to it and Harriet shivered, as she entered. It was a room reserved for high days and special occasions, and was, therefore, rarely used. In the centre of the room was an oval-shaped, polished walnut table, with two matching bureaus and a writing desk at the edges of the room. On the ochre walls were hanging an assortment of watercolours and oils, and in pride of place above the fire were hung the framed portraits of her boys.

Harriet dabbed her eyes with her handkerchief and pulled open her bureau. There, above two tins, labelled *Couttie's Assorted Biscuits,* were two neatly folded khaki uniforms, which had been returned in brown paper packets from the War Office. When Edward's had arrived, Harriet had taken to her bed, inconsolable, grasping his tunic to her chest until John had tussled it from her. The tunic hadn't smelled of Edward, and she had assumed that the War Office had tactfully removed the residues of war. However, six months later, when Malcolm's had arrived, she had been able to see that that had not been the case. Harriet could still see John now, as clear as day, standing by the front door, watching her with his arms folded, waiting for her to break down at the unforeseen sight of the horrific, indelible blood stains on his tunic. But she hadn't expressed her heartache and deep anguish; she had taken the kit, had wordlessly placed it inside her bureau and had made a cup of tea.

Setting the uniforms down on the table, she took the tins from the bureau and sat down with a long sigh at the table. She was exhausted, her heart was heavy and her head hurt, but at last the tears had stopped. She wiped her face and prised the lid from the tin: Malcolm's, she found. It contained the letters and postcards, which he had sent home—the paltry remains of the last two years of his life during which Harriet had no personal memories of him upon which to draw. Her memories ended on a cold afternoon, when he had stood on the doorstep, shaken John and her by the hand, and cheerfully strolled down the path. He'd taken one final glance back at her, then he had gone and all her memories of him terminated there. Of the next two years of his life, all that remained was contained in the *Couttie's Assorted Biscuits* tin on the table in front of her, which had become an unacknowledged metaphor for her emotions surrounding the boys' deaths, only ever opened when she was certain that John would be out of the house for some considerable amount of time.

She began to re-read Malcolm's first letter home, despite being able to recite it by heart: *Dearest Ma & Pa, I received your welcome parcel, yesterday. Thank you. Very pleased to hear that all at home are well. I am still in the best of health and training is quite all right. We're all eager to get out there and get on with it, to be frank. I've met some decent lads here. One of them, Timothy is from down the road in Bexhill. I shall write again when there is more news. Your loving son, Malcolm.*

His naivety at wanting to *get on with it* had astonished her when the letter had arrived, and it had astonished her afresh with every subsequent reading. What on earth had they been told in their training? John, of course, had nodded and grunted some sort of patriarchal approval.

She placed the letter on the table and picked out an embroidered postcard from the tin, admiring the attractive needlework. She ran her forefinger lightly over the coloured stitching, then paused, sitting up straight at the low familiar squeal of the front gate's hinges' being opened. She sighed, waiting for the door to be knocked. No doubt, it would be her sister, Naomi, coming to check on her. Or perhaps one of the neighbours. Maybe even one of her brothers or their wives.

She put the tin down on the table and stood up. Oddly, the anticipated rapping on the door didn't happen. She frowned and wandered over to the front window.

Someone was standing at her front gate, gaping at the house, yet not moving.

It was a man. A soldier.

The *Dead March*, repeating in her mind, finally petered out.

As though in a trance, Harriet walked to the door, pulled it open and drew herself slowly along the path towards this apparition.

'Hello,' he eventually said. His voice was so quiet and indistinct that she knew that he wasn't real.

'Hello,' she replied, playing along.

He stood, staring at her, his dark eyes empty, his face blank, saying nothing.

This wasn't the first time that this had happened, but this was the most vivid, the most real.

'I did my best to get here, but I was too late,' he said, this time his voice was louder and clearer.

Too late for what? she wondered, but didn't like to question him, lest he should disappear. She studied the detail of him, holding her breath and not daring to blink.

For a few long seconds, nothing happened. Neither of them moved. Neither of them spoke. Then, Harriet, in a breathless burst, asked, 'Do you want to come in?'

He nodded but still didn't move.

'Ma,' he whispered, reaching his hand out to her.

She didn't understand, yet found herself walking the last steps towards him, still very much entranced. She extended her hand to his, long before their fingers could meet.

'Ma,' he said again, almost childlike, as she drew nearer still.

The detail of his face was bewildering, like nothing her mind had ever conjured before. He was wearing his uniform, that of the Border Regiment. His boyish face and short hair made him appear younger than thirty years of age, but then she wondered if perhaps she was projecting him as he had been, when she had last seen him.

He was just inches away now, and Harriet reached out, touching the very tips of his fingers. She flinched, then moved in, quickly running her hand up his left arm, in those fleeting moments, feeling the detail of every fold and crease in the fabric until, at last, her hand came to rest on his warm face.

'You're…back,' Harriet mouthed, bursting into tears. She pulled him tightly to her, and, with his strong arms on her back, only then did she believe what her eyes had been trying to tell her; that her only surviving son, Fraser had returned home to her. 'Are you home for good?' she breathed, almost not daring to ask the question.

'Yes,' he replied. 'Demobilised today.'

'Oh, thank God!' she stammered tearfully. 'Come inside.' She released her grip on him, finally believing him to be real.

Fraser sighed, staring at the open front door of his home. 'You can't imagine how many times I've pictured this moment over the last four years.'

Harriet placed her arm around his shoulder and sobbed: 'Me too.'

She placed a hand in the small of his back and gently guided him towards the visible house interior. Under her hand she felt his rigid frame relax, as he took slow steps forwards.

At the front door he drew in a long breath, then entered inside with a noisy exhalation, a mixture, Harriet supposed, of profound relief, familiarity, but also uncertainty. Dropping his kit bag on the floor, he knelt down and removed his boots. He walked towards the sitting room with a nervous gait, one which suddenly reminded Harriet of the times when he had been that boy, creeping up the hallway, playing soldiers, anticipating an imminent ambush by his two younger brothers.

She followed him into the sitting room, where he faltered slightly, having been about to sit in John's armchair. He sat instead in the Windsor chair by the window, and she took her own armchair beside him and dried her eyes once more.

'It's so quiet,' he whispered.

Harriet listened for a moment. Now that the *Dead March* had ended, she could hear very little, just the almost indistinct, mixed shrill of birdsong from the back garden—bluetits and robins, they sounded like. 'Yes, I rather suppose it is,' she acknowledged.

'It's *too* quiet,' he complained. 'Can you put the gramophone on?'

'Yes, of course. Vivaldi?'

'Anything,' he said.

Harriet hastily got up and placed a record on the gramophone. As the music began to smother the silence, so Fraser visibly appeared to relax again.

'Would you like a cup of tea?' Harriet asked. 'You must be gasping for one.'

'Yes, please,' he replied.

'You just sit and relax,' she said, heading to the kitchen. Out of his earshot, Harriet steadied herself and let out a soft whimper. The sheer relief of having her Fraser home reignited the locked grief inside of her, and she felt the emotion rising once again.

'What happened in the end?' Fraser asked, startling her. She turned to see him, leaning on the doorframe. 'With Pa, I mean?'

The shock re-compressed her anguish, and she was able to swallow down her emotion. 'It was his heart,' she answered, filling the copper

13

kettle with water and placing it on the hot range. 'He became dizzy and short of breath. Doctor Johnson called on him several times and said it was beating to its own strange rhythm. Mitral heart disease—something to do with the valves. There wasn't much that could be done for him in the end… He died peacefully in his bed four days ago.'

'And was he still a miserable old bugger?' Fraser asked.

Disregarding the vulgarity of his vocabulary, the light-heartedness caught Harriet off-guard, and it took her a moment to reply: 'Well, he was never going to change, was he?'

'No, I don't suppose so. And how was the funeral?'

Harriet faltered at the question and answered before she had untangled her true sentiment. 'It was what he would have wanted: a full congregation; representatives from all the various organisations he had served with over the years; his favourite hymns and bible readings.'

A protracted silence fell between them, as she prepared the tea things, all the while contemplating Fraser's question. The painful truth was that the death of her two sons had conferred upon her an everlasting and numbing grief, which would forever eclipse any other pain or sorrow that she could ever know in her life; even that caused by the death of the man with whom she had been married for thirty-one years. She realised now that she had experienced John's death and his funeral that morning through the eyes of a detached stranger.

The kettle's furious whistle broke the moment and settled her indecision about whether or not to explain to Fraser that which she had just come to realise for herself. She removed the kettle from the range, filling the teapot with boiling water, and settled on, for the time being at least, not speaking about it any further. 'Do you want to go and get changed?'

Fraser shrugged. 'Into what?'

'I don't know… Shirt and trousers?'

'What for?' he asked.

She glanced at him and could see that he wasn't being facetious. 'To be more comfortable… To start to draw a line under it all… To forget the war…' She instantly regretted her choice of words, as if forgetting were as simple as removing his uniform. She braced herself for a deserved rebuke, but none came.

'Okay,' he said softly, and left the room.

Harriet made the tea, placed it onto a wooden tray with a plate of homemade lemon soufflé cakes, and carried it into the sitting room.

Vivaldi had finished and she thought it a good idea to have something playing before Fraser returned. She flicked through the ten-inch records, pausing briefly to consider each one in turn. Handel, perhaps? No, it would only remind her of the funeral. Brahms? No, his bearing a teutonic taint had far outweighed any of his musical accomplishments and he had not been played in their home for more than four years. Liszt? Yes, perfect choice. She carefully laid one of his records on the gramophone and lifted the needle into place.

The dramatic—perhaps *melo*dramatic—opening bars filled the sitting room, as Harriet sat down in her armchair and picked up her cup of tea.

Fraser entered moments later, wearing a white shirt and a pair of brown trousers, frowning. 'Is this *Dante's Divina Commedia*?'

Harriet nodded. 'I thought it would be pleasant background music...'

Fraser raised one eyebrow. 'You do know it's about a journey through hell and purgatory, don't you?'

The instant mortification stung Harriet. 'Oh, gosh, I'm terribly sorry...'

'It's fine, Ma,' he insisted, giving a fragile smile.

She couldn't quite meet his eyes, as she encouraged him to sit: 'Come and have some tea and cake.'

'Thank you,' he said, sitting opposite her and picking up his cup without the saucer. Harriet noticed him shifting slightly in his seat, and the fingers of his free hand fidgeting. She could but try to imagine actually how difficult it was for him. Time—she had been advised on many occasions by many different people—was apparently a great healer. Her duty, she saw clearly now, was to offer him routine and distraction.

'Your bedroom is exactly the way you left it,' she said.

'Yes, I noticed.'

A moment of silence stretched uncomfortably.

'Take another piece of cake,' Harriet encouraged.

And Fraser did, shoving it into his mouth in one go, devouring it without any hint of pleasure. Before he had even finished chewing, he asked, 'Is erm...Louise Ditch still about in the village?'

Harriet grimaced. 'Yes, she's still here. Helping her mother in the shop.'

'Oh, right.' Fraser sat up, trying to appear less interested than she actually knew him to be.

'She's engaged...' Harriet added quickly, '...to Peter Wolf from Whatlington.'

Fraser sniffed. 'Made it back, then, did he?'

'Yes, got back a week or so after the Armistice. He's working on his dad's farm.'

'Lucky him,' Fraser said. 'God only knows what I'm going to do with myself now.'

'You don't need to rush into anything,' Harriet said, trying not to look at him with pity. He had barely finished studying Civil Engineering at Goldsmith's College when war had broken out and, but for a short spell working alongside his father, he had had no time to fashion out a proper career for himself.

Fraser gulped down the rest of his tea, then asked, 'So, what's new in the metropolis of Sedlescombe, then?'

Harriet paused, pondering recent village news. All of it, without exception, was banal, trivial and inconsequential nonsense. She went to say so, but then reasoned that perhaps that was precisely what Fraser needed; to be helped to remember normality and to forget whatever horrors he had witnessed. 'Mr Metcalfe won the Utility Poultry egg-laying competition this year. Well—*he* didn't win—his pair of White Leghorns did. Nine hundred and thirteen eggs...' she began, tentatively testing his reaction to the absurdity of what she was saying.

'Nine hundred and thirteen? In a year?'

Harriet laughed. 'I know. Amazing.'

'Did you not enter your Sussexes?' he asked.

Harriet harrumphed. 'No chance with my ladies. They're far too moody and temperamental.'

'What else?' he asked.

'Let's see... The Sedlescombe Brass Band was donated two nearly-new cornets...'

'Wow,' Fraser enthused.

That he was finding something of interest from the triteness of her words heartened Harriet, emboldening her to explore the recent past for additional anecdotes. 'Oh, I know! The Choir and Ringers had their annual outing last Tuesday—a very pleasant day out in Eastbourne, so I gather—not getting back to the village until *gone midnight*.'

'Golly. What an adventure,' Fraser mocked.

'Quite. The summer fete was a thoroughly agreeable affair, by all accounts, raising much-needed money for the church and village hall.

Usual things: stalls, music, theatrics. The best part, though, was the pig-hunt for women.'

'Really?' Fraser asked.

'Oh, yes. Half the women of the village chasing this poor creature around the woods. Utter lunacy.'

Fraser smiled. 'I take it you didn't join in, then?'

'Not on your life! Mrs Selmes eventually caught the unfortunate creature,' Harriet said with a note of disapprobation.

'And what did she win?'

'The pig itself,' Harriet answered. 'The poor thing. I only hope for his sake that he went straight to the slaughterhouse; living with Mrs Selmes would be a fate worse than death.'

Fraser tittered at the story, and Harriet continued to rake over village news for his apparent enjoyment or distraction.

She looked at his face, as she spoke, imagining that she could see some degree of spirit returning to his eyes, as though such a thing might be possible in such a short space of time. In spite of herself, she refrained from asking the serious questions about what had been happening to him in the last years, resolving that, with time, perhaps the answers might be forthcoming.

Chapter Two

4th August 1919, Sedlescombe, Sussex

Four days had followed, where Fraser had slept for far longer than Harriet felt could be healthy for a man of his age. His sleeping patterns were erratic, to say the least, as were his eating habits. Unlike when he had been a child, he ate anything and everything put on a plate in front of him at any time of the day or night. Apart from those two things, he had sat languidly in the sitting room, staring into space, waiting for goodness only knew what—his next meal or sleep, she could only surmise. All the while, Harriet had busied herself closely in the background with a raft of household chores, many of them superfluous. On the fifth day, she was running her new Daisy Vacuum Cleaner along the hallway, pumping her right foot ten-to-the-dozen on the pedal, when she saw in her peripheral vision that Fraser was in the parlour, stooped over the table.

'What are you looking at?' she asked, gratefully setting aside the vacuum cleaner.

Fraser stepped to one side, revealing that he had emptied the two *Couttie's Assorted Biscuits* tins onto the table, which she had clean forgotten to put away.

'Is this everything you have of theirs?' he asked quietly.

'Yes,' she answered, dabbing her brow with her handkerchief and placing her hands on her hips. Given that he had taken no interest in the books or newspapers, which she had suggested he read over the last few days, she was somewhat heartened to see him take an interest in *something*.

'*Army Record Office, London, 14th July 1917,*' he read. '*Sir, It is my painful duty to inform you that a report has been received from the War Office notifying the death of Pioneer Malcolm McDougall, 159353, Royal Engineers 'P' Special Company, which occurred in the field on the 4th July 1917. The report is to the effect that he was killed in action. By His Majesty's command I am to forward the enclosed message of sympathy from Their Gracious Majesties the King and Queen.*' Fraser stopped reading and glanced at Harriet. 'Where's the message from the King and Queen?'

'Well...' Harriet began, 'It wasn't personal. Their Gracious Majesties probably don't even know that empty messages of condolence have been being sent out in their names… So, I threw it on the fire.'

Fraser raised one eyebrow, then continued to read: '*I am at the same time to express the regret of the Army Council at the soldier's death in his Country's service. I am to add that any information that may be received as to the soldier's burial will be communicated to you in due course.*' Fraser lowered the letter. 'Did you receive anything about his burial location?'

'No. I had to write a letter to the Imperial War Graves Commission, and they sent me this,' she said, handing him a small photograph that showed four wooden crosses. Taking a magnifying glass from her bureau, she held it over the image. 'That's his grave, there,' she said. Malcolm's name and date of death, etched on a small tin plate in the centre of the cross, rose enlarged from the otherwise dull, monochrome image.

Fraser sighed, as he stared at the photograph but said nothing.

'It came with details of the location: Essex Farm Cemetery in Belgium—just north of Ypres.'

'God…' Fraser said, and Harriet tried simultaneously not to rebuke him for using the Lord's name in vain but to infer meaning from that single word.

'I wish I knew more about what happened to them, Fraser,' she said, touching his arm, as he read one of Edward's postcards. What she didn't add, though, was that she wanted to know about *his* war, too. She pointed to the documents spread out on the table and said, 'I've got all this and yet it tells me nothing about what happened to them. You know…at the end. Is there any way to find out?'

Fraser blew his cheeks out. 'Official channels, maybe,' he ventured.

'I want to find out what happened to your brothers… Where they were before they died… *How* they died… And, since the Imperial War Graves Commission have outright banned repatriation, I want to visit their graves.'

'Really?' Fraser asked, incredulously. 'Malcolm died in Belgium, and Edward in Greece.'

He was right, of course: the task would be difficult. She had first mooted the idea to John soon after the Armistice but had been forbidden from taking any further action. But now she was free to do as she pleased. Then, a significant thought struck her: if she were to seek Fraser's help in her endeavours, it would serve the additional purpose of giving him something with which to occupy his time until such a moment as he would be ready to return to his career. 'We'll start with Malcolm,' she said, displaying a confidence, which she didn't really possess.

'*We'll* start?'

'Yes,' Harriet insisted with a smile. 'You're helping—at least until something more suitable comes along for you to do in the world of engineering.'

'I'm not even sure I want to be an engineer… What's the point in expending energy, planning, creating and building new bridges, roads… If you could see the state of the towns and villages in mainland Europe…'

'But they really need more people like you: young and bright with a good head on your shoulders,' Harriet countered.

Fraser shook his head and began to pick amongst the documents on the table. 'Talk me through what you've got for Malcolm, and I'll make my mind up about just how ridiculous a task this all is.'

Harriet scooped up a collection of more than twenty postcards. 'Well, he sent me all of *these*.'

He took the stack and quickly flicked through them. Choosing one at random, with a colourful bouquet of three roses on the front, he read the back: '*Dear Ma, hoping you are well, love Malcolm.*'

Harriet responded to his look of scepticism with a light shrug of her shoulders. 'Some of them are more *descriptive*,' she said, leaning closer and flipping through the cards. 'One of them…now where is it? One of them mentions his friends. Another of them has a photograph on the front, showing his location at the time.' She selected a card and held it in front of Fraser: '*Ypres Quai*,' she read from the front. The picture was a quaint depiction of two barges on a canal with several large wharf-like buildings standing beside it. Between the water and the buildings were several horse-drawn carts and men calmly going about their business. Harriet turned the card over and read: '*Dear Ma and Pa, A card to let know that I am quite well. Have not had too much time for writing just lately, so have had to send cards. We have had a lot of rain this last day or two & a big storm on Thursday night. Remember me to all at Sedlescombe. Love to all, Malcolm.*'

'When was it sent?' Fraser asked.

'June 1917,' Harriet answered.

'So, that was probably where he was killed, then, a month later.'

Harriet shrugged. 'Perhaps.'

Fraser picked up another postcard. This one was thicker than usual, and on the front was the emblem of the Royal Engineers, embroidered on a piece of lace. He lifted the decorative flap to reveal a dried blue flower. He turned the card over and read the brief message silently: *Dearest Ma, thought I would share the beauty of this blue poppy; think they would look rather wonderful growing amongst the hollyhocks in the back garden of Linton House. Love Malcolm.*

Seemingly, Fraser had seen enough. He sighed and looked at her. 'Ma, what you want to do is nigh-on impossible,' he said softly. 'I mean, *I* don't even know where to start.'

Harriet nodded. Seeing and hearing what little information she had about Malcolm's war gave her a sudden realisation of the enormity of the task, which she had been proposing. Besides which, she wasn't some special, exceptional case; there were millions of women in the country just like her with no knowledge of what had become of their sons. 'Yes,' she agreed, beginning to place all the documents into one neat stack. 'Your father said as much.'

Fraser reached out for her hand. 'Wait. I said it was nigh-on impossible, not *im*possible.'

'Really?'

'I don't mind *trying*, Ma, but like I said, I don't even know where to begin.'

Something, which Harriet couldn't immediately identify, changed inside of her. It was an indefinable lift, a lightening of her long-suffering heart, perhaps. 'Right,' she said, grasping her hands together, as she worked to contain the intense welling of hope inside. She moved across the room and sat at John's writing desk. She opened the lid and pulled out a sheet of white paper and his best silver fountain pen. 'You sit down and work your way through those postcards, making a note of anything that might give us a clue: friends, places he visited, people he met... He talks about a Timothy somebody quite often. Timothy Mogridge or Muggridge?'

'And what are you going to do, dare I ask?'

'I'm going to write to the battalion commander, or general, or whoever's in charge of the Royal Engineers and tell him I'm jolly well coming to see him.'

'Well, before you go and make yourself look a fool, you might do well to remember that he was serving with the Royal West Kents in the Pioneer Brigade. And it's the captain you need, not a commander or general.'

Harriet set the pen down and frowned. 'Yes, well, what does that actually *mean*? I was a little perplexed to read in the telegram that he was in the 'P' Special Company. Why so many dratted names? Companies, regiments, battalions, armies—it's all so very confusing. What was he actually *doing*?'

Fraser shrugged. 'The captain should be able to tell you more, especially now the war's over.'

'Let's get to work, then,' Harriet said, picking up the fountain pen and formulating her opening sentence.

Chapter Three

'I'll wait here,' Fraser said, suddenly drawing to a complete standstill.

Harriet looked at him with a moue. 'Why? What's the problem?'

Fraser's forehead scrunched up, as he frowned at her. 'I'm technically still in the army, Ma. The last thing I'm going to do is barge my way into a battalion office and demand to speak to the officer in charge. I'd be court martialled.'

'I'm not sure that's *technically* possible if you're in the reserves, but anyway…' Harriet replied, walking indignantly along Bank Street towards the headquarters of the 4th Battalion Royal West Kents. The day was hot, and, as Harriet strode along, she felt as though she were melting under her heavy, black, ankle-length mourning dress.

The building, which she sought, came into view. It was a large red-brick edifice with a low roof, pitched in the centre, reminding her of a typical Methodist chapel. The words *Corn Exchange* were carved into a white stone slab, set above the portico entrance. Beside the door were two long thin windows. It was thankfully a much less intimidating building than Harriet had feared.

She paused at the entrance, took a long breath in, then knocked on the white panelled door.

After a few moments, a young lady with pinched features opened it cautiously. She was wearing a rather fetching red front-buttoned dress with a wide V-neck and a rather less-fetching scowl on her face. 'Yes?' she said coolly.

'Good morning. I've come to see Major Sir Captain Cohen.' Harriet smiled and made a move towards the door, but the young lady didn't budge.

'I see. And do you have an appointment?'

'Strictly speaking, no,' Harriet answered. 'However, I did send him a letter last week, informing him that I would be coming today. Perhaps he neglected to tell you?'

'Well, I can assure you that Major Sir Captain Cohen does not have any appointments scheduled for today,' she asserted.

'Oh, how wonderful—plenty of time to fit me in, then,' Harriet said, taking a giant stride to the door and pushing against the secretary's resistance. Harriet found herself in a large vestibule with two desks, several potted plants and a run of metal filing cabinets.

'That is very much *not* what I meant, madam!'

Ignoring the lady's ongoing protestations and taking a hasty glance to the back of the room, Harriet could see three white doors with a central pane of obscure glass. Behind two she could see nothing at all and presumed them to be water closets or cupboards but, behind the right-hand one, she saw blurred movement and heard the low hum of conversation. 'This one, isn't it?'

'Madam, you really *cannot* just barge your way inside like this!' she called after Harriet. 'You must make an appointment!'

'Oh, but I did!' Harriet said pleasantly, turning the golden door knob and stepping onto the wooden block flooring of a long corridor, which served several closed doors. At the other end she could see a wide staircase, leading up to the first floor.

'Madam, please stop!' the secretary cried.

'It really won't take long,' Harriet said over her shoulder, as she marched down the corridor, glancing at the brass name plates attached to each door, as she passed. She reached the final one before the staircase to find that luck was on her side. *Major Sir Captain H. B. Cohen*, the black etched letters read. Harriet rapped hard on the door.

The secretary caught up with her and grabbed her arm. 'He's not *in* his office,' she said.

Harriet faced her, disliking the smug look that she found there.

'He's in a meeting.'

'Then I shall wait,' Harriet countered, spotting a chair and small table in the triangular space below the stairs and walking over to it in order to sit down. She pulled off her black suede piqué gloves and folded them into her raffia bag.

'He will be in meetings all day; he's a *very* busy officer.'

Harriet clapped her hands together. 'Not a problem, my dear. I've waited two years to find out what happened to my son, so another few hours won't make a great deal of difference. Oh, and if you're making a pot of tea at any point, I would *love* a cup. Thank you so much.'

The secretary, with her face flushed, thundered past Harriet and stomped up the stairs.

Harriet peeped up above her, half-expecting to see cracks in the plaster from the secretary's angry footsteps. She waited patiently, and, sure enough, just a few minutes later came the sound of two sets of shoes descending the staircase above her. One clearly belonged to the secretary, while the other sounded like a weighty, cumbersome pair of boots, in which Harriet hoped to find standing Captain Cohen.

The secretary appeared beside an officer in the uniform of the Royal West Kents. He looked like most of the army officers, whom she had ever encountered before—of similar age to her, grey hair, military moustache, florid face and no sign of a personality. She stood up and offered him her hand. 'Mrs McDougall,' she introduced herself, trying to ignore his damp, limp handshake. 'I wrote to you last week.'

One of Captain Cohen's springy eyebrows arched up, reminding Harriet of an excited caterpillar, which she had once found demolishing her brassicas in the vegetable patch at the rear of Linton House. A brown something-or-other moth. She couldn't recall the exact name just then, though Malcolm had told her it at the time, including its full Latin appellation.

'Madam, this is *most* irregular,' Captain Cohen reproved, receiving a firm nod of agreement from the secretary.

'Yes, it is rather,' Harriet agreed.

'There are other organisations, designed *specifically* for this task—have you tried the Red Cross?' he demanded.

'Yes,' Harriet lied, making a mental note to pursue this line of enquiry later. 'They directed me to you.'

'Did they, now? Well, they shouldn't have done. Most irregular.'

'It is also most irregular for seven hundred thousand British men to be slaughtered in the ludicrous assertion that war can end war. It is also most irregular, Captain Cohen, that a boy, whom I brought into this world and nurtured, cared for and loved beyond measure, is lying dead in a grave in a foreign land.' She added a thin smile to her diatribe and waited.

Captain Cohen drew in a lengthy breath and looked at the secretary. 'Perhaps if an appointment can be made for a week or so's time, we—'

'No,' Harriet interjected. 'That simply won't do. I shall be leaving here today with answers.'

'I'm afraid *that* simply will not be possible. Miss Tyler, please escort Mrs Dougall to reception to schedule an appointment. If she fails to leave, then for heaven's sake, telephone the police.' Captain Cohen huffed and scurried into his office.

'It's Mrs *Mc*Dougall, actually,' Harriet corrected, uncertain of what to do now, hearing what sounded like a bolt being driven across Captain Cohen's office door. 'Fine,' she conceded.

'This way,' Miss Tyler said, heading up the corridor with her head held high.

Back in the reception area, Miss Tyler took a seat at one of the desks and opened a large burgundy ledger. 'Now, let's see.'

'Anytime next week is fine,' Harriet said.

'No,' Miss Tyler said, shaking her head and dragging out the word to triple its actual length. 'The week after, and the one after that, are looking pretty busy, too. And then Captain Cohen will be on leave for ten days.' She continued to flick pages of the diary, shaking her head. 'Then he will be in Scotland for three weeks... I can *probably* squeeze you in on the 29th September?'

'That long away?'

Miss Tyler nodded and smiled sweetly. 'This is a *very* busy office, Mrs McDougall.'

'Then I don't think I will make an appointment, thank you,' Harriet said, equally sweetly.

Miss Tyler nodded and closed the ledger. 'Probably for the best.'

Harriet turned and began walking towards the door. She reached out for the handle and then turned on her heals to face Miss Tyler. 'Oh, could you just pass a *super*-quick message to the Captain?'

'What is it now?'

'Just to say that, should any suitable occasion arise to see me *today*, I shall be just around the corner, taking tea with Gladys at number six, Church Lane. Thank you so much.' Harriet opened the door to the sound of Miss Tyler's chair grating against the wooden floor.

'Wait!' Miss Tyler instructed. She glowered at Harriet, then hurried down the corridor towards Captain Cohen's office.

Harriet stood by the door, poised with one hand on her hip.

Seconds later, Captain Cohen marched towards her, looking one step away from exploding with anger. 'Come to my office now, Mrs McDougall.'

Inside his office, he closed the door behind them. It was a surprisingly large room, with bay windows facing out over a small rose garden. His enormous desk, covered in a scattering of paperwork, dominated the space. On the walls were hung various paintings of grey-moustached men in army uniform, and around the room were dotted an assortment of bookshelves, sagging under the weight of heavy military tomes.

'Sit,' he instructed, indicating a plain wooden chair in front of his desk, while he himself sat opposite her in a much grander leather affair. He laced his fingers together and leant over the desk. 'What is it you wish to know? Your son, was it?'

'His name was Malcolm McDougall and he served in your battalion.'

Captain Cohen's lower lip turned down and he shook his head. 'Don't remember him.'

'He was in the Special Brigade and died on the 4th July 1917. He was buried at Essex Farm Cemetery, and I would just like to know what happened to him at the end—how he died. So, if you could start by telling me the movements of the 4th Battalion, say from the beginning of 1917 through to July, that would be most helpful. Perhaps the brigade diary might help?'

'Mrs McDougall, what do you think this is? Even if I were so minded to, I could not possibly divulge strategic military movements, not yet even twelve months since the Armistice. Indeed, one would be hard-pushed to locate such information in the public domain on the *African* Wars twenty years ago. Good heavens!'

'Oh, don't be so preposterous. Malcolm was sending postcards home from some of the places he visited, for goodness' sake. I'm not in need of *strategic military movements*, just the names of the places he was serving in prior to his death.'

Captain Cohen emitted another giant exhalation, appearing to consider his options. 'I'll tell you what, I'll have Miss Tyler type up the names of the places where the unit was based in the month leading up to your son's death. And that, Mrs McDougall, is all.'

'Thank you,' Harriet said, watching, as he stood and made his way over to a filing cabinet behind his desk. 'Oh, and if you could tell me the names and addresses of any of the surviving soldiers, who served with Malcolm, that would be most wonderful, too.'

'Absolutely not. Confidential,' he barked, without turning around.

'Oh.'

'One tick,' he said, bustling past her with a thick bundle of papers out into the corridor.

Quickly, Harriet jumped up and rushed over to the filing cabinet, from which Captain Cohen had just pulled the papers, and opened the drawer. She hurriedly flicked through the dividers until she reached one

27

headed *4ᵗʰ Battalion Personnel*. It was a worryingly thin file, arranged in alphabetical order, and when Harriet examined a random entry, she found that it gave just the barest of details about each man: personal information, rather than the military movements that she had been hoping to find. Nevertheless, Harriet thumbed quickly through to surnames beginning with M and found Malcolm's file. It was a single sheet and every entry—name, address, age, next of kin—was already known to her.

Disappointed, she pushed the drawer closed and began to head back to her chair. Then she stopped, remembering the name of one of Malcolm's friends from his postcards home and hurried back to the filing cabinet. Timothy Mogridge. She found his entry easily, slid it out and looked at his address: *'Gulls Nest, West Parade, Bexhill on Sea, Sussex'*. Harriet repeated the information aloud to commit it to memory, refiled the paper and closed the drawer.

The sudden returning heavy clomp of footsteps in the corridor told her that Captain Cohen's arrival would happen before she could possibly regain her seat.

'Mrs McDougall, what are you doing?' he growled, as he entered the office.

Harriet slowly lowered her gaze from one of the portraits behind his desk, as if being roused from a daydream: 'Hmm?' She returned her gaze to the portrait. *'General Sir Charles James Napier.* Funny looking chap, wouldn't you say?'

'No. I would not say, actually. One of our great leaders during the Peninsular Wars,' Captain Cohen stated, pushing past her to reach his desk. 'Mrs McDougall, I really must insist that this meeting is over. I have nothing more I can offer to assist you in finding out what happened to your son. I'm sorry, but that is the fact of the matter. If you would kindly return to the reception area, Miss Tyler will have prepared the document for you by the time you get there.' He extended his damp hand towards her. 'Good day, Madam.'

Harriet shook his hand. 'Thank you,' she said, marching towards the door.

'And, Mrs McDougall...' he called after her. 'I do not know how you came by my address, or my wife's name, but the next time you threaten a member of His Majesty's Army like that, I shall have you arrested.'

'Very well and I am sorry to have done that,' Harriet said. 'It's just... I really did need to speak with you. And, well, there aren't many men, military or otherwise, who like to risk upsetting their wives. I gambled that you would imagine that she would side with me on the affairs of a mother's heart.' Having achieved her aim, she left the disgruntled army captain, headed smartly out of his office and back to reception.

'Here,' Miss Tyler said flatly, handing over a piece of paper, blank but for four typed place names in Northern France and Belgium. No dates or times, but it *was* a start.

'Much obliged to you,' Harriet said, taking the proffered paper and flouncing from the building.

She sighed, as she pushed the door closed and stepped out into the late-morning sunshine. She paused for a moment to catch her breath, then looked over the list of places. *Arras. Croisilles. Bullecourt.* The last name on the list, where Malcolm was said to have lost his life, sent a shudder through her: *Ypres.*

A light breeze wafted through the open kitchen door of Linton House, providing Harriet with a welcome waft of respite against the interminable heat of the day.

'There,' she said, sealing the envelope on a letter to Timothy Mogridge. Beside her on the table was another letter, addressed to the British Red Cross in London.

Harriet undid the top four buttons of her black blouse, fanned her collar for a few precious moments, then rebuttoned it to the neck. She carried the two letters through the house to the parlour, where she found Fraser poring over a map of northern Europe. Four red pencil loops denoted the places where Malcolm had been before he died.

'Have you found anything more?' Harriet asked him.

'Nothing of substance, no.'

'Hopefully something will come of these,' Harriet said, holding up the two letters, then making for the front door. 'Shan't be long! I'm just going to the Post Office, then calling to see Mrs Morris to ask if she might like to accompany me to London to see a medium.'

'*What?*' Harriet heard Fraser call after her, as she closed the front door.

Chapter Four

12th August 1919, Bermondsey, London

A deep uncertainty, which worried Harriet tremendously, coiled and twisted the insides of her stomach, as she stood on the doorstep to the tall house in front of her. A particular flat in this tenement belonged to one Mrs Leonard, a medium with whom she had made an anonymous appointment. The brick house was in a line of ten or so others, each as run-down as the next. Children with dirty faces and ragged clothes stopped their game of leaping over a pile of horse excrement in the middle of the street to stare at her.

She looked away, down at her trembling hands, wondering if she was doing the right thing. If Fraser, Mrs Morris and the Reverend Percival were to be paid heed, then no, most definitely she was not doing the right thing. The most critical opinion of the latter had been imposed upon her after she had told Fraser of her plans to seek out the help of a medium. He had immediately dashed out of the house, returning some time later with the reproachful vicar.

'That death is the end has never been a Christian doctrine, Mrs McDougall...' he had preached to her, the moment that she had allowed him inside Linton House, '...but this kind of interest in a premature reunion with the departed is, well, unhealthy, ungodly and leaves one susceptible to all kinds of opportunism. It pains me to cast aspersions but these people are nothing more than charlatans, preying on the weak and desperate.'

'Weak, Reverend Percival? Weak?' Harriet had replied, slightly astounded. 'Desperate, yes. Weak, no.'

'I think you understand my meaning, Mrs McDougall.'

'Perhaps, Reverend, you might feel differently, were you in my position,' she had retorted, before politely requesting that he should leave.

And now, standing here in this unsavoury neighbourhood, his words of warning prevented her from knocking on the door. And yet...

She couldn't shake the possibility of getting some answers. Her favourite author, Arthur Conan Doyle had publicly proclaimed an ability to communicate through a medium with his son, Kingsley, who had died of pneumonia following the Battle of the Somme; an ability as had also been reported by a good many other normal, respectable people.

What, she questioned herself, was the worst that could happen? That she would learn nothing more than that which she now already knew? Fraser, of course, suspected all kinds of fraud and trickery, and it was because of this that she had booked her appointment under a different name, giving no other personal information whatsoever.

She had to try.

Harriet knocked on the door, glanced again at the inquisitive children on the street, then stood staring at her black shoes until she heard the creak of the door opening before her.

'Mrs Catt?'

Harriet looked up and nodded. The lady in front of her was a good deal older than was she, with a hunched back. Her hair was so thin that Harriet could see large patches of her blotched scalp through the grey clumps that persisted. Her face was haggard, tired.

'I'm Mrs Leonard. You'd best come in,' she said, shuffling awkwardly around and moving inside the house.

Harriet followed, instantly but covertly turning her nose up at some foul-smelling odours emanating from the bowels of the house. The hallway was painted—a long time hence—in a dull brown, and the boards were bare, lending an oppressive feeling to the place, all of which only served to heighten Harriet's anxiety.

Mrs Leonard paused at the backroom and indicated that Harriet should enter first.

The room was small and lit by a single candle on a table in the centre. Shards of sunlight pierced through torn slits in a tatty blanket, hung in a clumsy attempt to cover the window.

'Sit down, Mrs Catt,' Mrs Leonard said pleasantly.

'Which chair?' Harriet asked, glancing between the two on either side of the table.

'Oh, it doesn't matter to me...or to the spirit world,' Mrs Leonard laughed. 'You just make yourself comfortable.'

Harriet sat at the nearest chair, not comfortable in the slightest.

'Now, Mrs Catt,' Mrs Leonard said, quietly reaching over and touching Harriet's left hand. 'I ain't givin' no assurances about who's out there for ya: might be someone, might be no-one. I have what's called a control, that be a person what's already on the other side and who talks through me. Her name is Kaifa. You can't speak directly to

31

her; she will talk if she can. Did you bring something of your loved-one's, what I can use to make a connection through Kaifa?'

Harriet nodded, not entirely sure of what she had just been told, and produced Malcolm's blood-stained tunic from her bag, which Mrs Leonard placed on the table in front of her, having no obvious reaction to the blood stains.

'Are you ready to proceed?'

'Yes,' Harriet muttered.

'Very well,' Mrs Leonard said, placing her hands down onto the tunic.

Harriet watched, as Mrs Leonard leant back and closed her eyes. Her mouth fell open, as if she had just dropped off to sleep and her hands, resting with palms open on the table, began to twitch. At that moment, Harriet recalled Fraser's warnings about the trickery and illusion employed by some mediums and she again questioned the validity of coming all this way to see this charade.

'I've got a young man with me,' Mrs Leonard suddenly ejaculated, in a high-pitched, squeaky voice. 'Rather above the medium height. He holds himself well.'

'Malcolm?' Harriet blurted out, instantly wishing that she hadn't just given herself away like that.

Mrs Leonard seemed not to react to the name. 'He has greyish eyes...or perhaps brown. Dark hair... Handsome...very handsome, I should say. A nice oval face...'

Even though she could have used his support right now, Harriet was glad that Fraser wasn't there; she could hear him, mocking Mrs Leonard's shrill voice and the description of a soldier, which could easily be applied to half the British Army.

'He's laughing at you!' she suddenly shrieked. 'He's struggling to speak for the laughter. He can't believe you of all people is 'ere!'

'Why, what's so funny about that?' Harriet demanded.

'He says you being here don't sit well with your beliefs. He's laughing at something else, too: your name. He says it ain't yours, it's someone else's...somebody close to you's.'

Harriet gasped. Mrs Harriet Catt had been the name of her grandmother.

Mrs Leonard went quiet for a few seconds, having the look of someone being told something complicated to remember, then she asked, 'He says find the poppy and the red star; it will help you with it all.'

'Help me with *what* all?' Harriet asked, wondering what on earth that could mean.

'He says, he's happy here and he's got lots of friends with him. He's losing his form now. He says he's got work to do—something with a laboratory—but if you look around for him, you'll see him... He's gone.' Mrs Leonard sat bolt upright, as though stung by electricity, and opened her eyes. In the voice with which she had first greeted Harriet at the door, she said, 'It was him, wasn't it—your son, Malcolm?'

A surge of conflicting emotions rose inside Harriet, and she stood, hastily rummaging in her bag for a coin. She tossed the money onto the table, grabbed Malcolm's tunic and dashed from the room, tears running down her cheeks. She hurried down the hallway and outside, gulping in large mouthfuls of fresh air, as she hastened along the street. At the end of the road, she turned to look back, seeing the haunting figure of Mrs Leonard out on her front steps watching her go.

'Did you get to speak to Malcolm?' Fraser called from the parlour, making no attempt to disguise his facetiousness. 'Or was he too busy to talk? Were Edward and Pa there, too, all talking over each other as usual?'

Harriet closed the front door, removed her shoes and blustered into the parlour, intent on rebuking Fraser, when she quickly stopped herself short. 'Oh.'

A man, wearing scrappy brown trousers and a dirty shirt, stood up from behind the table, where Fraser was studying a map of Belgium. The visitor smiled in the best way that he could, given that the complete left side of his face was terribly disfigured. Most of his lower eyelid was missing, revealing a hideous network of tiny bloody veins and the left corner of his mouth was pulled downwards, permanently defying its owner's obvious desire to smile. The skin in between mouth and eye was lumpy and uneven, as though hastily fashioned from soft wax.

Harriet cleared her throat and tried to look into his good right eye.

'Ma, this is Timothy Mogridge,' Fraser introduced.

'Hello,' he said. 'Very nice to meet you.' His voice—clear and well-spoken—was a complete mismatch for his appearance and took Harriet aback somewhat.

'Ah! Thank you so much for coming,' she managed to say, thrusting her hand in his direction, which he shook vigorously. 'Can I get you something to eat or drink?' she asked, casting a chastising glance to her son, who had obviously forgotten his manners in her absence.

'Erm, if you can spare something, that would be lovely,' Timothy answered shyly.

'Spare it? Good heavens, you've come all this way; it's the very least that I can do for you. I'll get you a nice cup of tea and some jam sandwiches. I've got some fresh Swiss roll, too. Or, at least I *did* have, before I left this morning,' she said with a playful nod in Fraser's direction. 'Come with me into the kitchen.'

She could hear him following on behind her and, as she walked, tried to regain her composure from the surprise at his appearance. The poor man and those terrible facial injuries, she thought, all the while determined not to show her shock.

'Make yourself at home,' Harriet said, directing him to the kitchen table. 'It's very good of you to come.'

'Thank you,' he mumbled, taking a seat.

'Tell me about yourself, Timothy,' Harriet said brightly, as she filled the kettle with water.

'Which self?' he asked.

Harriet paused and looked over at him. 'What do you mean?'

'Pre- or post-war me?' he answered.

She assumed from his somewhat cryptic answer that the changes—both mental and physical—wrought by the war had been sufficient for him to consider himself now a different person to that which he had been prior to 1914. 'Despite how incompatible they may seem to be, do your two selves not make a whole person, however damaged?' she asked gently.

Timothy considered her response, casting his eyes out through the back door to the garden. He turned back to face Harriet and shook his head firmly: 'No. We may share a name and a history, but the Timothy James Mogridge, who's sitting here now, is not the same man as the one who joined up in 1915.' He spoke matter-of-factly, as though he had long-since come to terms with the separation of his personalities. 'My wife and daughter can attest to that,' he added.

'Oh…' Harriet said, as she carefully spooned the tea into the pot.

'My daughter's four now and she has no memory of me before the war. During that time, she's become very much a mummy's girl and, what with me looking the way that I do, she generally bursts into tears whenever I go near her. Not that I can blame her, of course. And my wife, well, it's the mental damage that she finds the hardest to cope with…' His voice trailed off and he looked back outside again.

'But you survived!' Harriet exclaimed, spreading a thick layer of jam onto some sliced bread. 'If you can survive something so devastating, which claimed the lives of so many others, you can survive anything else that life might throw at you, no matter how impossible it might feel at the time.'

Timothy smiled, but it was the smile of a man tolerating a lack of understanding. 'Survived for what, Mrs McDougall? I've nothing. My wife and daughter don't want me—not who I've become anyhow. I can't get a job, which has meant that most of our possessions have had to be sold off, or pawned. We've been forced to leave our house and now live—for want of a better verb—in one room in my wife's parents' house, who have also made it clear that I'm a hindrance, and that, actually, it would have been better for everyone if I *hadn't* survived.'

'Oh, Timothy, that's a dreadful thing to say,' Harriet said. She stopped arranging the tea and sandwiches, about to go and place a comforting arm over his shoulder, but she saw in that moment that he wasn't looking for sympathy or consolation, he was simply relaying the facts as he saw them.

'It's fine, honestly,' he insisted. 'I spend a lot of time by myself now, thinking, walking…'

Harriet placed the sandwiches, teapot, plate and cups and saucers on a tray and carried it to the table. She set it down, then placed her hand onto his. This time she looked into his damaged left eye. 'You will get through it, I promise you.' She poured the brewed tea through the strainer into the three waiting china cups.

Timothy gave her another of his you-have-no-idea looks, then glanced down at the food. She heard the unmistakable groan of his stomach.

'Please, help yourself,' she encouraged, her heart aching for him.

He reached over for a sandwich and, ignoring the plate that she had placed in front of him, put it straight into his mouth. In two bites it was gone, and he was reaching for another.

'I can find you work—goodness me, there's *so* much to be done around here. Gardening, odd jobs, errands—things my late husband said he would do but never actually got around to doing. I could ask around the village, too. My brother, Herbert is the village builder. I'm sure he could find something for you.'

35

'Thank you, but no,' he said between mouthfuls.

'Well, if you—'

'So, then…' Fraser interpolated, bursting into the room with his map. 'Do we know more about Malcolm's work in the 'P' Special Company, yet?' he said, to nobody in particular. 'Swiss rolls!' he added, leaning over Timothy and shoving one straight into his mouth.

'Oh,' Timothy said, glancing between Harriet and Fraser. 'You don't even know what Malcolm was doing out there?'

Harriet shook her head. 'No idea. The Royal West Kents have been next to useless. Please, anything you can tell us—anything at all— would be most welcome.'

Timothy hastily swallowed the last bite of the last sandwich, took a swig of tea, then spoke: 'I was with Malcolm from the early days of the newly formed 4th Pioneer Battalion. We trained together—'

'But why did he transfer there in the first place?' Harriet interrupted.

'Because, like me, he had a degree in chemistry,' Timothy replied.

Harriet felt a heavy sinking feeling inside, guessing where this might be leading. 'Sorry,' she apologised. 'I interrupted. You were saying that you trained together?'

'That's right. We trained in various villages around Helfaut in France. And, around the usual military drilling and marching, we learnt about cylinder engineering, meteorological practice, and of course, the use and deployment of gas.'

Harriet sighed involuntarily at hearing the word *gas*, cursing herself for having taken Malcolm's side when he had gone against that field of study chosen by most other McDougall men in the family, that of civil engineering. Malcolm's two brothers, his father, grandfather and uncles had all pursued that career, having gained degrees in the subject from Goldsmith's University. Malcolm had wanted to study chemistry, and she had fought his corner for the right to study that which he ultimately chose. Perhaps he would have still been alive if—

No, she stopped herself. Edward had pursued civil engineering, but that, too, had got him killed. The boys could have studied anything, or nothing at all and would still be dead; that was the brutal truth of the matter.

'In mid-June 1916,' Timothy continued, 'we moved out to the front line. We left Helfaut as an intact Gas Brigade of sixteen cylinder companies, with two hundred and twenty-five men per company, but we arrived, separated and spread out across the full seventy-mile-long frontline, being used among the five armies, as circumstances dictated. A little disorganised, to say the least.'

'Then what happened?' Harriet asked.

'Then we did what we'd been trained to do: set up an integrated system of gas cylinders along the frontline of trenches and, when the weather conditions were just perfect, open the jets and watch the deadly vapour, White Star, roll across no-man's land towards the Bosche trenches.'

'White Star?' Harriet repeated, recalling what Mrs Leonard had said about finding a red star. Could she have made a slight mistake?

'It was the name of the gas we used: a fifty-fifty mixture of phosgene and chlorine. As I said, deadly stuff. One sergeant in our company received a slight dose, when he was disconnecting a four-way pipe. He paid no attention to it, seemed to be fine in himself, and carried on. The next day he collapsed and died.'

'It's so inhumane and barbaric,' Harriet commented. 'I can't imagine what Malcolm, with his love of science and nature, must have thought of it.'

Timothy shrugged. 'He just did what the rest of us did and got on with the job.'

'What about *Red Star*—does that mean anything to you?'

Timothy shook his head. 'No, sorry. Should it?'

'Where have you got that from?' Fraser asked her with a scowl.

'Nothing, don't worry,' Harriet said, having already decided to withhold most of what had occurred with the medium. 'Was it always awful?' she asked, the fear of the answer almost preventing her from asking the question.

A conspiratorial look passed between Fraser and Timothy, and she knew that they were silently agreeing to spare her.

'No, not always,' Timothy eventually answered. 'One of the biggest joys of working in the Special Companies was watching thousands of rats dying from the effects of the gas—that made us quite popular at times. Not that it really made a difference to their numbers, though, unfortunately.'

'Gosh…' Harriet murmured, not enjoying the mental picture forming in her mind.

'What next?' Fraser pushed.

'Well, to be honest, I wasn't always with Malcolm. As I said, the battalions were spread out all over the frontline, so I could easily go days or weeks without seeing him. I know at some point in late 1916, he returned to England for a brief spell—'

'England? Did he?' Harriet interjected. 'What on earth for?'

'He was a good chemist, Mrs McDougall, one of the best, and because of that they sent him to the Research Laboratory in Woolwich. I think he went there to advise on the practicalities and realities of gas warfare. You know, the view from the Western Front and all that.'

'Good gracious. I had no idea,' Harriet mumbled. She turned to Fraser. 'Did you know about this?'

Fraser shook his head. 'No, no idea.'

'How long was he there for?' she asked.

'I don't know, sorry. I saw him back on the front, though, in January 1917: a terrible winter, that was, the worst of the whole war. Ground as hard as iron, trenches flooded up to your armpits. You can imagine trying to lug one-hundred-and-eighty-pound gas cylinders through all that...'

Harriet felt sick. She desperately wished that Malcolm had been able to come home during his time back in England for one last visit. Heavens, Woolwich was only sixty-odd miles away from Sedlescombe. Then she wished that Malcolm had just stayed there, in the safety of the laboratory, quietly mixing his chemicals, while the war had happened hundreds of miles away without him. She wished...

'Do you know what happened?' Fraser asked. 'When he died?'

Timothy took a long breath. 'No, sorry. I wasn't actually there. I know he was treated at the Essex Farm Advanced Dressing Station before he died.'

'I see...' Harriet muttered.

'If it's any consolation to you, the last time I saw him, he was in very good spirits.'

Harriet didn't know if it was a consolation or not. To hear that her beloved son had returned to England and had not thought to mention it, never mind actually pay her a visit, wounded her deeply. She rose from her chair. 'More tea? More sandwiches?' she asked, glancing between the two men.

Both nodded.

'Right,' she said, heading back over to fill the kettle.

'So, do you know where the explosion actually happened?' she heard Fraser asking Timothy, pushing his map down onto the table between them.

Both men were leaning in closely over the map, studying it carefully. Harriet kept one ear trained on their conversation, as she made the tea and another round of sandwiches. This time, she made more. Fraser's insatiable appetite had not waned in the last few days, and Timothy seemed to be devouring the food, as though he hadn't eaten anything in several weeks. As she prepared the food, she thought about what she had just learned about Malcolm's death. It was certainly more than she had known previously, but still lacking in the finer detail of a first-hand account of someone present when he had died.

Having arranged the tea and sandwiches on a tray, Harriet carried them over to the table. Timothy and Fraser had created a rough chronology of the battalion's movements from July 1916 to Malcolm's death in July 1917.

'Tuck in,' Harriet said, and the two men wasted no time in grabbing a sandwich each. 'Can you think of anyone who might know more about that final day and…what actually happened?' Harriet asked.

'There is, actually,' Timothy answered. 'The Duchess of Westminster.'

'Pardon?'

'The Duchess of Westminster. She had her own hospital in Le Touquet. Officially it was the Number One British Red Cross Hospital, but it was known as the Duchess of Westminster's Hospital,' Timothy explained.

'So, Malcolm died in *Le Touquet*?' Fraser queried, opening the map out further and pointing to the French seaside town, miles from Ypres. 'That doesn't make any sense.'

'No, he wasn't sent to Le Touquet. For some reason the Duchess was nursing on the frontline at the time. I heard from a friend that he was being treated by her.'

'Good golly,' Harriet gasped. 'The Duchess of Westminster.'

Timothy shrugged, as he wolfed down another sandwich.

'It's not such a big deal, Ma,' Fraser commented. 'Lots of women like her did the same thing, or else turned their mansions into convalescent homes. It was some doleful attempt to *do their bit*,' he said with a note of cynicism.

'The Duchess of Westminster,' Harriet repeated pensively to herself, taking inexplicable comfort in the fact that this member of the aristocracy, about whom she knew nothing whatsoever, had been with her son shortly before his death.

'I'm sorry to say that I think that's all I can help you with,' Timothy said, drinking the last dregs of his tea. 'And I probably should be getting home.'

His words struck Harriet as apathetic and laden with a horrid melancholia. 'Listen, Timothy. Why don't you stay here? It can be for as short or as long as you need.'

'It's very kind of you, Mrs McDougall, but no, thank you.' He rose from his chair and shook Fraser's hand. 'If I think of anything else, I shall drop you a line.'

'Thank you,' Fraser replied.

Harriet led the way through the hallway to the front door, where she pressed a handful of coins into Timothy's hand. 'To cover your expenses...' she explained before any offence could be taken.

'You're very kind, Mrs McDougall,' he said, shaking her hand.

'My offer was genuine and will always be there,' she reiterated.

He nodded, opened the door and made his way outside.

Harriet stood watching him go, waving as he passed through the gate and out into the street. She pondered a moment on what his life might now hold. She took in a long breath and held it, as she looked over the village green.

'What was that all about?' Fraser yapped from behind her.

She hurriedly closed the front door and turned to face him, knowing full well the cause of his irritation, but decided to pretend otherwise. 'What was all what about?'

'Inviting a veritable stranger to come and *live* here, for goodness' sake!'

'He's a broken man, Fraser. Have a heart,' she retorted.

'Good God, Ma. Take a day-trip to any town or city and you'll see hundreds of men like him—the walking dead. Are you going to invite them all back here to live as your surrogate children?'

'Now you're just being absurd and cruel, Fraser.'

'What's happening to you, Ma? Visiting mediums, stealing confidential information from the army and now this? Maybe you should just let sleeping dogs lie.'

'Sleeping dogs?' Harriet cried.

'Sorry, not a good choice of idiom, but you—'

'No, not *a good choice of idiom*. They're my sons, Fraser—your brothers—and all the while I have breath left in my body, I will *not* give up finding out what happened to them.'

40

With her heart trying to thunder its way out of her chest, Harriet stormed through the house and out into the back garden. She jammed her hands onto her hips and sighed, as she tried to calm her thoughts. Hearing Fraser's diatribe of the behaviours, which were so very uncharacteristically hers of late, allowed a tiny niggle of doubt to enter into her mind for the first time. But then—

She spotted it in her peripheral vision at first, then it flew closer and closer, almost dancing in front of her eyes. It was off-white in colour, no more than an inch in length, and she recognised it immediately from Malcolm's sketches on his bedroom wall: a male Ghost Swift moth.

The moth continued to flutter in front of her, before leisurely flying over to the bed of lilac Michaelmas daisies beside her. After a short moment, he pulled open his wings in a grand gesture of display, and her subconscious reminded her of Mrs Leonard's words about seeing Malcolm if she looked around her.

Harriet smiled, and a tear ran down her cheek.

Chapter Five

Harriet withdrew a handkerchief from her sleeve and ran it slowly across her forehead. Needing some respite from the high midday sun, she slowly sauntered towards the shade given by the canopy of a pair of elders. The trees, along with a shed and a low picket fence to keep the chickens out, provided a natural separation of her vegetable garden from the long stretch of flower-bed-lined lawn, which led back to the house. She sat at one of a pair of white iron chairs and placed the trug full of produce, which she had just picked, onto the matching table and tossed her head back, grateful for the breeze meeting the nape of her neck. The purplish elderberries above her were plentiful this year and would soon be ripe enough to make a good stock of elderberry and blackberry jam, using her mother's old recipe. Harriet exhaled and looked at the house. This was a spot to where she would often retreat, when she needed a moment to escape the mayhem of running a household containing four oftentimes helpless men. She smiled at the amalgamation of memories playing and merging in her mind; memories, which seemed now to belong to a different lifetime.

Her recollections were interrupted when a Ghost Swift fluttered past her, braving the daytime instead of keeping to its usual rounds at dusk. It was yellow with brown hindwings: a female, Harriet identified. She watched closely, as it flew over her neat line of round lettuces, and was incredulous to see some tiny droplets being expelled over her vegetables. She leapt up, intent on chasing it away, realising that the moth was releasing her eggs. She would need to crush them before they hatched and devoured her lettuces. She marched over to the vegetable garden, keeping sight of the moth as she went. Then, she remembered the male Ghost Swift, hovering and practically dancing in front of her a few days ago, and she stopped. Her outrage suddenly and decisively softened, and she watched the moth disappear over the back fence into the meadow and woodland beyond.

She cursed herself and her irrational thoughts, which were jumbling in her mind and which were being irritated and heightened by the heat. She wiped her brow once again and went to return to the shade of the elder trees, when she heard her name being called from the house. She knew the voice and inwardly sighed. It belonged to Hannah, her sister-in-law. She was well-meaning enough but the bond between them really only existed because Hannah had married Harriet's brother, Herbert.

'Good afternoon,' Harriet called, not really in the right frame of mind. She picked up the trug of gathered produce and began a slow and reluctant saunter to the house. She presented a fixed wooden smile all the while she walked. 'Lovely day,' she greeted, as she drew close enough to be heard.

'Far too hot for me,' Hannah countered. She was sweltering in a long pale dress and straw hat, one of the few fortunate women of the village not to be enduringly attired in black. 'I wondered if you had time to spare for a cup of tea?'

'Of course,' Harriet replied.

'My! What a wonderful lot of courgettes and tomatoes you've picked,' she said, eyeing the trug, as she followed Harriet inside. 'Ours have been a veritable *disaster* this year.'

'Take some,' Harriet said. 'I've plenty.'

'Well, if you're sure.'

'Very sure,' Harriet answered, filling the kettle with water.

'So, how have things been with you since John's passing? Hasn't been an easy few years, has it?' Hannah asked, placing a hand on Harriet's arm, making it difficult for her to make the tea.

Harriet tried to ignore Hannah's blatant condescending tone, offering her a stony rictus. 'Not great, no, but I'm keeping strong, like everyone else.'

'Oh, you are *such* a brave thing,' Hannah said, pulling what Harriet supposed was a sympathetic grimace, but which left her sweaty and leathery face contorted like a grotesque. What her brother, an energetic and handsome man, had ever seen in her, Harriet had never been able to ascertain.

Harriet placed the teapot, cups and saucers and jug of milk onto the tray and headed towards the back door.

'Oh,' Hannah said, 'I rather thought we might stay inside in the cool.'

Harriet nodded her agreement and moved to place the tray down on the kitchen table.

'How about the parlour?' Hannah suggested. 'North-facing, it'll be lovely and cold.'

Harried looked at her sister-in-law with growing suspicion. Hannah had never, in the twenty-odd years of knowing her, suggested that they take tea in the parlour. As Harriet walked along the hallway towards the front of the house, her suspicion began to morph into a clearer idea of why she might have come.

'I've just seen Fraser loitering around the village green, staring longingly into *Ditch's* like a love-sick puppy,' Hannah commented with a laugh. 'Does he know that Louise is betrothed to Peter Wolf, I wonder?'

'He does, indeed,' Harriet confirmed, setting the tea things down in the one small clear space on the table not taken up by the paperwork surrounding the enquiries into Malcolm's death.

'Good Lord above!' Hannah exclaimed when she spotted the raft of documents. She pulled off her hat, wafting it in front of her face, as she leant in for a closer look. 'What on *earth* is all this?' Her gaze flitted quickly between all the maps, photographs, postcards, letters, notelets and official military paperwork, then she stared at Harriet, waiting on the answer.

Harriet knew now that somebody—probably Fraser—had told Hannah about her investigation, but for now she played along with the pretence that Hannah was discovering it all for the first time. 'I'm trying to find out what happened to Malcolm, and all of these—' she gestured to the table, '—are the jigsaw pieces that I need to help me build a picture of his last days.'

'*Notes from the medium, Mrs Leonard...*' Hannah read, immediately shooting a disbelieving look at Harriet. 'Good Lord, Harriet. A *medium*? Surely not?'

'Yes.'

'And what did this *medium* tell you, for heaven's sake?'

'All kinds of things,' Harriet answered, pouring the tea into two china cups.

'So, you believe in all of that now, do you—this *spiritualist* nonsense—that's risen up, as if from nowhere, since the end of the war?' Hannah enquired, not attempting to hide her own misgivings on the subject.

'I... I'm not sure. Maybe, yes.' The truth was, Harriet didn't know what she believed anymore. Her feelings on the matter were a tangled and complicated mess. The visit to Mrs Leonard had left her unsettled and more confused than ever. The mention of finding a red star and a poppy was just bizarre and made no sense. The physical description of Malcolm, however, was accurate but, as she had thought at the time, could just as easily have been applied to any number of men. The

44

obvious identifying scar above Malcolm's left eye, sustained following a fall from a tree when he had been nine years old, had conveniently gone unnoticed by Mrs Leonard and Kaifa, her strange alter-ego. But then there was the fact that she seemed to know that Harriet had visited her under a false name. 'So would anybody with half an ounce of sense,' Fraser had later scorned. 'What fool would turn up to one of those impostors using their real name?' She had wanted to say Arthur Conan Doyle, but had not thought it a great defence and so had kept her mouth shut. The one thing, which Mrs Leonard *had* imparted and which had really shaken Harriet's equilibrium, had been the reference to a laboratory. A reference, which in itself was a very specific detail that had taken on much more significance since Timothy Mogridge had divulged the precise nature of Malcolm's wartime work. 'I'm a sceptical believer,' she had explained to Fraser, following their discussion into the matter. 'Well you can't be; it's an oxymoron,' he had replied. 'It's like saying you're an Atheist Christian.'

Now Harriet noticed Hannah raise her eyebrows disapprovingly at the revelation.

'Hmm… What else have you got here, then?' she asked, prodding a finger at the table.

Harriet picked up a document, drawn up by Fraser, which pulled together everything, which they had gleaned so far, into a working chronology of Malcolm's last months, and used it to explain everything to Hannah up to the point that they had now reached. Yesterday's post had returned Harriet's own undelivered letter, which she had written to the gas laboratory in Woolwich: she had surmised that the end of the war had thankfully brought about its closure, but that still left her enquiry unanswered.

Hannah smiled. 'Well, now you know what you know, you can put the matter to rest.' She picked up her cup and saucer and took a sip of tea, wandering towards the front window.

'What do you mean? I've barely started,' Harriet retorted.

'Goodness, ought you not leave things as they are?' Hannah asked, spinning around.

'No,' Harriet said, smiling politely. 'Perhaps if you'd lost two children, Hannah, you'd understand.'

'Perhaps,' Hannah seemed to concur, drinking more tea and evidently considering Harriet's statement. 'But we've all lost *something*, haven't we?'

The question was pointed, demanding a counter-question from Harriet, since, as far as she knew, Hannah had not lost anybody close to her in the conflict. Neighbours, extended family, yes, but her own children or husband, or brothers, no. 'Everybody?' Harriet pushed.

'Look at Herbert and me—with the shortage of young men out there, there's no hope of our Dorothy and Mercy ever getting married…and with that denial of matrimony comes the loss of Herbert and my ever seeing any grandchildren. Our line of the family, I am very certain, Harriet, will end when our spinster daughters leave this life for the next.'

Her sister-in-law's insensitive comments stung Harriet's heart. She stood from the table and took a deep breath. She hurried towards the door and, without turning around, said, 'Will you see yourself out, Hannah? I've suddenly come over all funny and need to have a lie down.'

'Yes, of course. Do you need me to fetch anything?' she called after Harriet. 'Water? A doctor?'

'No.'

'Shall I take some tomatoes and courgettes off your hands?'

'Yes,' Harriet shouted back, rushing up the stairs into her bedroom and closing the door. She collapsed onto the bed, her thoughts black and thunderous, yet more determined than ever to pursue her search.

'Ma?' a quiet voice said, with an accompanying tap of the door.

The word lacked the rougher Scottish edge of John's voice; it had to belong to one of the boys.

'Ma?' he repeated.

Of course, it had to be one of the boys; John wouldn't be calling her *Ma* now, would he. It sounded as though it could be Fraser but, their being born only a year apart, she often confused the sound of his voice with that of his brother, Malcolm.

Then, like the collision of two steam engines in her mind, her thoughts reassembled with a thud, which made her wince and sit up sharply. There was, of course, only one person left in this world to whom the voice could belong: Fraser.

'Yes?' she answered, taking stock of herself. She was fully dressed, lying on top of her bed in broad daylight. Then she remembered why she had gone there in the first place: her sister-in-law's unsolicited visit.

'I thought you'd like to know the second post's been—there are a couple of official-looking letters you might wish to see.'

'I'll be down presently,' she replied.

She heard the floorboards outside her room groan, as Fraser crossed the landing to the staircase. Harriet took a few seconds of breathing deeply, then stood up and made her way downstairs. She gingerly stuck her head into the parlour, sighing with relief to find it mercifully devoid of her thoughtless sister-in-law.

She found Fraser reading the newspaper at the kitchen table, the second post stacked beside him.

'Did you put your Aunt Hannah up to coming here and prying?' Harriet asked, doing a good job of masking her annoyance, as she approached the table and picked up the post. The top envelope had been stamped with the words: *RED CROSS*.

Fraser looked up and frowned. 'Of course not, why would I?'

Harriet shrugged. 'Maybe the same reason you informed the Reverend Percival about my visit to Mrs Leonard?'

Fraser rolled his eyes. 'Ma, you might not like it but you're the talk of all the village.'

'Am I, indeed?' Harriet muttered with a wry smile, sliding John's bronze paper knife into the back of the envelope.

'Any number of people could have put Aunt Hannah up to snooping around. I'm past caring,' Fraser informed her.

Harriet withdrew a single sheet of paper, headed with the details of the International Red Cross: '*Dear Mrs McDougall,*' she read aloud. '*First of all, we would like to express our deepest sympathies with you and the unenviable situation in which you find yourself. As an organisation, we strive to do all we can to assist family members seeking answers about their loved ones' actions in the Great War. I have searched our extensive archives, which cover various institutions, including the Voluntary Aid Detachment, British Red Cross Convalescent Hospitals in the United Kingdom, the Red Cross Wounded and Missing Department and copies of records from the International Prisoner of War Agency in Geneva. I regret to inform you that these searches have not borne a successful result in providing details of your relative. Owing to the nature of the conflict, the International Red Cross does not consider the records in our care to be in any way complete. Therefore, an unsuccessful search of these archives does not guarantee that your relative did not come into contact with these agencies. On behalf of the International Red Cross, we wish you well in your endeavours...*' Harriet mirrored Fraser's look of disappointment.

'What about the other letter?' he asked.

Harriet briefly examined the grand swirling handwriting on the front and felt the quality of the envelope, before carefully running the paper knife through the top of it. She saw the address detail at the top of the embossed letter and emitted a light gasp. 'The Duchess of Westminster!'

'What does she have to say?'

'*Dear Mrs McDougall, Thank you for your letter. You are correct in your assertions about my wartime employment. Indeed, I was away from my usual post at the Number One British Red Cross Hospital at Le Touquet in early July 1917. If my memory of this feverish time serves me correctly, then I was based briefly at the Essex Farm Advanced Dressing Station. As I am sure you will appreciate, however, the vast number of men passing through my care often precludes me from individual recognition—*'

'Well, thanks very much,' Fraser interjected.

'I haven't finished,' Harriet responded lightly, her eyes having read ahead, '—*I would suggest that you arrange a convenient time to visit me, bringing along a picture, should you have one, of your son. Yours respectfully, Lady Grosvenor, Duchess of Westminster.* Well, I never did!'

'I don't suppose she'll remember him,' Fraser commented.

Harriet ran her fingers through her hair. 'I must send her a telegram at once,' she said, hurrying down the hallway. She began to form the wording of the telegram—brief and concise—in her head, as she marched to the parlour, when someone knocked on the door, startling her and making her lose the words intended for the telegram. 'Now what?' she mumbled under her breath, as she tugged open the door, half-expecting to see her sister-in-law back to check that she was feeling better.

'Sorry, Mrs McDougall. I had nowhere else to go.' It was Timothy Mogridge, wearing the same ratty clothes, his eyes red, swollen and moist. In one shaking hand he held a lit cigarette, in the other a small brown suitcase. A tear escaped down his cheek, and he hurriedly removed it with his shirt sleeve.

'Come in, dear Timothy. Come in.'

Chapter Six

24th **August 1919, London**

Grosvenor House on London's Park Lane was like nothing Harriet had ever seen before. It was palatial, a sprawling stone edifice of varying architectural style, but unquestionably truly magnificent. As she stood at the bottom of the wide stone steps, which led to the front door, she took a look down at herself, all at once unexpectedly feeling wholly inadequate. She had purchased a new black dress and black straw hat specifically for this visit, hoping that a chic, sophisticated appearance might somehow endear her to the Duchess.

'Mrs McDougall?' a voice enquired.

The front door was open—goodness only knew for how long it had been that way—and behind it stood a solemn-faced footman, dressed immaculately in black and white livery. He was young—in his early thirties, Harriet guessed—and a scarred hairless gully above his right ear silently articulated some past inexpressible horror.

'Good morning,' Harriet beamed. 'I've an appointment with the Duchess of Westminster,' she added, all at once unsure of exactly how she should address her upon coming face-to-face.

The footman smiled. 'Please, come inside. Lady Grosvenor is expecting you.'

As he closed the door behind her, with a heavy-sounding *clunk*, Harriet had to stifle a minor gasp at the interior of the hall. Dominated by an ornate mahogany staircase, which rose, separated into two, then curled around to a stone balustraded first floor, the hallway was monumentally vast. Light poured down from a domed glass roof, illuminating a range of exotic tapestries and oil portraits, all of which adorned the walls.

'This way, Mrs McDougall,' the footman said, striding across the polished wooden floors to an open door on the far side of the hallway. He stopped, stepped backwards and indicated that Harriet should go in.

She stepped inside what must have been the drawing room, with large bay windows overlooking Hyde Park. The Duchess rose from a chaise longue.

'Ah, good morning. Mrs McDougall, I presume?' the Duchess said.

Harriet was suddenly taken with the idea of curtseying but couldn't quite decide if it was indecorous or not. Instead, she smiled and offered her hand.

The Duchess was a tall slender woman with an impossibly thin waist. She was strikingly handsome and wore her dark hair in an American close-cropped-wave style, which Harriet had only previously seen in *Woman and Home* magazine. Marcel waves, they were called, if she remembered rightly. A little *too* modern for her own taste.

'Lovely to meet you, Mrs McDougall,' the Duchess said. 'Would you care for some tea?'

'That would be lovely, thank you,' Harriet replied.

'Tea for two,' she instructed the footman, who nodded, smartly scuttled from the room and closed the door. 'Come and sit down.' The Duchess pointed to a long dark-wood table with an elaborate floral centrepiece, around which were positioned half-a-dozen chairs, upholstered in a deep burgundy colour and embroidered with ornate white roses.

Harriet sat down, knitting her fingers together on the table, then quickly retracted them, fearing to display incorrect etiquette. She straightened herself in the chair and cleared her throat.

'Relax, Mrs McDougall, please,' the Duchess said pleasantly, having evidently noted that she was feeling on edge. 'Did you have a good journey to London from good old *Sussex by the sea?*'

'Yes, thank you. A very pleasant train ride,' Harriet answered. 'I don't suppose I shall ever tire of travelling through the High Weald—such beautiful countryside.'

'Indeed—a truly magical place. I appreciate simplicity and tranquillity of life all the more these days.'

'You must have witnessed some awful things,' Harriet commented.

'Yes, I saw the absolute *worst* of humanity out there,' she agreed. 'But, do you know what, Mrs McDougall... I consider my time out there as a privilege, for I also got to see the absolute *best* of humanity. Acts of bravery, acts of kindness, acts of heroism the likes of which one could never imagine.'

The skin on Harriet's arms prickled with this unexpected elucidation that somehow goodness could be found among the brutality.

'So, tell me about Malcolm,' the Duchess said gently.

Harriet cleared her throat and began to repeat the trite phrase, which had become so familiar to her: 'He joined the Royal West Kents in—'

'No, tell me about who he was *before* the war,' the Duchess expounded. 'Men in khaki is all I've known, Mrs McDougall. Regiments, battalions, ranks, service numbers—none of it about the man inside the uniform. One of my great lamentations—working out there, in the field—was that there was no time to get to know anybody. I should like to know who Malcom McDougall really was, if you don't mind.'

The question threw Harriet, and she took a few moments to extract the child, whom she had raised, from the man who had gone to war. 'He was a happy boy,' she started. 'Always adventurous and keen to explore. He went to Blackheath Proprietary School in Greenwich and he—like his two brothers who also attended there—did very well. Academia seemed to come naturally to him, and he was generally a well-behaved boy.' Harriet grinned at the returning warm memories. 'The only time—to my knowledge, at least—that he got into trouble at school was for conducting his own scientific experiments in his dorm. The last one—making white phosphorous by boiling his own urine in a test tube—had him suspended for two weeks...'

Harriet wondered if she had said too much, or if the reference to urine had been rather too vulgar, but the Duchess let out an unexpectedly raucous laugh, just as the footman returned carrying a silver tray. 'Boiling his own urine! What a lark!' she cried.

Harriet smiled, noting the footman's disconcerted expression, as he carefully conveyed the tea things from the tray to the table.

'Thank you, Simmons,' the Duchess said, pouring tea from a silver pot into the two cups.

'And he simply loved the natural world,' Harriet continued, sensing a genuine interest from the Duchess and enjoying sharing Malcolm with her in this way. 'He would spend *hours* upon hours in the woodlands surrounding our home, making detailed observations of flowers, insects and birds. He'd sketch, make notes, take cuttings, collect bird eggs... He was a true lover of life and the natural word.'

'He sounds a true delight. You must be very proud of all that he was.' The Duchess added milk to the two cups, then slid Harriet's across the table.

Harriet thanked her and nodded, finding it a refreshing change that someone should think to talk about Malcolm's successes *before* the war.

51

Most people—even close friends and family—would focus on the sacrifice, which he had made for his country, a vacuous statement devoid of any real meaning or, for that matter, truth.

'Did you bring a picture of Malcolm?' the Duchess asked. 'I cannot retain names for toffee...but I never forget a face.'

'Yes, I did,' Harriet replied, opening her bag and withdrawing a postcard. On the front was a photograph of Malcolm, taken in 1916 in his uniform, and on the back was written, *Dear Ma & Pa, something to remind you of what I look like! Love, Malcolm.* Harriet passed the postcard across the table.

The Duchess squinted and studied the image for some time without speaking, leaving Harriet unable to interpret clear meaning from her facial expressions. She supposed from the time that it was taking, that despite what the Duchess had said about not forgetting a face, she was indeed struggling to extract his image from those of the thousands of men, whom she must have encountered. Finally, she smiled and looked across to Harriet. 'Yes. I treated him, undoubtedly—a lovely boy and such a shame.'

'Really?'

'Oh, yes, without question,' the Duchess confirmed, giving an assertive nod of her head. She sipped her tea, then continued: 'He was a charming man, and I remember him being quite excited that he had seen some blue poppies—would that be right? *Blue?*'

Harriet's reply caught in her throat and she had difficulty answering. She nodded, taking a drop of tea.

The Duchess smiled, evidently pleased with her successful recollection.

'How was he?' Harriet managed to murmur.

'All things considered, he was well,' she replied. 'Do you know much about the Advanced Dressing Station at Essex Farm?'

'Nothing at all.'

'It was the terribly unattractive functional kind of building, which one might expect from a dressing station so close to the frontline, hastily dug from a bank beside the Ypres Canal: cold, dreary and windowless. But we did our best to make it comfortable for the men. There was an officers' mess, a latrine room, a kitchen, a room for convalesced soldiers ready for evacuation and then there were the two medical wards: one was for walk-in cases; the other was for stretcher cases brought in by field ambulance. Malcolm, along with two other engineers, was a stretcher case.'

'And what had happened? What was wrong with him, exactly?'

'They were all suffering from the effects of gas poisoning,' she answered.

Harriet nodded, slightly exasperated that people around her seemed so inclined to spare her the detail, which she so desperately craved. As horrible or as awful as the truth might be, she simply had to know it. 'Please, I want... I need to know everything. Don't hide any details from me.'

The Duchess nodded. 'I understand. I lost my boy, Edward, when he was five years old. I hadn't been there at the time and I had to know absolutely everything. One can't grieve fully and completely without the truth.'

'That's exactly how I feel,' Harriet agreed. 'Although people around me keep telling me to leave things well alone...as they are.'

'I shall tell you everything as I remember it. Malcolm and his two comrades were brought to us by ambulance. I knew as soon as I spotted the brassards on their arms—red, green and white for the gas units—what their ailments would likely be. They were all conscious but suffering considerably from the effects of the gas. Malcolm also had a nasty, but treatable gash on his upper arm. Their faces were jaundiced, and they were coughing constantly: an unpleasant hacking noise, which produced a foamy green froth.'

Harriet's determination to remain stoically impassive was crushed. The image, which the Duchess had just revealed, was foremost in Harriet's mind, displayed there as clearly as an authentic recent memory. She began to sob quietly.

'Oh, Mrs McDougall,' the Duchess intoned, standing up and moving around the table to place a comforting arm around her shoulders, an act of kindness that surprised Harriet and made her cry all the more.

Harriet dabbed at her eyes with her handkerchief, mortally embarrassed. 'I'm so sorry.'

'There's really no need to apologise. I should have been more sensitive.'

Harriet shook her head. 'No, I asked for the full truth and the full truth, however unpalatable, is what I would like.'

The Duchess returned to her seat and drank some more tea, waiting for Harriet to have regained her composure fully.

'Please, go on,' Harriet said.

'Are you sure?'

'Yes.'

'Very well. In the early days of gas attacks, chlorine was used. The effects were almost immediate and really quite ghastly. Then phosgene began to be deployed. Ten times more lethal than chlorine but the effects would take longer to become evident and, if such an appalling and incongruous thing can be said of it, it was kinder at the end. Malcolm and his two comrades simply slipped into an unconsciousness from which they did not wake.'

'Thank you for your honesty,' Harriet said quietly.

'The three men were buried, as was the general rule, that night in the cemetery attached to the Advanced Dressing Station. The *curé* read a burial service over the graves, each being marked by a simple wooden cross.'

Harriet sighed, taking strange consolation from the detail of Malcom's final hours.

The Duchess smiled. 'As I mentioned, the effects from the phosgene took some time, and so, once we had made him comfortable, he was able to converse with me. He was really quite enamoured by those blue poppies he had seen. He wanted to try and sketch them. He slept a great deal...' the Duchess looked upward, as though trying to coax more from her memory. 'Oh, and of course, he spoke of his only having been back at the front for a matter of days.'

'Really? Where had he been?' Harriet asked.

'Home on leave,' the Duchess answered with a smile and an accompanying look, which said that she clearly expected it to hold some resonance with Harriet.

'I beg your pardon?' Harriet said.

'Oh,' the Duchess said, her cheeks reddening sharply.

'I think you must be mistaken.'

'Yes, forgive me,' the Duchess stammered.

Harriet studied the Duchess carefully, noticing how she was struggling to regain her equanimity. She clearly *didn't* think that she was mistaken at all but was pacifying her. 'Tell me.'

'Look, I dealt with thousands of men during the war, in various states of consciousness and lucidity and—'

'Please,' Harriet interrupted.

The Duchess sighed, wriggling in her chair. 'I'm *fairly* confident that Malcolm said he'd been back to England on leave. I can't recall any additional facts from the conversation, except that he had been to Woolwich, and the reason I remember it is because he talked about his staying in a guesthouse not far from where one of my nurse-friends lived.'

'Woolwich?' Harriet blustered. 'So, Malcolm used his *one* yearly eight-day pass to go to Woolwich? Whatever for?'

The Duchess flushed again. 'I'm afraid that I really could not say. He might have told me at the time, but I honestly cannot bring it to mind. As I said, I might very well be wrong on this point…'

'It'll be those damnable gas laboratories,' Harriet seethed, her hands beginning to quiver. 'If only he'd come home… I'd have seen him…just before he died. It's just not right.'

'No, it isn't, Mrs McDougall. My experience found very little, if anything at all, that was right with the Great War.'

'Where was this guesthouse that he stayed in?' Harriet asked.

'I don't remember, except to say that it was not too far from the Royal Artillery barracks.'

'Right, thank you.'

'Try not to take it to heart, Mrs McDougall. There could be any number of reasons why your son was back in England and unable to visit you.'

'Yes,' Harriet agreed absent-mindedly, though not able to imagine a single one. 'Is there anything else that you can remember him saying?'

'I'm sorry, but I think that's all,' the Duchess apologised.

'Thank you very much for taking the time to see me,' Harriet said, drinking the last of her tea, and rising from her chair. 'It really is very good of you.'

'It's the very least that I could do, but I rather feel that I have only made matters worse,' the Duchess said with an enquiring grimace.

'Not at all; I appreciate your candour,' Harriet said, tucking Malcolm's photograph back into her bag. 'Good day to you,' Harriet said, extending her hand out towards the Duchess.

'Good day, Mrs McDougall, and the best of fortune with your quest.'

The half-an-hour walk back to Charing Cross was somewhat of a blur for Harriet. She was walking through Green Park, mulling over what the Duchess had told her, when a young man wearing a shabby and dirty khaki uniform stepped onto the path in front of her. His face was haggard, his eyes puffy and bloodshot and he was missing his left ear. He held his head to one side, like a curious dog and thrust forward a tin cup. 'Spare change, lady?'

Harriet was taken aback at the sight of him.

'Sorry, I didn't mean to scare you,' he stammered.

Harriet fumbled in her purse and handed the poor wretched man some of her loose change.

'God bless you, madam,' the man said, with a nod of his lop-sided head. He moved off the path again, out of her way and slumped down onto a pile of grubby blankets—his home, she presumed.

At the station, whilst she waited for the return train to Hastings, Harriet was approached by another former soldier. He sloped towards her, as though it were an effort to walk, his two hands forming a cup. His appearance was grotesque but at once almost farcical, as though he had just scrambled out of his own battlefield grave. His uniform, if such a filthy and bedraggled tunic and kilt could be described as such, belonged to the Seaforth Highlanders. His unpleasant odour reached her before he did, and Harriet could see through his dark beard that he had several teeth missing.

'Can you spare a few pennies?' the man slurred in a heavy Scottish accent.

Harriet gazed into his rheumy eyes, wondering how life had taken him from fighting for his country to begging in Charing Cross train station. And why was he continuing to wear the uniform of his regiment, nine months after the Armistice? Surely, he'd had opportunity to change his clothes since then? Or was he perhaps wearing the uniform as a reminder to the public of his sacrifice?

'Thanks, anyway,' he mumbled, turning and wandering off in the direction in which he had just come.

'Wait!' Harriet called.

The man stopped and turned to face her.

'What's your name?' she asked.

'Danny.'

'How old are you, Danny?' Harriet questioned.

'Twenty-eight,' he replied.

His answer shocked Harriet. 'Where are your family, Danny?'

'What's with all the bloody questions? It don't matter me name, me age or me family. None of it matters, lady; not to me and certainly no' to you.'

'But it does,' Harriet countered. 'Someone out there is missing you terribly and wishes you to come home.'

The man laughed loudly.

'Here,' Harriet said, handing him the last of her change. 'People care.'

'Aye, sure they do,' he said, waving a dismissive hand. He held up the money. 'Thank you.'

'I care,' Harriet insisted.

'You care to a point, lady, aye, but you'll be getting on your train back to your nice wee home. In a few days, you'll nay remember me.' The man pointed behind Harriet. 'You'd best be going.'

She hated that he was so completely right. She had to catch that train home and she would, in time, forget all about him. But what could she do? As Fraser had been so very keen on pointing out, she could hardly invite every displaced soldier to live with her at Linton House.

Harriet sighed, as she watched him lumber away towards a smart-suited gentleman, who shooed him away like a street dog.

'Golly,' Harriet said to herself, as she walked up the front path. Fraser had evidently been hard at work in the front garden. All the rose beds had been weeded and the edges of the lawns trimmed neatly. She smiled, pleased at how it made the garden look, but more pleased that Fraser had taken the initiative to do something to keep himself occupied. Having seen the raft of poor dispossessed men today, she feared what might become of him were he to lapse into apathy.

Inside the cool house, she sat down on the monk's bench in the hallway and removed her shoes with a groan of satisfaction at the feeling. Then, she noticed the smell. Not unpleasant, as such, but certainly strange. She padded along the hallway, the odour increasing as she neared the kitchen.

'Welcome home,' Timothy greeted. He was standing at the kitchen sink, peeling potatoes and wearing, as she had told him to do, one of John's old outfits, topped by an apron of hers.

'Thank you,' Harriet said uncertainly. 'What's going on?'

'I'm cooking dinner,' Timothy answered. 'Your niece—Mercy is it?—she called around with a couple of rabbits. Something about a swap for courgettes or something similar. One's hanging in the larder, the other I took the liberty of skinning and preparing for our dinner: rabbit pie.'

'Oh, right.'

'Sorry, I hope I haven't overstepped a line,' Timothy said.

'Gosh, no. Not at all,' Harriet replied, sitting at the kitchen table. 'It's just...a first, is all.'

'What's a first?'

'Someone in this house cooking me dinner,' she laughed.

'Oh!' he said. 'Really?'

'Yes, really.'

'And did you have a productive day?' he asked.

That was a question Harriet had mulled over for much of the train journey home. 'Yes, I suppose so. The Duchess of Westminster was very kind. She remembered Malcolm perfectly. A curious thing, though: she said she was almost completely certain that Malcolm used his one yearly eight-day pass to return to Woolwich—to those wretched gas labs.'

Timothy stopped peeling and stared at her. 'That is odd. If they'd wanted him back at the labs, then he wouldn't have needed to use his pass for that.'

Harriet shrugged. 'Only one way to find out, I suppose: a trip to Woolwich. Do you know where Fraser is?'

'No, haven't seen him all day. He set off out not long after you.'

'Oh. Did he say where he was going?'

'No, I just heard the front door go, and that was that.'

'So, it was you who did the front garden, then?'

'Yes. Again, I hope I haven't overstepped a line.'

'No,' Harriet answered. 'Thank you.' She had been about to protest at the amount of work, which he was doing, but then she realised the sense of purpose that it must have given him, and, for the first time, he appeared to be something close to happy.

A light knocking came from the front door, and Harriet went to answer it.

She inwardly sighed upon seeing her sister-in-law, Hannah standing there. 'I just wanted to check that you got the rabbits,' Hannah said, barely audibly and straining her neck to look over Harriet's shoulder.

'Yes, thank you very much.'

'Only, Mercy said that there was a *man* here...'

'That's right, yes,' Harriet said.

'A friend of Fraser's, is it?' Hannah pushed.

'That's right, yes,' Harriet agreed, thinking Hannah undeserving of a wider explanation and enjoying the slow drip-feeding of information.

'Oh. Mercy seemed to think that he was *living* here.'

'Yes, he is.'

'Right,' Hannah said, clearly puzzled.

A few seconds passed where neither woman spoke.

'Well, I'd better get on, then,' Harriet said finally, moving to close the front door.

Hannah raised her index finger and lowered her voice even further to the point that Harriet could barely hear her: 'There was one other thing.' Slowly and deliberately, Hannah peered over her shoulders. 'Young Fraser was seen this morning, getting on a coach.'

Now it was Harriet's turn to look perplexed. 'And?'

'And...' Hannah whispered, '...and he was with *you-know-who.*'

Harriet shook her head. *She* didn't *know who.*

Hannah mouthed, with great exaggeration, two words: 'Louise Ditch.'

Harriet didn't wish to show her dismay at this news. 'Oh, that, yes,' she said loudly, as though the whole village could be privy to this news, should they wish to eavesdrop. 'Nothing untoward going on there.' She found herself emitting a very odd high-pitched laughter, with which she surprised herself as much as it did Hannah.

Hannah nodded doubtfully. 'Well, cheerio for now.'

'Goodbye,' Harriet said, closing the front door. She exhaled noisily and closed her eyes for a moment. What on earth was Fraser thinking? Malcolm, or even Edward, come to that, would never have done such—

No, she couldn't think like that. The boys were all different, none of them perfect.

Harriet and Timothy were sitting together in the garden, just beginning to eat their dinner, when Fraser returned home.

'That looks delicious,' Fraser commented, when he saw the pie.

'*Timothy* made it,' Harriet said pointedly.

'Oh,' Fraser replied.

'Yours is being kept warm in the oven,' Timothy added.

Fraser began to head back into the house, and Harriet called after him: 'Only, we didn't know how long you'd be cavorting with Miss Ditch...'

Fraser said nothing, as he continued into the house.

'That was a little churlish,' Harriet remarked to herself.

'I wasn't *cavorting*,' Fraser said upon his return to the table. 'Louise is a friend, one of a very select few of my friends, who are actually still living. Or, because of her gender, am I to be denied her companionship, too?'

'Of course not,' Harriet replied. 'It's just—'

'*What will people say?*' Fraser interrupted.

'Just be careful, is all,' Harriet said, setting down her cutlery. 'Life is changing, Fraser—goodness me, I can *vote* now—but it's changing so very slowly. We live in a small village within a society where a man's friendship with a woman engaged elsewhere is viewed at *best* with distaste and disparagement.'

'I don't much care,' Fraser said. 'I'm thirty years old. I will see whomsoever I please. Does it give you a distaste?' He stared at her, unblinkingly, waiting.

She herself had just said it: life was changing. The prevailing Victorian attitudes were gradually receding, making way for goodness only knew what new norms of morality. Five years ago, she would have been mortified beyond belief and would have taken firm action to prevent his ever seeing Louise Ditch again. Now…now, like so many other areas of her life, she just didn't know any more. 'Just be careful, Fraser,' she eventually said.

Fraser turned his attention back to his food, and the heated moment passed, allowing the mood to simmer back down to quietness.

A minute or so later, Harriet said brightly, 'I need to book a trip for us.'

Fraser groaned. 'Where to, now?'

'Woolwich,' she replied, then proceeded to tell him all that she had learned from the Duchess of Westminster.

Chapter Seven

31st August 1919, Woolwich, London

The day was miserable. Heavy rain had greeted Harriet and Fraser, as they had left Linton House and had continued to plague their entire journey to London. They arrived at Woolwich Library with their sodden clothing stuck uncomfortably to their skin.

In the library vestibule, Harriet paused a moment to shake off as much as she could of the water from her black coat. 'I feel like the wreck of the Hesperus,' she complained, turning to face Fraser, who was standing beside her, clutching a small suitcase in each hand. They had travelled to London by train, then taken a taxi directly to Woolwich Library, having absolutely no idea where the day was going to take them, or indeed, where they would be sleeping that night.

'You look like it, too,' he replied.

'Thank you, Fraser,' she said, striding into the overly warm library. 'Do come along.'

Harriet spotted the sign for the lending desk and called to the elderly gentleman standing behind it: 'Reference section, please.'

'First floor,' he barked back, frowning at the puddle of water pooling around hers and Fraser's feet.

'Much obliged,' Harriet said with a nod of her head, aware that she was attracting attention due to the curls of steam now rising from her clothing, as though she were on the verge of combusting.

On the first floor they were confronted by wall-to-wall shelving and several triangular islands of wooden bookstands.

'You look over there,' Harriet directed, pointing at the back wall, 'and I'll look at these.'

Fraser strutted off to the back of the room, while Harriet cast her eyes over the nearest bookstand. 'Local history, local history, local history,' she muttered, peering around each of its three sides. 'Next.' She marched purposefully to the following stand and checked its contents. 'War—well that's the *single* last thing I would wish to read about...'

'Can I help you, madam?' a voice said from beside her.

A young prim lady, with neat curled hair and a pleasant face, was standing beside Harriet, holding a stack of books.

'Ah, yes, thank you. I'm looking for something that will give me a list of guesthouses near to the Royal Artillery barracks in 1917,' Harriet said with a smile.

'That's very specific,' the lady commented with a light chortle. 'Let's see what we have. Follow me.' She led Harriet to one of the bookshelves, close to those where Fraser was seemingly taking an age to check a single shelf. 'Right, here we are—*Kelly's Directories.*'

In front of the lady was a run of fat red tomes, dating back to the last century. She ran her index finger over the dates etched on the spine in gold lettering. 'Here,' she said, extracting it with the care and precision expected of a librarian, before placing it delicately into Harriet's hands.

'Thank you so much,' Harriet said.

Fraser wandered over to Harriet, making no attempt at haste, while she flicked open the book and began quickly thumbing her way through.

'Guesthouses!' Harriet declared, thrusting her index finger at the page. 'Go and ask that nice young lady if she's got a map of Woolwich. Quick, before she disappears...'

Fraser ambled off on the trail of the young librarian. Harriet let out a muted laugh at the sight of her son, still copious amounts of steam rising from him and trailing a dwindling puddle, as he walked with the two suitcases in hand. She watched, as he reached the librarian and smiled courteously, properly removing his bowler hat to speak. The lady reciprocated his smile, then led him to one of the bookstands out of Harriet's line of sight.

Harriet waited impatiently. After a few moments, he returned, carrying a large map of the area.

'Let's go to that table over there,' Harriet suggested, noticing a cluster of empty desks.

Fraser opened the map on the desk, then began to scan it for the Royal Artillery barracks. 'There!' he said, prodding a finger forwards. 'We're looking for anything close to Repository Road...'

Harriet began to read through the twenty-three guesthouses listed in the directory, with Fraser checking off each one as she read. In the end, they had noted down six potential locations, all of which fell within a half-mile radius of the barracks.

'Well, that wasn't very conclusive,' Fraser complained. 'Now what? I am really going to need a nice hot bath and a decent hearty meal, later.'

Harriet tapped the piece of paper on which she had just written the six addresses: 'Well, with a spot of luck, we'll be able to get rooms in whichever one it was that Malcolm stayed in when he came here. That way, we'll get a roof over our heads and some information about what exactly he was doing here.'

'What if he stayed in some God-awful dive?' Fraser asked disdainfully.

'That's enough of that language, thank you very much,' Harriet snapped. 'Let's go: the sooner we get moving, the sooner we can settle in somewhere for the evening.'

'Number eighteen,' Harriet said, hastily re-pocketing the now soaked piece of paper with the six addresses. This guesthouse, like most properties in the surrounding streets, was a modest two-storey brick affair.

'Doesn't look too awful,' Fraser commented, as Harriet knocked on the door.

'Let's hope it's this one, then' she murmured, as the rain continued to heave down. She was now wetter and colder than she had believed it was possible to be; even her under-garments were now entirely saturated. Given the atrocious conditions, which Fraser must have endured, though, she thought better of it than to complain to him.

The door was pulled open with a suddenness, which startled her.

'Yes?' said a small woman in a dirty apron. She was in her forties, had olive skin, long black hair and incongruous piercing blue eyes.

Harriet smiled. 'Terribly sorry to trouble you—'

The woman noticed the suitcases in Fraser's hand and instantly smiled, as she opened the door. 'Come, come, come!' she said, practically singing.

'Thank you,' Harriet said, sighing with gratitude at even a moment's respite in from the rain.

'Two rooms, yes?' the lady asked. 'How many nights?'

'Well,' Harriet began, unsure of the best way to explain that in fact they would not be staying at all, if Malcolm, too, had not stayed there two years previously.

'We're looking for where my brother stayed,' Fraser stepped in. 'He stayed somewhere nearby in June 1917. Could it have been here? Do you keep a register, or something similar?'

The woman looked between them, evidently very confused. 'So, you don't want rooms, no?'

'Well, it all rather depends on whether my son stayed here, or not,' Harriet said. 'It's all rather complex. If he stayed here, then yes, we will, too.'

The landlady sniffed hard, an action that signified a distinct shift for the worse in her demeanour. 'Wait here.' She walked off, rocking from side to side on oscillating, bulbous hips.

'I'm not sure that I do want to stay here, now,' Fraser whispered behind her.

'Sshh.'

The woman re-appeared with a scowl, holding a thin ledger. 'Name?'

'Malcolm McDougall,' Harriet said, enunciating the word very carefully. 'He was a soldier with the Royal West Kents and worked in the gas labs in—'

'Nope,' the woman said, snapping the book shut definitively, and gesturing that they should now leave the house.

'Thank you very much for looking,' Harriet managed to say, before the woman had gained on her and, by her ample proximity, forced her to turn and bump into Fraser's back. 'Come on, move.'

The door slammed smartly shut behind them.

'That went well,' Fraser said, placing his long-inadequate bowler hat back on his head.

A heavy wind was now whipping up the rain, driving it into their faces.

Harriet ignored his sarcasm and quickly pulled out the piece of paper with the blurred addresses. 'The next one is just at the end of this road,' she remembered, just as the wind caught the sodden paper and tore it into two. She hurriedly stuffed the two pieces into her raffia bag and led the way along the deserted street.

In under a minute, they were standing in the doorway of a house similar in design to the last one. They read a handmade sign written on a piece of card in the front window: *Rooms to rent. Short / long term stays.* Harriet rapped with the iron knocker twice and waited.

A lady of a similar age to Fraser, with a small child propped on her hip, opened the door and smiled. 'Rooms?' she deduced, standing back to admit them inside.

'Before we come in,' Harriet said, having learned her lesson, 'I must quickly explain: my son, Malcolm was killed in the war and, before he died, he came to stay at a guesthouse in Woolwich, and we— that is, my son, Fraser and I—are trying to find in which guesthouse it was he stayed. When we find it, we will stay there. Do you have anything that might say whether or not he came here in June 1917?'

'Come in and I'll have a look for you,' she said pleasantly.

Harriet thanked her and entered the house, followed by Fraser.

'This is Kate,' the woman said, suddenly handing Harriet the toddler in her arms.

'Oh, goodness me—it's been a while since I've held one of these!' Harriet said with a laugh.

The girl seemed quite used to being passed from pillar to post and simply stared unblinking at Harriet. She didn't even seem to care that Harriet was soaked to the skin. The woman, whose house it was, went upstairs and Harriet could hear her talking to herself.

'Aren't you a marvellous little thing?' Harriet said to the girl, rubbing the end of her nose. 'Isn't she, Fraser?'

'Hmm?' Fraser said, apparently unaware that she was holding a child.

Harriet remembered, then, what her sister-in-law, Hannah had said about not having grandchildren. The possibility was still there for her, she supposed, but Fraser had never shown any inkling of wanting children before. Maybe her family line, too, was one destined to be extinguished within a generation; an idea, which saddened her so very much.

'June 1917?' the woman clarified, appearing on the stairs before them. She shook her head. 'No, I had three long-terms here—Belgian women—and that was it for June. Sorry.'

'Oh…never mind. Thank you so much for looking,' Harriet said. 'Onwards and upwards.'

The woman regained her daughter from Harriet and said, 'I lost my husband in the war, too. Good luck finding what you're looking for.'

Harriet smiled sympathetically, stroked the little father-less girl's cheek, said thank you again and goodbye.

Once again, they found themselves standing on the pavement in the street, as a thick curtain of rain thrashed around them.

Harriet removed the two pieces of torn paper, managed a quick glance at them just before a violent gust of wind ripped them clean from her hands, instantly whirling them high into the air.

She and Fraser silently watched the two pieces of paper rise, fall and dance at the whim of the wind, neither one making any attempt to go chasing after them.

With the paper taken from sight, Fraser turned to her, his wet face expressionless.

Harriet held up the two torn corners of paper still in her hand, entirely blank. 'I saw the road of the next one but not the number in time. It was the one on Love Lane—do you recall what it was?'

Fraser shook his head glumly.

'Come on, then. Best foot forward!' Harriet chimed, summoning the last of her strength and positivity for both of them, as they headed up the sodden street to goodness only knew where.

They reached Love Lane: an assortment of housing types, ranging from poor tenements to more substantial detached homes.

'You take this side of the street,' Harriet instructed, 'and I'll take the other.'

Fraser looked abjectly miserable. 'What if there's no sign up? Or what if they've since stopped renting rooms? What if—'

'Then we find the first place we can to spend the night and return to the library in the morning to write out a fresh list further afield,' Harriet answered.

'This is just...' his sentence trailed off, as he turned and began to trudge the length of the street, which fortunately was not a long one. Harriet crossed over and started to check each and every house for a sign that it was now, or had ever been, a guesthouse.

As she walked, she contemplated again the question, which had so troubled her since speaking with the Duchess of Westminster: why had Malcolm come here and said nothing to her? Goodness, even if his work at the gas laboratories had been so demanding to the extent that he couldn't have left Woolwich, then she would have travelled here to see him without a second thought. Now that he was gone, she couldn't bear to think of him in an ill light, and this internal conflict left her with a horrid, sick, tugging feeling in her stomach.

She continued to walk, but her pace had fallen to that of some doddery woman twenty years her senior and she could feel the last dregs of her resolve draining away.

'Ma!' Fraser called to her from across the street. He had stopped in front of a decent-looking house, set back slightly from the street behind a low stone wall and black metal gates. 'Forge House?'

Forge House, Love Lane. That was it! 'Yes, that's the one! Do they have rooms to rent?' she shouted.

'Yes,' he replied.

In that moment, her priorities shifted. The search for the guesthouse, in which Malcolm had stayed, could wait until tomorrow. For now, they would call it a day and get some rest. If good fortune were on their side, there would be hot food, a warm bath and a comfortable bed for the night, and they would be restored for another attempt tomorrow.

Harriet trotted across the street to the opposite pavement to meet him. Fraser had opened the gates, and together they rushed towards the front door, as though they were competing for the finish line of a marathon. The house was fairly modern in design and, despite the historic-sounding name, looked as though it had only been built ten or so years ago.

Fraser hammered hard on the door, making Harriet flinch and wince with embarrassment.

A middle-aged lady with brittle grey hair appeared at the door, wiping her hands on her floral apron. 'Goodness gracious me—get inside!' she said.

'Do you have two rooms, please?' Harriet said, unable to find the energy with which to explain their convoluted story and current predicament.

The lady shook her head and grimaced. 'No. Terribly sorry, but I don't.'

'Oh, my goodness!' Harriet cried, quite melodramatically.

'But the sign outside...?' Fraser pressed.

'I've got *one* room. Two single beds, four and six a night with breakfast.' The lady held her hands open and palms-up, implying that the decision was over to them.

Harriet and Fraser looked at each other, saying nothing. Sharing a room with her snorer son was so very far from ideal, but right now she would happily have shared a room with the Kaiser himself.

They nodded with a simultaneous reluctance.

The lady clasped her hands together. 'Marvellous. Let me take your coats.'

Harriet and Fraser handed her their overcoats with great relief.

'Follow me,' she said, leading them to a room on the first floor, then stepping back to allow them inside. 'Will you be wanting a dinner? I'm making beef and kidney pie, greens and crumbed potatoes.'

'That would be so perfect,' Harriet said. 'Heaven, actually.'

'Yes, please,' Fraser agreed. 'And is there any chance of a hot bath?'

The woman laughed. 'What, now?'

Fraser nodded tentatively, sensing that there was something amiss.

'A strapping lad like you. Yes, you're most welcome to a bath... But I should probably warn you, though, that the bath is in the kitchen, where I'll be doing the cooking.' She laughed again, and Fraser flushed bright red, mumbling something about waiting until later after all.

The lady disappeared off down the stairs, leaving them both standing in the room, dripping wet.

Harriet looked around the pokey space. There were two beds with emerald bedspreads, with one bedside table and a narrow walk-way between them. Beside one of the beds was a thin wardrobe and a sash window, from which she could see nothing but great torrents of rain and grey skies. At that moment in time, it felt to her as though the window were mirroring her very soul.

'I'm going to go outside and use the WC,' Fraser informed her. 'So, why don't you get changed first, then me?'

Harriet nodded and, when he had left the room, slid the brass bolt across to the doorframe and began to peel off her soaked clothing. She stripped entirely naked, her clothes creating a big, wet pile at her feet. She popped the dual clasps on her suitcase and opened it up. From the selection of drab, black clothing, she chose a light dress and a thick cardigan.

Moments later came a knock at the door, startling her.

'Ma, are you decent?' Fraser called from the other side.

'No, not yet,' she answered, flustered.

When she was finished, she slid the bolt back and opened the door. 'Is it far?' she asked.

Fraser nodded. 'Bottom of the garden, I'm afraid. A bit gloomy in there, too. There's an umbrella leaning by the back door.'

'Wonderful,' Harriet muttered. 'I'll wait and go and speak to Mrs Whatever-her-name-is instead.'

She walked sluggishly downstairs, following the scent of cooking into the kitchen at the rear of the house.

Mrs Whatever-her-name-is smiled, as she entered. She was standing at the sink, scrubbing carrots. 'Everything in order?' she asked.

'Yes, thank you, Mrs...?' Harriet prompted.

'Mrs Lawrence,' she said, offering her her wrist to shake.

'Mrs McDougall,' Harriet said. 'May I sit down?'

'By all means—make yourself comfortable. I'll put you in the guest register after dinner, if that's ok? I've got a fresh pot of tea brewing, just now. You look like you're in dire need, Mrs McDougall.'

68

'Oh, I really am.' Harriet sat at the kitchen table and emitted a small sigh.

'So, tell me, Mrs McDougall, what brings you and your fellow to my door in these wretched conditions?'

Harriet baulked at the use of the word, 'fellow'. Did she think that she and Fraser were here as a couple? Good heavens! And she hadn't even asked if they were married! Harriet quickly explained their relationship and the reason for their stay in Woolwich. 'I don't suppose you would have kept your guest records from back in June 1917?'

'No need for the register,' Mrs Lawrence replied. 'I remember Malcolm, alright. A lovely lad, he was. I'm so, so sorry to hear that he didn't make it through the war.'

'Do you really remember him?' Harriet stammered, quite taken aback.

'Yes. He was here a good few days—possibly even a week,' Mrs Lawrence said. 'Funny thing, you know, he stayed in the room you and your other boy are in now. How about that, then, eh?'

Harriet saw Malcolm, as clear as day, lying in one of the beds—the one by the window, which Fraser had chosen, she thought—after a long day or night mixing gasses or whatever it was, which he did at the laboratories.

'I suppose you didn't see much of him, though?' Harriet said.

Mrs Lawrence laughed. 'No, not much. But you know what these youngsters are like when they're in love.'

'Pardon me?' Harriet broke in. 'In…love? In love with whom?'

'Oh. I presumed you knew…' Mrs Lawrence said. She stopped scrubbing the carrots, hands poised in mid-air over the sink, and turned to look at Harriet. 'A girl called Lina.'

'Lina?' Harriet parroted. She searched her mind for any mention of the name, but nothing was forthcoming. 'Lina what?'

'Lina Peeters.'

'She sounds foreign,' Harriet replied uncertainly.

'Belgian,' Mrs Lawrence confirmed.

Harriet sighed. Nothing was making any sense to her. 'Please, would you mind awfully just starting at the beginning?'

'Let me make this tea, and I'll come over and tell you everything.'

Harriet grudgingly agreed and had to wait several interminable minutes for Mrs Lawrence to dither around the kitchen, preparing the two cups of tea. Finally, she sat down opposite Harriet and passed her a cup.

'There you go. That'll warm you through,' Mrs Lawrence said. 'Right, now… Lina. One day she knocked on my door, asking if I had any rooms for her manfriend, who would be coming over from the trenches on leave. I told her I did and, sure enough, a week or two later, he showed up on my doorstep with her, as arranged.' Mrs Lawrence sipped her tea, then continued. 'They spent most of the time together and—'

'But surely he was busy working at the gas laboratories?' Harriet interrupted, entirely confused.

Mrs Lawrence curled her lower lip, as though the idea were preposterous. 'No. I just said: he was here on leave. They went to the music hall, the theatre, the park, the swimming baths, but no mention of any laboratories, no.'

'It sounds like he was jolly well on holiday!' Harriet cut in.

'Yeah, I suppose he sort of was.'

'Good heavens. And what was *she* doing here, for goodness' sake?' Harriet asked.

'Like the rest of the Belgian refugees… Making ends meet.'

Harriet had a vague recollection from the start of the war of thousands of Belgian refugees settling in England, mainly in London, but she herself had never encountered any. At least, not that she knew. There certainly weren't any refugees in Sedlescombe. She drank some tea, giving her brain a moment to catch up with this latest revelation. It was even worse to know that he'd come here on leave and had not bothered to communicate with her, much less see her. There really was no excuse at all.

'And where is this *Lina Peeters*, now?' Harriet asked.

From her facial expressions, Mrs Lawrence didn't seem to know the answer. 'I presume she did what the rest of them did and went back home when the war was over. Our government welcomed them here with open arms, even grateful for the extra help they gave with most of the men being away and that, but when the end of the war came, and the men returned, they weren't so keen to have them staying and really did all they could to get shot of them.'

'Could she still be living here, in Woolwich, Mrs Lawrence?' Harriet asked. 'It's really most important that I speak with her.'

'I couldn't say. I'm fairly certain she lived among a little community of refugees all around the Woolwich New Road area. If you went there, I'm sure someone would be able to tell you one way or another.'

'Right,' Harriet said, instantly determining and then, just as quickly, dismissing the vague notion of going there and making enquiries right at that very moment.

'That feels much better,' Fraser announced, entering the room in clean, dry trousers and a shirt. He sat down beside Harriet. 'Have you asked about Malcolm?'

Harriet raised her eyebrows. 'Oh, yes. He came to Woolwich for a lovely holiday, by all accounts.'

Fraser frowned. Harriet repeated what she had learned, and across the room Mrs Lawrence quietly made another cup of tea for her guests.

That night, Harriet was sitting up in bed in her silk camisole, rubbing Vaseline into her cheeks. Fraser was in the next bed, already sound asleep and thankfully not snoring. As seemed normal with him since his return, he could fall asleep within moments of getting his head down.

She slowly pulled all the pins from her hair, then carefully fed it into a hairnet. She looked around her, still unable to believe that Malcolm had stayed in this very room just a month before he had died. Such a curious and upsetting state of affairs, she thought.

Now that she was here in the quiet darkness, she hoped that Malcolm had slept in the bed, which Fraser now occupied; there was something very different between falling asleep on his bed at home and willingly climbing into one in a strange place, and in which he had slept just weeks before he had died.

Harriet took a long breath in and laid her head down on the pillow, then reached over to the lamp and fumbled to switch off the light.

The following day could well have been the following month for the complete change of weather. The heavy, grey clouds had absconded overnight, leaving a perfectly clear, blue sky in their wake. The sun, too, was making a good effort to dry the rain-soaked streets. Harriet, with Fraser in her shadow, walked down the stairs to the kitchen, with a positive spring in her step.

'Good morning,' Mrs Lawrence said, taking a glance at the wall-clock. 'Well, I say morning, but you're not far off afternoon.'

Harriet half-smiled, embarrassed at the late hour at which they had woken. Although, when Harriet herself checked the clock and found that it was just gone half-past-ten, she thought Mrs Lawrence to be exaggerating somewhat. Still, it was far, far later than her usual wake-up time at home.

'You obviously needed the sleep,' Mrs Lawrence added warmly. 'I've got hot cocoa, boiled eggs and bacon for breakfast. Take a seat and I'll bring it right over.'

Harriet and Fraser sat either side of the table.

'I wonder what our resident vagrant is getting up to at home…' Fraser mused provocatively, one eyebrow arched.

'Mowing the grass, weeding the garden, fixing the fences and undertaking general repairs I shouldn't wonder,' Harriet replied pointedly.

'Give the man a medal,' Fraser responded.

'Give the man a chance.'

'Here we go, two mugs of cocoa,' Mrs Lawrence said, presenting them with their drinks. 'The food will be ready any moment.' Mrs Lawrence returned to the stove, from where the enticing smell of fried bacon began to waft around the room.

'What are your plans today, then?' Mrs Lawrence asked.

'Going door-to-door along the Woolwich New Road until we find Lina Peeters, or at least someone who knows where she is,' Harriet replied.

Despite all that Harriet had explained about their quest, Mrs Lawrence seemed surprised to hear this. 'And what will you do, exactly, if you find her?'

'Torture her with questions,' Fraser answered.

Mrs Lawrence sniggered, which Harriet didn't find particularly helpful.

'Talk to her,' Harriet corrected. 'I just want to understand what happened in those last weeks of his life and to know if he was happy…'

'Oh, he was certainly happy when he was around Lina,' Mrs Lawrence said. 'Walked around with a permanent smile on his face, he did. To look at him, you wouldn't think that a few days before he'd been in the trenches on the Western Front.'

'And a few days later he was dead,' Harriet added sorrowfully, instantly regretting it. As she feared it might, this last utterance made things awkward and brought their conversation to silence.

Mrs Lawrence brought two plates to the table: each contained two slices of well-cooked bacon, a piece of toast and a boiled egg. 'I'll leave you to it,' she said, beating a hasty retreat from the kitchen.

'Well that was subtle of you,' Fraser whispered, leaning in across the table.

'Oh, just be quiet and eat your breakfast. We've got another long day ahead of us.'

'Joy.'

The Woolwich New Road looked like any other in London. From the description, which Mrs Lawrence had given, that the Belgians had created their own *sub-community*, Harriet had been expecting something different. What that was, precisely, she now couldn't say. Perhaps people wearing noticeably different clothing, or the houses dressed in a different manner. But it was in every way ordinary. It was a busy road with several horses and carts vying with impatient automobiles, as was slowly becoming the norm in the cities and larger towns nowadays. A motorbus, heaving with passengers rattled noisily past. People were going about their business, just as they were on every other street in the area. A long run of shops, with their canopies extending out over the pavements, saw a steady flow of customers coming and going.

'Ma, we're not really going to knock on every door in the street, are we?' Fraser groused.

Harriet didn't know what they were going to do, actually. She watched the passing traffic and thought for a moment. If someone arrived in Sedlescombe looking for her, where would they start? The answer was suddenly obvious. 'Follow me!' Harriet directed, setting off with great strides.

They walked a short distance along the road, then waited for a suitable gap in the motor traffic, before hurrying across to the other side.

'Oh, I see,' Fraser said, looking up and seeing the building in front of them.

It was a grand stone edifice with the acronym, 'G.P.O.' carved in large letters on a long plinth, which divided the ground floor from the two upper floors. If anyone knew where Lina lived, it would be someone working at the General Post Office.

Harriet bound up the steps and into the building, entering a large room with a high, ornate ceiling. A long wooden counter-top ran almost the entire length of the rooms and was divided into small kiosks, at which stood half-a-dozen men wearing suits and ties.

'You wait here,' she instructed Fraser.

'Gladly,' he replied.

Three of the assistants were available. Harriet made a quick assessment and chose a man young enough to have served in the war. She approached him with a wide smile. 'Good morning.'

'Morning. What can I do for you, madam?' he asked.

'Well,' Harriet said earnestly. 'My son, Malcolm, was tragically killed in the war—' she paused briefly to see if her words had struck a chord with the young man, which they did not seem to have done, '—and, just before his death he wanted me to give something to his friend in Woolwich. But, for the jolly life of me, I *cannot* find what I've done with her address.' She met his grey eyes, hoping that he might interject at some point to assist. When he didn't, she continued: 'Her name was Lina Peeters—a Belgian girl—and I know it was somewhere around here, possibly even this very road, where she lived.' A short titter, then another pause, but still nothing was forthcoming from the teller. 'So could you be a gem, my dear, and just jot down her address on a piece of paper for me, please?'

The young man shook his head. 'No.'

'Pardon me?'

'I said, no. Addresses are private, madam. I suggest you consult a residents' directory of the area.'

'Hmm. And, in your professional opinion, do you think it likely that *Belgian refugees* would be listed in such a residents' directory during *wartime?*' Harriet asked incredulously.

The man shook his head again. 'No.'

'Thank you for your time and understanding!' Harriet said, spinning on her heels and marching to Fraser with her head in the air. 'Useless place. Useless. That's the difference between villages and cities…' She paced past him and out of the building.

On the pavement outside, Harriet took a moment to consider her options. Then, she spotted what in Sedlescombe was the very heart of provincial gossip: the butcher's shop, *T. Thomas & Son. Purveyors of Home-Fed Meat.* 'There!'

'Ma, do you really think the *butcher* is going to have Lina's address?' Fraser quietly scoffed, as they padded around in sawdust, waiting in a small queue.

'No, but I'll bet my hat that he knows someone who does,' Harriet replied, running her eyes over the range of animal corpses suspended from hooks in the ceiling.

When she reached the front of the queue, Harriet wasted no time dithering about with the convoluted story or even with the much

74

simpler half-truth, which she had just stated at the G.P.O. 'I'm looking for a Belgian girl by the name of Lina Peeters and it is of the utmost importance that I speak with her,' she asserted.

The butcher—in a white hat and blood-stained, white coat—seemed to take her diatribe in his stride. 'Don't know that name, my love, I'm afraid, but if it's a particular *Belgian* you're after, try Miss Yavuz at number eight. She's got loads of houses in the area and used to rent them out to the Belgians before they all went back home. She'll know of her, if anyone does, I'm sure.'

'Thank you very much—most kind.'

'Any meat, while you're here? Glazed ox tongue on special offer this week, or how about some English hams—cooked and dressed?'

'Perhaps later,' Harriet lied with a wave, as she left the shop.

'Ma,' Fraser said, reaching for her arm and drawing her to a standstill. 'Where's this going to stop?'

Harriet looked into his eyes, instantly understanding his worry that they would endlessly be sent from one place to the next, procuring the tiniest scraps of information on Malcolm's final movements. It was a question, which she had considered herself, too. 'I just think, as his mother, that I will know when the time comes to stop.'

Fraser exhaled, dissatisfied with the answer.

Harriet smiled. 'Right now, though, we're going up to see this Miss Yavuz at number eight.'

'Fine,' he accepted. Then, as they walked towards the house, said, 'Yavuz. It doesn't sound terribly Belgian, does it?'

Harriet shrugged.

The house was a rather large and impressive Victorian building, set back from the bustle of the main road behind a long and well-tended garden. It was detached with a central front door and two adjoining pitched gables above. If Miss Yavuz was the owner, then she was clearly very well-off indeed.

They walked to the front door and Harriet hammered twice with the knocker, a fierce-looking, silver tiger-head. Behind the obscure glass, she saw movement approaching.

'Someone's coming,' Fraser said, needlessly.

The door opened and a toffee-skinned lady peered warily out, wearing an exotic headscarf and some kind of oriental wrap-around-style dress, the likes of which Harriet had never seen before.

'Good morning—so sorry to trouble you,' Harriet began, sensing a need for haste from the woman's attitude. 'My son, Malcolm, was killed in the war and, before he died, he became friendly with a young Belgian girl, who lived around here. I'm trying to track her down—her name was Lina, Lina Peeters and I understand you used to rent out your properties to them.'

The lady nodded, said nothing, but motioned for them to enter the house.

They entered a hallway, surprisingly bright considering the range of striking tapestries, rugs and oriental adornments covering almost every visible part of every wall.

'My goodness!' Harriet exclaimed, feeling as though she had just stepped into an Arabian courtyard house.

'Do you like it?' Miss Yavuz asked, evidently pleased by Harriet's reaction.

'I've never seen anything quite like it,' Harriet said tactfully, studying a stuffed tiger's head, proudly mounted on the wall beside her, baring its great white teeth in perpetuity.

'My father shot it in Bhutan,' Miss Yavuz explained.

Harriet was entirely confused. Here was a woman of middle-eastern appearance, wearing oriental clothing, surrounded by eastern décor, living in Woolwich and renting out homes to Belgians.

'It's certainly *exotic*,' Harriet exclaimed.

'So, you've come about one of the Belgians, yes?' Miss Yavuz asked.

'That's right, Lina Peeters.'

'I remember her, yes. She lived at number ninety-six, on this road.'

'Ninety-six,' Harriet repeated, tapping Fraser's chest, as she spoke.

'But she's gone now,' Miss Yavuz said with a laugh. 'One year ago, I had four houses, all of them filled with Belgians. Now, I have four houses with unemployed soldiers unable to pay the rent.' She rolled her eyes and sighed. 'But, such is life.'

'Do you know where Lina went?' Harriet asked.

'She, and the family she shared the room with, went back to Belgium very soon after war ended.'

'She shared her room with another family?' Harriet said.

'Oh, yes. The Van De Veldes—nice family. Lina lived with them in their room.'

Harriet was mortified at the idea of so many people squashed into one room. She could only imagine that it was the same for the entire house. 'Do you know which part of Belgium they went back to?'

Miss Yavuz thought for a moment. 'Ypres.'

'Are you certain about that?' Fraser pushed.

Miss Yavuz nodded vehemently. 'Very sure, yes. But I'm sorry, I don't have a specific part or address.'

'Can you tell me any more about this girl, Lina?'

'I didn't really have too much to do with her, other than to collect the rent. She worked as a charwoman, I think. She was very pretty, about his age—' she pointed at Fraser, '—and quiet. Spoke very good English by the end of the war, though.'

'When did she come here, exactly?' Fraser asked.

'Oh, right at the beginning; when they all came.'

'Did she want to go back to Belgium?'

'I don't think many of them did, to be honest. Go back to what? Their homes, businesses…all gone. They had lives here. They had their own schools, shops, churches, newspapers—even their own hospital. But, the government wanted to get rid of them. Business contracts were terminated, good hard-working men and women lost their jobs overnight, replaced with the torrent of soldiers returning from the war. Then the government offered free one-way tickets back to Belgium for a limited time only and most went. Now you'll be lucky to find ten percent of them left here. It's very sad,' Miss Yavuz said, shrugging her shoulders. 'They were nice people who paid their rents on time.'

The ending of the war had brought an end to the ceaseless deaths, but the repercussions and the profound sadness had not ended for so many. Harriet often had cause to wonder if there was a single person alive, who had not suffered in some way because of the war: she doubted it very much.

'Thank you, Miss Yavuz,' Harriet said. 'One final question, if I may: did Lina, or any of the other Belgians ever mention my boy, Malcolm McDougall?'

'I don't think so, no. I don't recognise that name; I'm very sorry.'

Harriet thanked her, took one last look around at the extravagant house, wishing she could spend more time examining all the wonderous artefacts, then they headed out into the sunshine.

'Well, I wasn't expecting that,' Fraser murmured, as they headed down the path to the main road.

'Neither was I,' Harriet concurred. 'Let's go and take a look at ninety-six… Just to have seen it.'

'Then what?' Fraser asked.

'Home, I suppose, to pack for our next trip…to Belgium,' Harriet answered, forestalling any likely protestations from her son by moving off swiftly.

Chapter Eight

Two large, brown trunk cases, strapped up and locked, waited by the front door of Linton House. Harriet entered the parlour and stood, with her hands on her hips, gazing around the room. Had she remembered to pack everything, which they would need? The walnut table, which had been covered in documents pertaining to the investigation for what felt to Harriet like a long time, was now empty and appeared strikingly odd with its current lack of purpose. The parlour, for the time being at least, had returned to its previous seldom-used incarnation. As she stood there, she thought of what Miss Yavuz had said, about all those poor Belgians' being crammed into one room or the soldiers returned from war, struggling just to pay the rent. And here she was, owning a large house with this room, used only on high days and holidays, *and* a completely empty bedroom. The thought, though, of packing up the boys' belongings was a step too far for her. Besides, what would she do with all their things? Throw them away? Give them away? Tuck them away in a cupboard or in the loft, never to be seen or touched again? As ideas, they were all equally horrific and unconscionable.

Now satisfied that she had indeed taken everything from the parlour, which they might need on their trip, Harriet walked along the hallway to the kitchen, where Timothy and Fraser were polishing off the final slices of her Victoria sponge with their usual unrestrained gusto.

'You're sure you've packed all the papers?' Fraser asked, his mouth full of cake.

'Fraser, close your mouth when you're eating,' Harriet admonished. She had overlooked a lot of these vulgar behaviours, which he had apparently learned from the war, but it was time to draw the line at the very worst of them.

Without commenting, Fraser finished his food. 'Mother, have you packed all the papers?'

She ignored the sarcastic undertones and replied: 'Yes, I have.' She had placed all the documents in her raffia bag, which she had also checked twice more since. She walked over to Timothy and placed her hand on his shoulder. 'Now, are you *sure* you don't want to come, too?

I'm certain it wouldn't be too late and we could use the extra help, I don't doubt.'

'I know but I'm very sure, thank you, Mrs McDougall,' Timothy answered. 'I'll never go back. I'd sooner visit—' he searched for a more fitting, slightly less awful alternative, '—hell, if I'm being completely honest.'

Harriet squirmed slightly from the bluntness of his comment. She glanced at Fraser, wondering whether he too might hold similar feelings and she might have corralled him into a trip, which he really didn't want to make. He hadn't really complained. Or had he, and she had ignored it? She looked at him, gazing into his cup of tea, in a world of his own. She wasn't even certain that he had heard what Timothy had just said.

'And you'll be alright here, by yourself?' she asked Timothy.

'Oh, yes. I thought I might go and get some paint from your brother and re-paint the fences at the back of house.'

'There's no need...really,' Harriet countered, taking another look at Fraser, hoping that he might have caught Timothy's offer and become more open to such jobs himself, but still he just gaped absentmindedly at his drink. 'If you wish to do it, Timothy, then please go ahead, but I beg you not to do it on my account. Really, it just isn't necessary.'

Timothy smiled. 'It keeps me out of trouble.'

'Have you heard anything from Nell, yet?' she asked of his estranged wife.

Timothy shook his head. 'I thought I might write her a letter.'

'What a good idea! There's plenty of paper and envelopes in the bureau—help yourself.'

'You're very kind, Mrs McDougall.'

'Nonsense,' she said, giving a dismissive wave of her hand. She left the room, wanting to check her bedroom one last time, when someone knocked on the front door. 'Oh, glory! Fraser, the taxi-cab's here already! He's early! Come on!' Harriet suddenly felt flustered and rushed, not quite ready to head out on their expedition. She tugged open the door, her mind leaping from one thing, which she still needed to do, to another. Then... 'Oh.'

'Well, that's a charming greeting,' Hannah said, expressing mock offence, which might have betrayed her true feelings slightly.

'Sorry, I was expecting it to be our taxi-cab,' Harriet explained, making no effort to invite her inside.

'So, it *is* true,' Hannah said, her eyes widening, taking in the readied luggage. 'You *are* going to the continent.'

'Perfectly true,' Harriet replied.

'How long are you going for?'

'As long as it takes, I suppose,' she answered with a wooden smile.

'As long as *what* takes, Harriet?' Hannah asked, thrusting her hands on her hips.

'My investigations,' she said enigmatically. 'I really must go now and make the final checks before we depart. Was there anything else, Hannah, dear? I'm awfully pressed…'

Hannah shook her head and Harriet began to close the door.

'Are you leaving *that man* here?' Hannah whispered, shoving her hand forward to prevent the door from closing.

'Timothy? Yes, absolutely. He'll be looking after things for me,' Harriet said. 'Good day to you.' She closed the door with an inaudible sigh. 'That woman…' she mouthed to herself through clenched jaws.

Fifteen minutes later—just enough time for Harriet and Fraser to finalise their preparations—a Charron taxi-landaulet arrived. It was dark blue with white striping and operated by a small-but-growing company in Battle. As Harriet and Fraser climbed onto the leather seats, the driver carefully strapped the two cases to the luggage rail. They drove out of the village more slowly than Harriet would have liked, receiving inquisitive stares, as they proceeded, being the only motor transport on the road. There were Mrs Honeysett and Mrs Selmes standing at the gate of River Cottage, watching on. Harriet knew from their knowing expressions that they were fully aware of what she was going off to do. Harriet waved and smiled with an expression that showed clearly her antipathy for their judgmental nosiness.

Out of the village centre, the driver accelerated somewhat and they made it to Battle train station with plenty of time to spare, before the first train of the morning to Hastings was due. The taxi-cab drew to a lurching halt outside the station, flinging both Harriet and Fraser from their seats.

Fraser offered her his hand, helping to haul her back onto the seat, just as the side door opened and the driver's grubby face peered inside. 'Sorry 'bout that,' he apologised with a sniff. 'Some little urchin ran straight out in front of me, the little…'

Harriet nodded, and Fraser scowled at the man's explanation, as they climbed out beside the car. The driver clambered onto the footplate and took down the two trunks, handing them over to Fraser. 'There you go, mate.'

Fraser said nothing but took the cases and walked off.

Harriet paid the driver, thanked him, then followed Fraser into the building. It was small and heavily gothic in style, of which Harriet had never approved. If such an idea were possible, it felt to her like the station was an *anti*-church, as though some murky, heretical practices might happen there after dark. Absurd, of course, it was just an architectural style, seemingly favoured by the designers of Wealden train stations, but that was the conclusion, which she had drawn many years ago and it had stuck.

They were the only ones on the Hastings-bound platform and took their seats on a bright-green, cast-iron bench and duly waited.

'Do you not think we stand any chance of finding this Lina girl, then?' Harriet said after some time of conspicuous silence.

Fraser drew in a long breath and turned to face his mother. 'If she's in Ypres, I expect we can find her,' he answered, placing his hand on hers.

'She must have been quite special to him,' Harriet said, still not able to accept nor comprehend that Malcolm had used his pass to return to England but had not been to see her, his own mother.

Fraser's muttered agreement merged with the distant rumbling of the approaching train.

'Up you get,' Harriet said.

The South Eastern and Chatham train—comprising the steam locomotive and three dark crimson carriages—rumbled towards the station in its usual, noisy, angry way, as if reluctant to stop, and Harriet wondered for a moment whether it actually might well not. Then it began to slow down, heavily and grudgingly, as if taking a great effort to do so. With one final heave, it stopped.

'All aboard!' the guard boomed, stepping down from the middle carriage and looking up and down the platform at his joining and alighting passengers.

'Excuse me,' Harriet called. 'Which is First Class?'

'The Pullman at the end,' the guard said with a foul sneer.

Harriet nodded at the obnoxious man, remembering and comparing this to her wartime train journeys, when almost every guard had been a woman. She recalled the peculiar sight of the women operating the signal boxes, plate-laying, shunting the trains and fixing the tracks; every one of them had silently handed their jobs over to the men, when the end of the war came.

Fraser led the way along the platform to the end carriage, opened the first door, and they stepped inside. Harriet sat straight down, placing her bag on her lap, whilst Fraser bundled the two trunks into the wire cradle above the seats.

Three minutes later, the train staggered forwards and out of the station for the first leg of their journey—the short distance to Hastings.

After a short wait at Hastings Station, they boarded the continental express train to Dover. This, Harriet felt excitedly, as they entered the first-class cabin, was a much more glamourous and modern train. They exchanged 'how do you do?'s with the other well-dressed passengers, then took their seats opposite one another beside the window.

After a noisy announcement from the steam whistle, the train pulled out of the station and began to trundle at a decent, yet leisurely pace through the verdant Sussex countryside.

Harriet watched with great interest as they passed through small towns and villages interspersed with uninterrupted valleys of fields, farms and woodland, crossing the seamless border between the counties of Sussex and Kent.

When the coast came into view for the first time, Harriet sat up with a start and tapped Fraser on the leg, quickly realising, from the way that his bowler hat was on the verge of falling from his dipped head, that he was fast asleep.

She muttered an apology to the unfortunate lady sitting beside him with a bowler hat pressed to her shoulder, then turned back to the window, gazing out at the calm seas gently stretching up to the black stripe of seaweed, which indicated the most recent high-tide line. Across the water, some twenty miles away, she could just make out the hazy white cliffs and green hills of the undulating French coastline; the soil upon which so, so many had recently lost their lives.

The train eased up a little, as it entered the Admiralty Pier at Dover, a wide stone jetty, which extended out into the sea, and the terminus of which was the Marine Station.

'We're here,' Harriet said, nudging Fraser's calf with her foot.

He sat up with a start, and Harriet feared that he might shriek out from the sudden look of horror on his face.

'We're just pulling into Dover,' she said gently, bringing him to his senses.

'Right...right.' Fraser squinted hard, stretched, then stood up. 'I must have...nodded off.' He reached up and removed the two trunks from the wire rack, setting them down at his feet.

The train reduced to a veritable crawl, as it entered the gaping, arched mouth of the grand station building. Seconds later, it stopped, and through the open windows came a high-pitched whistle, quickly followed by the clattering of multiple doors opening and the chatter and bustle of people disembarking the train.

Fraser extended his hand out of the window, reached for the handle and opened the door. He placed the two trunks on the ground, then turned to offer Harriet a hand down from the carriage.

'Thank you, kind sir,' she said, taking a moment to absorb her surroundings. The building was alive with activity, such as she had never witnessed before: hundreds of travellers, scurrying in all directions like confused ants; porters, pushing carts heavily laden with cases; commercial travellers, dragging their wares to and fro the waiting ships. 'Good golly—what a place!' she murmured. 'Have you ever seen such a thing?'

Fraser didn't answer and Harriet noticed the vacant expression, which she had seen so often in the past days, return to his face. She traced with her eyes to where he was looking but couldn't tell—apart from the amassed crowds before them—what exactly had captivated his attention so. His face changed somewhat, now with an edge of palpable anticipation or nervousness. Perhaps even...panic? He was seeing something very different to that which was actually in front of them. She placed her hand on his arm, and said quietly, 'Fraser?'

He exhaled sharply, as though he had been holding his breath for some time to that point, and he met her gaze. 'Sorry. I was...day-dreaming.'

'Were you ever here...in the war?' she asked, now understanding.

Fraser nodded. 'It was packed, absolutely jam-packed with soldiers.' He let out a short laugh, fringed with bitterness. 'Nobody seemed to see what I was seeing—the paradox, the irony, it was just bizarre.'

'What do you mean?'

'In one direction, slowly drifting off the ships, were the hundreds upon hundreds of wounded soldiers: some on crutches, some on stretchers, some with limbs or parts of their faces missing. And standing watching them disembark, somehow not seeing, as I did, the flash of their own futures, were the thousands of fresh-faced young recruits, waiting to embark on the same blood-stained ships bound for the Western Front... I heard later how many of our wounded men came through this very building: one million, two hundred and sixty thousand, all told.'

'Gosh,' Harriet said. 'Unimaginable.'

Another laugh from Fraser. 'But they were the lucky ones, of course.'

'Yes,' Harriet agreed. 'Although I'm not sure poor Timothy, or some of the other unfortunate men I've encountered, would say the same thing.'

'Look. Look over there,' Fraser said, pointing at the foot-passenger entrance to the station.

'What am I looking at?' Harriet asked, just seeing an endless sea of people walking in and out of the building.

'The beggars,' he clarified.

Then she saw them, ten or more men, sitting in a row on a pile of blankets; all wearing the filthy uniform of their regiments, all in various states of distress, all of them desperately begging of passers-by.

'My goodness,' Harriet gasped, raising her hand to cover her mouth. 'Why is nobody helping them?'

'Why don't you invite them to live with us?' Fraser mocked.

'Fraser! Just look at the poor devils.'

'I know, it's dreadful.'

'We need to help them,' she said, rummaging in her bag for her purse.

Fraser reached for her hand. 'Stop, Ma. They're on every street corner of every town. The *government* needs to do something about it. It's not for individuals like you, tossing down a shilling every time a wave of philanthropy takes a hold of you.'

'Don't be so critical and dismissing of the actions of an individual, Fraser: one person can make a big difference,' she rebuked.

Fraser snorted, bent down to pick up the cases, and said, 'Come on, let's get on this jolly ship.'

They walked to the far end of the building, heading to a sign with the word *CALAIS* painted in large white letters over an arched doorway. Beneath the sign, a steadily moving queue of stylishly dressed men and women ran out of the building. Harriet craned her neck, but all she could see was a line of bobbing and dipping bowler hats. She turned to Fraser, trying to see from his expression how he was feeling at being back here under such very different circumstances. 'Are you alright?'

He nodded: 'I think so.' Then the queue in front shuffled forwards, and he added, 'There's our ship.'

Harriet stepped out of the building, and saw, moored to the stone jetty by coils of giant rope, a huge paddle steamer boat, more than three hundred feet in length. Her name, *Victoria* was painted in small letters on the black hull. 'What a thing!' she exclaimed, leaning over the white, metal railing, which ran along the quayside to the gangplank, to fully take in the boat. This would be her first time sailing and, as she glanced down at the inky water below, she felt a sudden wrench of anxiety. Her stomach and head, as though linked by an invisible thread passing through her body, seemed unexpectedly decided and united on the matter that this was an entirely barmy endeavour. What if it ran into trouble halfway across the Channel? Or, were it to hit an as-yet-undiscovered, errant mine left over from the war... Everyone knew about the naval minefields on this side, never mind the mines laid by the Germans on the other side! The Navy had lost its largest vessel ever, the HMHS Britannic, to a mine. And goodness! Not even to mention that the Britannic was the sister ship to the Titanic.

'Come on, Ma!'

Harriet looked up from the water to see that the queue had moved significantly forward. Fraser was standing at the gangplank looking at her, as though she had gone quite mad. Maybe she *had* gone mad to even consider boarding a ship, when the closest that she had ever come to swimming was dipping her toes into the sea on a daytrip to Hastings beach. But really, as she told herself, it was too late now for such worries and qualms. She straightened herself up, hoisting her eyes from the water, and walked towards Fraser.

'What were you doing back there?' he whispered, as she drew up beside him. 'You looked like you were maybe considering jumping in.'

Harriet rolled her eyes. 'Well, I can tell you now, that would have been the *absolute* last thing going through my mind.' As they took their first steps onto the gangplank, she went to ask Fraser again if they were doing the right thing, but she decided to hold her tongue. As she had discovered at several key moments in her life, it was only *after* having pursued a certain course of action, that it could be judged as having been the right one, or not.

'We're on the boat!' Fraser declared, taking a look around him. 'Out or in?'

'Pardon?' Harriet questioned.

'Do you want to stay *out*side and see the glory of the White Cliffs from the back of the boat, or do you want to go *in*doors and find somewhere to sit in the warm?'

Her instincts, which lately had guided so many important decisions, told her that indoors would be for the best. If she couldn't see the waves, or see how jolly far away from land on either side they actually were, then she could trick herself into believing that she was in some random building—perhaps a church or, better still, a village hall. But then! What if the worst *did* happen? Surely, they would stand a much better chance of survival if they were outside, where the lifeboats were?

'Oh, I don't know...' she dithered.

'Outside it is, then,' Fraser said decisively. 'It's a smashing day, and it would be a terrible shame to spend your first time on a boat crammed inside. Come on.'

Harriet followed him obediently, clinging to the edge rail, which ran along the complete perimeter of the boat. It felt vast; actually, too big and heavy to be able to sail anywhere. At the rear, most of the seats had already been taken, and they were forced to sit in front of each other in parallel rows, which enkindled her apprehension. She glanced to the young lady beside her, who appeared not to be accompanying the decidedly older gentleman sitting on her other side.

'Good afternoon,' Harriet greeted.

The lady turned and smiled. 'How do you do?' She had a soft, warm face and startling, emerald eyes. Like Harriet, she was dressed in black but her dress was one of the more modern, high-busted types worn without a corset. She guessed the woman to be in her late twenties or early thirties.

'A little nervous, actually,' Harriet answered. 'My first time on a boat.'

The young lady seemed amused and quite taken aback. 'Is it really? How charming. And where, pray tell, are you going?'

Just as Harriet went to speak, the loudest, most infernal noise, which she had ever had the misfortune to hear, boomed from somewhere close by behind her. She jumped with alarm, and roughly grabbed the wrist of the lady beside her.

Fraser's bowler-hatted head appeared between Harriet and the young lady. 'It's alright, Ma. It's just the departing horn. Means, we'll be off in a jiffy.'

'Marvellous… That's marvellous,' Harriet said, noticing that her hands were still attached to the lady's wrist. 'Oh, I do apologise.'

The lady laughed. 'No need…really.' She extended her right hand in Harriet's direction. 'Mrs Luckhurst.'

'Mrs McDougall.'

'Nice to meet you, Mrs McDougall. I think you were about to tell me where you are headed, before we were so rudely interrupted.'

'Oh, yes, that's right.' She took a breath, holding it longer than she might have otherwise done, as she felt the boat beginning to move. Better not to think about it, she told herself, and willingly conveyed the purpose of their visit, if only as a distraction from the sensations and experience of the voyage.

'That's what I'm doing, too,' Mrs Luckhurst said dryly. 'My husband was killed in service with the Royal Naval Air Service—shooting down those wretched zeppelin things.'

'Oh, I am truly sorry to hear that,' Harriet said.

Mrs Luckhurst sighed heavily, as she raised her shoulders and eyebrows simultaneously.

'Look, Ma!' Fraser said from over her shoulder.

'What?' Harriet asked, turning awkwardly to see to what he was referring.

'The cliffs—just look at them!' he said.

The boat—now steaming along at what Harriet imagined to be full power—was sufficiently distanced from Dover to show the sheer scale of the White Cliffs. Something about them was breathtakingly beautiful. Perhaps it was the pristine white, glinting like burnished marble against the blue skies, which so struck her with wonderment. Or perhaps it was just their ancient simplicity, that they had stood there impassively, while all around them the world crumbled into turmoil.

'Simply stunning, aren't they?' Fraser said. 'Enough to bring a whole ship of returning men to reverent silence.'

'I can well imagine,' Mrs Luckhurst said. 'A symbol of home. A reminder of the past and a hope for the future…' Her voice quivered on the final words, and she swiftly turned her head windward to the side.

Harriet heard Fraser shuffle backwards in his seat. A stillness settled around them, now, nebulous and bitter-sweet, made all the heavier by Mrs Luckhurst's emotive observations, for which none of them had been prepared. Still Harriet stared at the cliffs, watching as they expanded in breadth, yet diminished in height; the further they sailed from the coast, the more it felt to her, as though she were looking at little England through a magnifying glass.

'Do you want to explore the ship, Ma?' Fraser asked after some time.

Harriet shook her head. 'No, thank you, but you go ahead.'

Fraser grunted a response and wandered off towards the front of the boat.

'He seems a nice chap,' Mrs Luckhurst said, watching him leave.

'Yes, I rather suppose he is,' Harriet said, before hastily inserting a retraction of her poor choice of words. 'I mean, I don't *suppose* he is; he *is* a jolly decent lad.'

Mrs Luckhurst grinned and Harriet flushed red with embarrassment, which, when she evaluated its cause, she thought to emanate less from that, which she had just said, and more from a realisation that perhaps she had given Fraser insufficient consideration since his return home.

'Did he see much action?' Mrs Luckhurst asked.

Harriet thought for a moment. She had been asked this question by strangers an inordinate amount of times since the war had ended. At first, she had reasoned that it was polite chitter-chatter or an instant way of finding common ground; after all, everyone had something to say on the subject. But the more the question had been asked, the more sceptical she had become. Were they asking—*checking*—to see if he had actually fought and not objected? The first time that this thought had occurred to her, she had rushed to his defence, listing all the places to which he had been sent: Africa, Hong Kong, Calcutta, Constantinople. The reaction, oftentimes patronising, went along the lines of 'Oh, he was *over* there. *How fortunate.*'

'...Or not?' Mrs Luckhurst said in response to Harriet's silence.

'Do you know,' Harriet said, gazing back at the shrunken shoreline of Kent. 'I do so wish, now, that my three boys had been conscientious objectors. The very idea of having 'a war to end all wars' is patently absurd, and all those millions of young men sacrificed to the fallacy.' She sounded more indignant than she had intended, and she looked up at Mrs Luckhurst, expecting to find contempt or astonishment in her eyes. Instead, she saw tears.

Mrs Luckhurst smiled. 'It's so refreshing to hear someone say that. I feel exactly the same for my husband... I even suggested it to him when he was home on leave, once. I begged him not to go back. I said we'd find some remote place to hide, some tiny village in the middle of nowhere to see out the war together… Oh, the look he gave me.' Mrs Luckhurst laughed through her tears at the evoked image of her lost husband. 'I might as well have suggested he fly on an elephant to the moon.'

Harriet laughed, understanding fully. 'But they didn't object, did they? They bravely answered their country's call and carried out their duty. And here *we* are, the ones left behind who must repair, rebuild and find a way forward…somehow.'

Mrs Luckhurst squeezed Harriet's hand. 'Yes, indeed, we must. That, now, is *our* duty.' After a short moment, Mrs Luckhurst stood up. 'We shall be docking in twenty minutes or so. I'm going to have a wander around the ship. Would you care to accompany me?'

'Thank you, but I'll stay here. Go ahead, and if you see Fraser on your travels, do check he's not getting up to any mischief.'

Mrs Luckhurst laughed, as she walked away, then repeated Fraser's name, as though it were a peculiar or foreign word.

Harriet sat among the crowds, alone. In front of her, England was now all but a hazy distant outline. Behind her, France would no doubt be clearly discernible. She should get up and look, but the sea was rougher now, and the ship was markedly rocking from side to side. Half-panicked, she looked around at her fellow passengers but none of them appeared the least bit troubled by the vessel's sudden jerks and shudders. She closed her eyes and took herself back more than thirty years, to early September 1887. Specifically, to John's and her honeymoon in Cambridge, where, after several attempts, he had managed to persuade her to take a boat ride along the River Cam. It had been a giddy, pleasurable experience, although she had clung to the gunwale for the entire duration, much to John's amusement. She was there, now, in her mind. The pitching and swaying of The Victoria, upon the bottomless English Channel, was actually that little rowing boat, whose name—if she had ever known it—she had now forgotten, gently bobbing along the River Cam.

Harriet's thoughts roamed and rambled from the honeymoon to the wedding itself. Time had scrubbed much detail of the day from her mind, but the feelings, which rose concomitantly with these reminiscences, were those of peace, contentment and happiness. They'd loved each other, certainly, but the war had wrought such deep unalterable strains on their marriage that, by the time of John's death, she had no longer known what they had meant to one another. She compared the man, beside whom she had stood at the altar of West

Malling church, to the man whom she had laid to rest in Sedlescombe churchyard, and concluded that they had been the same person in name only. Her mind rehearsed the singular event of John's funeral, of the—

'Ma? Ready?'

Harriet opened her eyes. Fraser was standing over her with Mrs Luckhurst beside him.

'We're here, Ma. Are you alright?' He laughed, stooping down to pick up the trunks. 'Not got your sea legs, yet, then?'

He was mocking her, gently. She smiled, stood up and glanced to the side. They had docked. Dry land! Whistles were being blown, men were shouting instructions to and from the ship and a general restlessness pervaded the passengers, as they began to shuffle towards the gangplank.

Fraser turned and joined the slow-moving queue off the boat. Mrs Luckhurst followed immediately behind him, and Harriet noticed her placing a hand on his elbow, as a child might do, who didn't want to be separated from its mother.

A surge from behind suddenly buffeted Harriet in a different direction from Fraser and Mrs Luckhurst. 'Fraser!' she called, but he didn't hear her. The queue heaved and jostled forwards, off the ship and into a cramped room, where her small folded passport was checked by an officious gentleman behind a counter, before she was released out onto a busy stone causeway. The jetty jutted out over the water, providing an embarkation point for both the ships and the railway, and directly in front of her, passengers were pouring from a recently arrived train, creating utter chaos.

'Good golly! Fraser!' Harriet called, searching the sea of bobbing bowler hats for which might be his. 'Fraser!' she called, but her voice was lost to the elevated cacophony created by an impossible muddle of languages. It really was no good, Fraser had vanished, and standing there was just causing her to be bumped and pushed in all manner of unwelcome directions.

Harriet braced herself and defiantly pushed through the crowds towards the train, where she climbed the steps of the nearest carriage, and used her raised position to survey the madness and try to find her son. A swarming throng of whirling movement and oh, what a ludicrous number of hats!

There! He'd managed—willingly or otherwise—to find himself close to the front of the ship. He was searching for her, looking desperate.

'Fraser! Fraser!' she shouted, but it was quite useless. She tried waving, but he wasn't looking in her direction. 'Fraser! For goodness' sake!' She waved again, and this time he did see her. He nodded in acknowledgment, yet appeared to continue looking among the crowds. 'Fraser! I'm here!' He huffed—she was certain that he had huffed! But at least now he was coming towards her like a salmon swimming upstream against the current to reach her.

'What a place!' Harriet called out, as he drew close enough to hear.

'Did you see where Emily went?' he asked, unable to stop himself from looking this way and that.

'Emily? Who the dickens is Emily?' Harriet asked.

'Emily Luckhurst,' he clarified.

'Swept up in a tide of Frenchmen, I shouldn't wonder.'

Fraser sighed, seemingly unwilling to be deterred and not stopping his search of the crowds. He propped himself up on tip-toes to get a better look over the hordes of people, eventually giving up. 'Right. Shall we push through and find ourselves a *chambre d'hôtes*; there must be plenty nearby for travellers and tourists.'

'Just hang on a jiffy,' Harriet said. 'I overheard in all this commotion that this—' she indicated the train in which she was standing, '—is the last train to Lille. It wouldn't be such a terribly late time to arrive there and look for a guesthouse, would it?'

Fraser looked at his pocket watch and shrugged. 'Won't you be tired from all that travelling?'

'Goodness me, Fraser. We've only travelled from Sussex to Calais; I hardly think I need to have a lie down just yet. Now hurry and fetch the tickets,' she said, passing him some French francs.

She watched, as he disappeared once again into the madness of the port. He glanced constantly around him while he walked, as though checking for an unseen assailant. She lost sight of him, as he entered the terminal building, and she turned to enter the carriage, empty but for one solitary man, sitting upright beside the door with his gloved hands pressed around the tip of a walking cane.

'*Bonjour, Monsieur*,' Harriet said to him.

He nodded but said nothing, his little black moustache twitching, as if he were disgruntled to have to share the carriage.

Summoning what little French she could recall from her time at Sedlescombe School, Harriet made certain that this was the '...*train pour Lille*'.

'*Oui*,' he replied, without evening looking her in the eyes.

'Wonderful,' she exclaimed, taking a seat opposite him.

An out-of-breath Fraser arrived moments later: 'Done,' he said, holding up the tickets, before taking a seat beside Harriet. 'If this train makes good time, we could even take a taxi-cab straight to Essex Farm tonight. It'll be light for a good few hours yet. If you want to, that is...'

'I'd like that very much,' Harriet responded. Even though she had waited a long time to visit Malcolm's grave, the difference between seeing it today or seeing it tomorrow morning seemed an interminable chasm.

As time pushed on lethargically and the train remained stationary, Harriet became increasingly restless. She blew out her cheeks and fiddled with the window clasp.

Next to her, Fraser was once again asleep. She didn't know how he did it. All he seemed to need was somewhere to perch his bottom and he was off. It didn't seem to matter a jot how uncomfortable, or how noisy his surroundings might be. Now he was listing comically, like a ship about to capsize. She nudged her elbow into his side and he sprang awake, just like that.

'What?' he asked.

'You were asleep,' she scorned under her breath.

'And what of it?'

'It's embarrassing—you're on a *train*, for heaven's sake.'

'Do you actually care what a funny little Frenchman thinks?' he said, not even bothering to lower his voice.

Harriet shot a glance to the man opposite her. From his lack of reaction, she guessed that he couldn't speak English. Thank goodness.

From outside, a whistle pierced the air, and the train began to creep out of the station.

'Oh, at last,' Harriet said, turning to ask Fraser how long the journey would take. She opened her mouth to speak, but he was asleep.

At this, the Frenchman smiled, to which Harriet felt obliged to reciprocate. 'He's very tired,' he said, in accented but perfect English.

Harriet felt the blood rush to her cheeks. 'Yes,' she agreed, mortally embarrassed by Fraser's earlier comments.

'Are you travelling on from Lille?' he asked.

It took her a moment to regain her composure, but then was grateful to steer the conversation on from what he clearly must have heard Fraser saying about him. Choosing her words with care, and speaking more slowly than usual, Harriet explained to where they were headed and the reasons for the trip. For the most part, he listened impassively, saying little and, by the time they reached Lille, she was grateful to have had someone with whom to talk to pass the time.

'*Au revoir.* I hope your trip is a successful one, *Madame*,' he said, tapping the front of his hat with his cane, then stepping from the train.

'Cheerio,' Harriet said. She stood up and looked beside her. As their journey had progressed, Fraser had leant further and further over until finally his head had met with the seat, loosening his bowler hat, which had at some point tumbled to the floor. 'I've a good mind to leave you here,' she said, hands on hips, before raising her voice: 'Fraser, get up!'

Just like a sprung wooden toy, he pinged back up in his seat, wide awake. Without a second's hesitation, he bent down, returned his hat to his head, and picked up the two suitcases. 'Ready?'

The train station was mercifully much quieter than Calais. Outside of the main building, were three waiting taxi-cabs and several horses and carriages.

'Modern or antiquated?' Fraser asked.

'Modern,' she replied, and they climbed into the first car.

The journey seemed to take forever, and Harriet questioned whether they had made the right decision in going straight to the cemetery, given that they had yet to find anywhere to stay for the night.

Within minutes, Fraser was asleep, and for a while Harriet gazed out of the window, but the obvious scars of war—derelict buildings, trees shucked of their branches and Imperial War Graves cemeteries, littering the endless barren fields—left an unpleasant feeling in her stomach. From her bag she removed her copy of E.R. Tingle's *Guide to Flanders*, flicking to the *Helpful Words & Phrases* section at the back of the book.

'*Goeiemorgen*,' she rehearsed to herself. '*Hoe gaat het met jou?*'

As they continued through the destroyed Belgian countryside, Harriet read and practised several stock phrases.

'*Zalig kerstmis*,' she muttered, evidently more loudly than she had intended.

'What?' Fraser demanded.

'I said 'Merry Christmas' in Flemish,' she replied.

'Oh, well that will really come in handy in the middle of September, won't it?' he scorned.

'Sorry, *mijn nederlands is niet zo goed*,' she said with a smile.

The taxi-cab suddenly slowed down.

Harriet looked out of the window and gasped. They were here. Unquestionably, they were here. Rows and rows of wooden crosses—hundreds of them in neat lines—in a field beside the main road.

A painted sign at the entrance read: *ESSEX FARM CEMETERY*.

A sudden sensation, that her heart was being squeezed, overwhelmed Harriet and she struggled for breath.

'Are you alright, Ma?'

Chapter Nine

11th September 1919, Essex Farm Cemetery, Belgium

Harriet gripped Fraser's forearm. It was taking all of her strength to stay upright. The muscles in her legs were quivering, threatening to give out at any moment. She was taking short, insufficient breaths, and she suddenly felt stiflingly hot.

'Do you need to sit down, Ma?' Fraser asked, concern contorting his face, as he placed his hands under her elbows to steady her.

Harriet shook her head. 'No, I'll be fine. Just give me a minute.'

'What is it?'

It was a consuming fusion of emotions, which were hard enough to disentangle, never mind try to define or explain. Tiredness was certainly playing an insidious part; despite her earlier protestations, it *had* been a very long day. Foremost in her mind, however, was the overwhelming sensation of being just yards from her son's grave. She knew, and had accepted long ago, that Malcolm was dead and was never coming home, yet actually being in the cemetery brought with it the categorical finality that he would remain here under Belgian soil for all of eternity.

Harriet pulled in a deep breath, wiped her eyes, and said, 'I'm alright. Let's go and find him.'

Threading her arm through Fraser's, they walked slowly along the side of the road until they reached the entrance, pausing there to glance up at a tall white cross, raised imperiously on four stone plinths. Behind it, cowering low in the sky was an orange sun, setting on the distant horizon.

Harriet withdrew her arm from Fraser's, and silently surveyed the cemetery, surprised by several things at once. First of all, it wasn't at all how she had pictured it. It was long, almost rectangular in shape, and, as they had entered at the very top corner, they had a view down the cemetery of almost every grave, denoted by a neat wooden cross. She found it just too neat, imagining that a cemetery, created during the chaos of war, would be much more disordered and higgledy-piggledy. The second surprise to strike Harriet was that it was much less peaceful than she had thought it would be. Its situation beside the main road bestowed upon the grounds a constant low-level rumble of motor and equine traffic. The last surprise was what she saw at the base of every grave: the most beautiful displays of flowers and shrubs. A few rows away, a shirtless young man—possibly a gardener—was on his knees tending to some magnificent giant daisies. To find such deliberate beauty here, shocked her.

'What's the grave number?' Fraser called back to her, having wandered a short distance away.

Harriet saw that he was standing in front of a map of the cemetery. 'Plot one, row N, grave five,' she replied. She was certain that the reference number would be etched in her mind for as long as she lived.

Fraser pushed his face closer to the map, then turned and pointed vaguely into the cemetery. 'Just down there.'

As she followed him down a path running towards the left of the cemetery, Harriet felt the contradictory muddle of never wanting actually to reach the grave and the acute desperation to get it over with, to settle once and for all that part of her mind, which refused to believe that Malcolm was actually gone.

Her legs suddenly weakened once again at the impossibility of what she was now seeing in front of her.

Fraser had stopped and was indicating to a particular grave. 'Here.'

But she knew which one it was before he had spoken. At the base of the grave to which he was pointing rose a striking display of flowers: blue poppies, to be precise. Harriet looked urgently around the cemetery, spinning on her heels and checking other graves nearby. Then she looked further into the grounds, her eyes not finding what her brain was telling her *must* exist…

But, no! Impossibly, the only place in the entire cemetery, where blue poppies were growing, was at the base of Malcolm's grave. This flower, which he had sent to her and had mentioned to the Duchess of Westminster, was here, growing from his grave and his grave alone. What did it mean? Mrs Leonard had said that, if she found the poppy, it would help her. Did she mean that in finding his grave it might provide her with the resolution, which she needed?

She walked slowly towards Fraser, noticing that he had turned his head away from her, subtly trying to dab his eyes with his handkerchief. She reached his side, placing her hand gently in the small of his back, finally allowing her eyes to drop down to the grave itself. Like the rest, it was a simple wooden cross with an oval tin plate pinned to where the two perpendicular parts intersected. The words written there suddenly became illegible and watery. Then the cross itself blurred, as Harriet sank to her knees with her hands clasped together in front of her.

Malcolm. Dear, dear Malcolm. Her beloved boy, who would never willingly have hurt another human being, was lying here…alone…gone. Twenty-eight years of life…gone…snuffed out. All that he had been and all that he might have been…gone.

'I miss you,' she wept, 'so very, very much.'

Her eyes were stinging, and she tried to stem the flood of tears, but she just couldn't stop her mind from bringing to the fore oddments of happiness from Malcolm's childhood. One flickering snippet of memory leapt unaccountably to the next, and the next; all of them different mini-narratives but with the same ending, repeatedly wrenching her heart from pleasure to pain in an instant.

Time passed. How much, she couldn't be certain, but the snippets replaying cruelly in her mind had abated somewhat, the pauses between them increasing, as though themselves aware that the torments, which they brought with them, were simply unsustainable.

The nightmarish visions ceased as suddenly as they had begun. Harriet opened her eyes again, blinking the tiny beads of residual tears from her eyelashes. She wiped the thin dry, salty lines on her cheeks with the back of her hand and stared at Malcolm's name. She looked at it for a prolonged period, barely blinking, her mind too exhausted to reach the anguish-filled depths of her heart.

Then she noticed the poppies once more, pale blue with dusty yellow filaments in the centre. She reached out and held one, still unable to comprehend how it could be that the flowers were growing above Malcolm's body—no, *from* Malcolm's body—and nowhere else in the entire cemetery. She carefully ran her fingers down the length of the flower closest to her, snapping the stem at the base. From her raffia bag, she withdrew her diary, carefully sandwiching the flower among the centre pages, then shutting the book on it.

Harriet rose, feeling entirely drained. She realised, then, that Fraser was no longer by her side. She glanced around the cemetery and saw him talking to the man, who had been tending to the plants when they had arrived. She bent down and gently kissed the top of the cross, closed her eyes and found herself praying, something which she had not done for many months.

'Ma! Over here!' Fraser called, waving her over. From his body language, whatever it was that he had learned from the other man, didn't sound overly urgent, so she took her time walking to them, taking in all the names, ages and regiments of the graves, which she passed. Such a waste of life, and to think that this cemetery was but one of hundreds around the world. She'd read somewhere that at one cemetery alone, Tyne Cot, there were the graves of almost twelve thousand soldiers. Twelve thousand! She tried to imagine what twelve thousand people together looked like, but she simply could not: it was an unfathomable number.

'Ma, this gentleman is a gardener and knows something of what went on around here during the war,' Fraser explained.

'Bonjour...*hallo*,' Harriet greeted with a smile. She began to formulate a sentence in her head when Fraser cut in.

'He's English, Ma.'

'Oh, glory,' Harriet said. 'I see. Sorry.'

'Bonjour,' he answered with a titter. 'Most of us Imperial War Graves Commission gardeners are English,' the shirtless man revealed in an accent, which Harriet couldn't quite place. East End of London, or Essex, perhaps? He looked to be in his mid-twenties with short blond hair and a tanned muscular physique. He wiped his right hand on his trousers and offered it to Harriet. 'Joe,' he said.

'Mrs McDougall,' she answered, shaking his hand. 'Could you answer a question about this cemetery for me, please, Joe?'

'Well, I'll give it a go, yeah,' he said with a grin.

'Why are there blue poppies growing on my son's grave, but not on any other?' Before he could answer, she quickly added, 'It's not a complaint; they were a favourite of his. I just don't understand, is all.'

'I don't know, to be honest. We certainly ain't put 'em there. When we started off plantin' here, it was all fairly basic: blue cornflowers, white camomile, yellow charlock, *red* poppies... Now we've got our own nursery up and running, we've got dwarf lupins, nasturtiums, linarias... But what we ain't got—anywhere—is them blue poppies.'

'I see,' Harriet said. But, actually, she didn't see at all.

Joe laughed. 'We quite like it, really. One of the bigwig 'orticulturists came over from Kew Gardens, demanding to know how they'd got there and wantin' us to dig 'em up, but us gardeners 'ad a right old barney with him, saying that we didn't need to know 'ow they got there; someone or somethin', or nature or whatever had put 'em there and that was good enough for us. He stormed off in a right 'uff but let us keep 'em.'

'That's very good of you,' Harriet acknowledged. 'Thank you.' After a moment, she said, 'So you were here in the war and yet you chose to stay on afterwards?' She tried, but knew that she had failed, to hide the astonishment from her question.

'Na, I didn't stay. Most of us gardeners, who are here now, went home after the war. But our jobs had gone. I tried lookin' for a few months, but there just weren't nothin'. Then I saw the Imperial War Graves Commission was offering jobs out 'ere and, well, I applied and 'ere I am.'

'That must pose some difficulties,' Harriet said, casting her eyes over the cemetery, finding it enormously hard to comprehend how these men, having been forced away from their families for months or years on end, would *choose* to return to somewhere so far from home.

'It was 'ard at first, being back 'ere, yeah,' Joe answered. 'But these men—' he motioned to the graves around him, '—they was me family for nearly four years, you know. It just feels right to be back 'ere, looking after 'em, when their families can't, like.'

Harriet nodded, realising then that he had taken her mention of difficulties in working here to mean simply being back at a place where such despicable acts of inhumanity, such devastation, such hell, had occurred. The haunting, dramatic opening bars of Liszt's *A Symphony to Dante's Divina Commedia* played in her mind and she remembered Timothy's insistent refusal ever to return to the Western Front. She found the bravery in these gardeners, their returning to the now-empty trenches and silent battlefields, utterly extraordinary.

'So, were you actually *here*...in the war?' Fraser questioned.

'Not 'ere, exactly, na. Wipers. Somme...' he said matter-of-factly, as though he were casually describing previous holiday destinations. 'A mate o' mine, Arthur, who shares me billet was 'ere, though, with the Royal Engineers. When was your lad 'ere?'

'He died from gas poisoning on the 4th July 1917,' Harriet answered.

Joe thought for a moment. 'D'you know, I'm sure that's when Arthur was 'ere. He *should* be back at the billet sometime today. He's a bit of an odd one, but a very good 'orticulturist. Where you stayin' tonight?'

'Now, there's a question,' Fraser replied. 'We've got no idea.'

'Pretty sure the landlady of me billet, Mrs Tillens will be able to put you up for a night or two. She's got a farm'ouse outside Boezinge. God only knows 'ow it survived the war. Mrs Tillens swears it's because of the life-sized bullet-ridden Jesus she's got guarding the entrance.' Joe chuckled, then quickly stopped. 'Sorry, er, no offence meant if you're religious or—'

100

'It's fine,' Harriet reassured him. The days of her feeling the need to take offence at religious mockery had been long since confined to the past. 'Do you think she might have room for us?' Harriet asked.

'As long as you ain't precious about where you sleep—it's pretty rough—just to warn ya.'

'Oh, Joe,' Harriet said, becoming overwhelmed once more. 'That's so terribly kind of you. Thank you. I think the way I'm feeling right now, I could quite happily sleep in a field.'

'Yeah, done that a few times, too,' Joe said. 'Ready, then? I'm done 'ere for the day.'

'Yes, yes, absolutely,' Harriet said, casting a quick eye to Fraser, who nodded his agreement.

Joe bent down and picked up a rucksack, which rattled and clanked with the variety of tools inside. As he led them back towards the entrance, Harriet noticed for the first time that darkness had crept upon them. She turned to see Malcolm's grave, but it was lost in the shadows. 'Goodnight,' she whispered to him.

'Here we are,' Joe said, when they arrived at a Rover Sunbeam, parked beside the cemetery entrance.

Harriet stared at the vehicle, wondering how on earth they could have missed it on their way in. It was a battered, old automobile with two seats at the front, behind which was a section covered by a canvas painted in army-green. A circular emblem on the side, which revealed its previous incarnation, had been poorly painted over in a different shade. The words *Imperial War Graves Commission* had been hand-painted—again, badly—across the side.

'War ambulance,' Joe said. 'The old bone-shaker we call her. Hop in.'

Once Harriet and Fraser had squeezed into the passenger seat, Joe started the engine and Harriet could feel her insides jangling before he had even removed the handbrake. 'Is it far?' she asked with false brightness.

'Just a couple of miles,' Joe responded, pulling the former ambulance out onto the main thoroughfare.

They rumbled along at a speed with which Harriet was not particularly comfortable, swallowing down several gasps, as Joe swung the vehicle out into the oncoming carriageway in order to overtake several slow-moving horses and carriages.

'Nearly home!' he announced, pulling the old Sunbeam off the road and onto a dirt track at a speed which suggested that he had almost missed his turning.

'Glory!' Harriet yelped, grabbing on to Fraser's arm, as she slid sideways, banging into Joe.

'Sorry,' Joe said with a grimace.

Harriet managed a laugh, as she straightened herself up and looked out at the new landscape unfolding before them.

From their elevated position, Harriet looked out across the countryside. One barren field merged into another for as far as the eye could see. She could just make out one property, a farmhouse at the end of the track upon which they were now driving.

As the farmhouse drew closer, Harriet could see that it was dilapidated with crumbling out-buildings, broken walls and fences, and small hillocks of assorted debris dotted around the overgrown garden.

Joe pulled up just outside the white boundary wall and switched off the engine. 'It don't look like Arthur's back just yet.'

Harriet climbed out after Fraser, grateful to be free from the confines of the Sunbeam's cab. She followed Fraser and Joe to the gate.

Jesus came into view. He was, as Joe had suggested, standing at the entrance on a stone shelf, looking down upon them. Apart from being painted in somewhat garish pastel colours, he indeed resembled the Jesus depicted in Harriet's family bible: bearded, with a headdress, arms by his side with his palms open, facing forwards and outwards, as though he were inviting them inside. This Jesus, however, had several bullet wounds to his neck and chest. Rather awfully for the owner, Harriet thought, somebody had desecrated the statue, crudely adding trickles of red paint to the bullet holes.

Harriet sighed. Really, after all that had gone on in the world, had people no shame?

Joe noticed that she was staring at the effigy and intuited her thoughts. 'Mrs Tillens *swears* it's blood,' he whispered. 'Don't go correctin' her, for God's sake.' He glanced up at the statue. 'Sorry.'

'Right,' Harriet said.

The front door was ajar and Joe, with Fraser and Harriet close behind him, entered the farmhouse. Fraser removed his bowler hat, struggling to carry it alongside the two cases.

Harriet was shocked by the devastation that she saw in the room; some kind of sitting room, she supposed. Every wall was covered in a complicated pattern of spidery lines. As they passed through the room, it took her a moment to realise that they were cracks in the plasterwork, like those in a shattered mirror still held in its frame. Some were hairline, others were large enough to fit all one's fingers inside. Where some of the cracks had merged, deep islands of plaster had dropped from the walls and were now lying—exactly where they had fallen, goodness only knew how long before—on the floor. In the room itself were five chairs, all with torn fabric, and a wooden dresser, fiercely scratched and tarnished. Between the chairs were... *What* were they? Bits of tangled metal? Was that a pile of bullet shells? Then there was an upturned rusty bicycle with no wheels. Beside that was a collection of well-worn military hats, some of which she recognised as being British, others she presumed to be German.

'What *is* all this?' Harriet murmured.

'Crap she's constantly finding 'round the farm,' Joe uttered. 'War memorabilia. She found an 'and once—fingers an' all—and put it on the mantelpiece for a while.'

'Oh, my good godfathers!' Harriet shrieked.

'Ma,' Fraser chastised. 'Shush!'

Harriet glowered at Fraser's back. 'A *hand*, though!'

The room, which they entered next, had the same fracture lines dominating the walls and ceilings, and Harriet wondered what on earth could be left holding the house up, and how on earth anyone could live in such a place. There was a very old stove, a few mis-matching cabinets and a wooden butcher's block in the centre of the room, upon which a small army of flies were cavorting. This was the kitchen, Harriet supposed, making a mental note not to eat a single thing while they were here.

'Mrs Tillens?' Joe called out. He moved to the far end of the kitchen, from where an open staircase ran upstairs. He stood on the bottom step and craned his neck sideward to try again: 'Mrs Tillens?'

'*Wat?*' an old woman snapped, suddenly appearing at the open back door. Harriet was quite startled and, without thinking, took a step backwards. She had hair far longer than Harriet had ever seen on a woman before. Long, grey and lank, and her face was shrivelled and shrewish. She wore a long dirty apron and, in one hand, was holding a flapping chicken upside down by its legs. She eyed Fraser and Harriet suspiciously. 'Who is it, these people?' she asked Joe in pidgin English.

'They'd like a room,' Joe replied. Then, looking to Harriet: 'How many nights?'

'One,' Harriet and Fraser replied in unison.

Mrs Tillens scowled. '*Joat*—Yes. You have one night,' she confirmed.

'Thank you,' Harriet said.

'Dinner will be more francs,' Mrs Tillens said, promptly raising her other hand to the chicken's neck and, in one downward thrust, broke its neck. '*Kieke...Kip.* You eat chick'n?'

Harriet shuddered but somehow managed to maintain her veil-like smile. She said, 'No, we're full, thank you,' at the same time as Fraser attempted something from his stock phrases: '*Nee. Dank uwel!*'

Mrs Tillens shrugged. 'It no problem.'

Harriet conjured a not-especially-convincing yawn. 'I think we just need our beds. It's been such a jolly long day…'

'I'll show you to your room,' Joe said. 'Follow me.' He took them upstairs, where the damaged walls, messy floors and broken furniture continued. 'That's our room, in there,' Joe said, cheerfully pointing inside a small room, clogged with seven or eight beds.

Harriet struggled to elicit sense from her addled brain. 'Is it… Do you find it…?'

'It's alright,' Joe answered. 'Try sleepin' in a trench waist-deep in water with bombs going off around your ears.' They moved across the hallway and he said, 'That'll be your room.'

'Thank you, Joe,' Harriet said. 'You've been terribly kind.'

'That's okay, Mrs McDougall. I 'ope Arthur'll be back by mornin' to talk to ya.'

'Where is he, then?' Fraser questioned, saying the very thing which Harriet had been about to ask.

'He's one of the mobile gardeners. A driver, a cook and half-a-dozen gardeners head off in a lorry for a few days at a time with camping gear, cooking equipment and tools; the lot. They go off into the wilderness, tendin' to the cemeteries what are closer to the old front lines. I do it meself sometimes, but I don't like it much. Eerie and you don't very often see another soul all the while you're gone.'

'How awful, but oh, how good of those men,' Harriet commended.

'It's a job, ain't it. Anyway, 'opefully he'll be back before you 'ead off tomorra.'

'Well, good night, Joe, and thank you again.'

'Night,' he said, heading back to the stairs. He paused at the top. 'Can't get you a nightcap, can I? She does make a very good genever.'

'No, thank you,' Harriet replied, not sure what a *genever* might be.

'Yes, please,' Fraser said.

Harriet went to speak, to rebuke him, but she caught herself before the first words came out of her mouth. She said nothing and followed him inside their room.

'Well, this is nice,' Fraser said, setting the cases down beside him and tossing his bowler onto one of the two beds.

Harriet scowled at him, breathed deeply to try to unwind from the day, and glanced around her. This was going to be a long night, she feared. The room contained two wire beds with a straw mattress and a dishevelled blanket on each, presumably left unchanged from the last visitor. But for the two beds, the room was entirely empty. No dresser. No wardrobe. No washstand. No coat hooks. No lamp. Not even any curtains. Nothing. Part of her wanted to let go of her resolve and just cry. Part of her wanted to walk right away from this forsaken place and never return. Two things kept her from leaving directly, though: one, was the chance to talk with Arthur; two, was her acute tiredness, which was likely also intensifying her emotions. In truth, she wouldn't have the energy to walk back to the main road, never mind trying to find another place to stay. No, this would simply have to do for this one night.

She sat down on the other bed, removed her coat and then removed her shoes, hurriedly pulling her feet up from the dirty boards. She unpinned her hat, then began the laborious task of carefully removing all the pins from her hair, almost tempted for the first time in her life to leave them in.

'There we are. 'Ere you go, mate,' Joe said, entering the room with a small glass of apple-coloured liquid.

'Cheers,' Fraser said, taking the glass. He inhaled a great vulgar sniff, then sipped at the edge. 'Wow, potent. Quite warming. Nice. Thank you.'

'Enjoy. See you in the mornin'. Mrs Tillens does a really smashing breakfast, by the way.'

'Great,' Harriet said, already set on not partaking. 'Good night.'

'Night,' Joe answered, pulling their bedroom door shut.

Fraser set the glass down on the floor between the two beds, took off his shoes and coat, then picked up the glass and offered it to Harriet.

She shook her head vehemently: 'Absolutely not!'

'Try it, Ma. It'll help you sleep, at least. Medicinal.'

'No, Fraser,' she said, eyeing the glass, as though it might contain poison. Well, it did. But Fraser didn't take the glass away. It just stayed there between them.

'Try it,' he insisted. 'One mouthful. And I promise I won't tell Reverend Percival, if that's what you're worrying about.'

She scowled, both at him and at herself. Her resolve was weakening, and she saw herself reaching out and taking the proffered glass. *She* actually had a glass of alcohol in her hand! Was this the first time? Yes, surely it must have been. John was never much of a drinker, and on the rare occasion that he did have a pint, it was in a public house; never at home. Of course, he had become teetotal just prior to the Great War, when Harriet, alongside some other villagers, had established the Sedlescombe Temperance Tea Gardens.

'Go on, then,' Fraser urged.

She took the glass to her nose and inhaled, almost choking on the repellent fumes, at which display Fraser roared with laughter. She wanted to hand it back to him and go to sleep but, instead, she placed her lips to the coolness of the glass and took a small swig.

'Oh, my godfathers!' she shrieked, her head lurching about of its own volition, as the hot bite of the alcohol made its way down the back of her throat. She thrust the glass back in Fraser's direction and let go, not caring if he had taken hold of it yet, or not. She went to say, 'What the dickens is it made from?' but, when she opened her mouth, nothing came out but a feline hiss.

Fraser was laughing such as she hadn't seen him laugh in a very long time. Seeing him like this softened her compulsion to tell him off. She smiled begrudgingly and lay down on the bed, surprising herself at how comfortable it actually turned out to be.

Her eyes were unexpectedly heavy and she closed them for a moment. She thought of those days, which she had found so purposeful, so determined, running the Temperance Tea Gardens. She had firmly believed alcohol to be the devil's poison, which would doubtlessly lead the consumer onto a slippery slope to eternal damnation. But now? Just like her faith, just like her dabbling with the paranormal, just like her belief in the fundamental goodness of the human race, it was a great swirling mass of confusion, contradiction, conflict and ambiguity.

She was suddenly back in the tearooms, talking with Mrs Selmes and Mrs Davison about how they could get their message through to all the men frequenting the Coach and Horses and the Queen's Head night after night. They were eating jam sandwiches and Victoria sponge cake, drinking tea. Mrs Selmes had a suggestion but Harriet couldn't hear her properly, her voice was surprisingly distant and faint. Through extended shrouds of blackness, Mrs Selmes and Mrs Davison vanished and Harriet found herself quite alone. The tearoom was deserted. But directly opposite, a huge single-file queue had formed at the door of the Coach and Horses. Everybody, whom she knew from the village, was there; even Reverend Percival himself was waiting to get inside. It was all so hopeless. Another stretch of blackness pulled her away and she tried to discern some inaudible sounds that didn't seem at all to fit where she thought that she was. Harriet tried to call out to them, to save them, but nothing would come out of her mouth.

Chapter Ten

12th September 1919, Boezinge, Belgium

There it was again: a sort of tapping sound. This time, Harriet opened her eyes, having absolutely no idea of where she was. She followed one of the squiggly lines above her head until it met with another line. She followed that one to the floor and abruptly sat up with a start, remembering, with a suddenness which made her flinch, exactly where she was. 'Goodness me,' she mumbled, her heart thumping inside her chest. Daylight streamed in through the windows. What time was it? Was it morning? It must be.

On the bed beside hers, Fraser was on his side, his legs curled up to his chest under the woollen blanket, sleeping soundly.

A knock came from the door and Harriet recalled that familiar tapping sound, which had woken her.

She cleared her throat. 'Yes?'

Fraser stirred at the sound of her voice.

'Mrs Tillens is doing breakfast,' came Joe's voice from the other side of the door. 'And Arthur's 'ere. You both comin' down?'

'Lovely, thank you,' she croaked. 'Yes… Be right there.'

Fraser groaned and tugged the blanket over his head.

Harriet swung her feet down onto the floor, quickly retracting them, when she remembered how filthy it was. She carefully slid into her shoes and stood up, detesting the feeling of having slept in her same clothes. She longed for a hot bath and a clean dress, but that would just have to wait. First, they needed to get out of this condemned place. She pulled the blanket away from Fraser's face. 'Come on. Wake up. We need to get a move on. We've a busy day ahead of us.'

He grunted and sat up, looking dreadfully dishevelled, also having not changed out of his clothes. Harriet tentatively touched her hair, then promptly withdrew her hand, preferring not to dwell on her appearance.

Fraser exhaled, as he squeezed his feet into his shoes, evidently with some difficulty. He stood up, sighed again and walked over to the door.

Harriet followed him downstairs to the kitchen, where she found Mrs Tillens washing dishes in filthy grey water. She greeted them with a nod of her head. Joe was sitting at the table, pressing an entire boiled egg into his mouth. Harriet smiled warmly, thought of how Timothy would likely be doing the same right now at home, and said good morning.

Joe acknowledged Harriet and Fraser with a wave and pointed at the man sitting opposite him, chewing furiously on his mouthful in order to be able to speak.

'Please,' Mrs Tillens said, thrusting two tin cups at Harriet and Fraser, which looked suspiciously as though they might have been retrieved from the trenches.

'Thank you kindly,' Harriet said, staring at the muddy liquid.

Fraser thanked her, seeming not to have noticed the state of the receptacle, and sipped the drink with slurps of enjoyment.

Harriet tried, with a subtle nod of her head and a widening of her eyes, to point out the poor condition of the mug, but he was blissfully oblivious.

'Mrs McDougall,' Joe finally managed to say, 'this is the one and only, Arthur Dooley.'

Arthur—a tall unhealthily thin man with a blotched, crimson face and a clump of black unkempt hair—stood up and saluted: 'Arthur Dooley at your service.'

'Lovely to meet you, Mr Dooley,' Harriet greeted, unsure of how to take the man.

'Please, step into my office,' Arthur said, pointing to the vacant chair beside him. 'And call me Art. Or Arty. Or Arthy. Or Ar. Or whatever you fancy, really.'

Harriet carried the cup of coffee to the table and sat down, trying to ignore his eccentricity. Fraser wandered over and leant on the wall behind Harriet, at the same time sending a clump of plaster to the floor.

'Ey!' Mrs Tillens called.

'Sorry…'

'So,' Harriet began, 'I believe you served with the Special Brigade in the war?'

His eyes narrowed, as though he were deep in thought. 'The war?'

Harriet shot a look at Joe, and then at Fraser. Surely, he hadn't forgotten it…had he? 'Yes, the Great War.'

Arthur's eyes widened madly. 'Oh, the *Great* War! Yes! It *was* great, wasn't it!' He made a sudden loud explosion-noise with his mouth and throat. 'Guns. Bombs. And gas. Oh, the gas! Gas, gas, gas…' His voice jumped an octave and he pulled his wiggling fingers to just below his chin. 'The cute little rats all scurrying along and then—' he made another similarly guttural explosion-noise and then did his best impression of a rat dying, '—dead!' He picked up Harriet's mug and gulped her coffee down in one go, for which action she was unexpectedly thankful.

'And you were in P Company?' she said, trying to exert a firm steer on the conversation.

'The *Suicide* Company,' Arthur corrected.

'Pardon me?'

'That's what we were called: The Suicide Company.'

'Right,' Harriet said. 'Do you remember my son. He was called Malcolm. Malcolm McDougall.'

Arthur nodded quickly, continually, excitedly.

'And is there anything you can tell me about him, particularly towards the end?' she pushed, uncertain of this Arthur's having the ability to converse seriously on the subject.

Arthur made a further explosion-noise and then repeated his parody of the dead rat. For several bizarre seconds his head was tipped to one side, his tongue hanging loosely from his mouth.

'Art, stop playin' silly buggers and tell Mrs McDougall 'bout her son,' Joe said, kicking him hard in the shin under the table.

Arthur yelped, looking genuinely offended, like a scolded dog, and gazed at Harriet, as if unsure of what more needed to be said on the matter.

'He was a good one,' Arthur said, his tone having changed completely to one of a sincere and coherent adult. He nibbled on his thumbnail for a moment, gazing at the floor. 'One of the best, actually.' His fingers became twitchy again, dancing in front of his face, as if of their own volition. 'Chemicals! Chemicals! He would sit in the trenches working on the formulas that we had to follow.'

'Was that the reason he went to the laboratories in Woolwich?' Fraser asked.

Arthur nodded furiously again. 'He was one of the best; oh, yes!' He looked directly above him and pointed, making everyone else in the room turn and also look up, including Mrs Tillens, who was apparently trying to follow the conversation with great effort and interest. 'Thirty percent chloropicrin, seventy percent chlorine: YELLOW STAR! Sixty-five percent chloropicrin, thirty-five percent hydrogen sulphide: GREEN STAR!' His fingers burst open above his head with a mini-explosion. 'All the stars, so bright. He tried to make them human. Hello, I'm a star! No, *humane*.'

All things humane and matters concerning gas-warfare, did not, in Harriet's book, coexist naturally. 'What do you mean?'

In a peculiar, yet vaguely familiar voice, which Harriet deemed to be a poor impersonation of Malcolm's, Arthur said, 'If we're going to kill the buggers, let's at least try to do it quickly and *humanely*.' He dragged out the final word of the sentence, tilting to one side, as he did so. 'Phosgene. Smells like hay. Makes you choke on your own blood.'

The words were Malcolm's, of that Harriet was certain. Despite Arthur's obvious idiosyncrasies, hearing from him that Malcolm had tried to use his knowledge of chemistry for some good touched her, settled her in some way.

'What about Red Star?' Harriet asked.

Arthur frowned sternly. 'Red Star? Red Star?' He shrugged. 'No idea.'

'Are you sure?' Harriet persisted. 'You've never heard of it?'

Arthur filled his cheeks with air and shook his head. 'Red Star? Red…Star?'

'For goodness' sake,' Joe said sharply. 'Art, 'ave you 'eard of Red Star before, or not?'

Arthur shook his head. 'Nope, there's no Red Star. Lots of pretty colours, but not red.'

'And what about what happened just before he died?' Fraser asked.

'The Bosche sent over a mortar bomb. BANG! Gas! Gas! Gas!' Arthur mimed putting on a gasmask, then he flopped back in his chair, pretending to be dead.

'*Before* that bit,' Fraser said.

Harriet frowned at him, seeing from Fraser's face and composure that he was losing patience with this man.

'Working on the front line…' Arthur recalled. 'Malcolm noticed it… 'Ah, look, some of the gas batteries are broken." Arthur turned around to address Fraser. 'Circuit breakages. Malcolm: 'I'll carry the exploders up'. He climbed the parados in broad daylight—'

'Parados?' Harriet interrupted.

'Top of the trench,' Fraser explained. 'Parapet in front, parados behind.'

'I see,' Harriet said. 'So, he climbed out of the trench in *daylight?*'

'Yes, indeedey,' Arthur confirmed. 'Out of the trench, connecting exploders, getting the batteries fired. Boom!' He put on a squawky, bird-like voice and added, 'They work! They work!' His voice switched to exaggerated German: '*Hallo! Ich kann dich sehen, weisst du*! Bang!'

Harriet didn't know quite what to say. Thankfully, Fraser was holding his tongue. She looked at Arthur, folding a large piece of bread into his mouth, his recollection evidently over.

'Is that it?' Joe asked.

"Get them on a stretcher! Take them to the Dressing Station!' Bye, Malcolm...not coming back,' Arthur said through a mouthful of bread.

'Anythin' else?' Joe pushed.

Arthur shook his head. 'Didn't return.' Then his head flopped backwards with his mouth open.

Joe looked embarrassed and mouthed the word 'sorry' to Harriet. After a short pause, he asked her, 'D'you still want me to show you the Dressing Station and all that gubbins?'

'Yes, please. If that's okay,' Harriet replied.

"Course. We'll need to be headin' off in about twenty minutes, though—is that alright?'

'Absolutely,' Harriet confirmed, rising from the table and making her way towards the door.

'Not eat?' Mrs Tillens said.

'Not eat, thank you,' she answered.

'I can probably 'ang on for you to get some quick breakfast,' Joe said. 'She don't take long to cook it.'

'No, no,' Harriet insisted. 'It's quite alright. I'd sooner get on if it's all the same to you.'

Joe shrugged and said, 'Meet you by the wagon, then.'

'Perfect,' Harriet said, desperate to leave this awful madhouse behind. 'Come on, Fraser. Let's get our things together.'

"I'm taking a G.S. Wagon into Poperinge!" Arthur called, sitting upright again. "Don't let on."

Harriet paused. Arthur was using the mimicking voice, which he had just used for Malcolm. She turned around, noticing that Fraser had also picked up on it. 'Is that what Malcolm said? Did Malcolm say that?'

Arthur looked from one person to the next, as if he were in trouble. 'No. Yes. I'm not supposed to let on.'

'He's dead, you know,' Fraser responded impatiently. 'It doesn't matter much, now.'

Arthur raised a finger to his lips and whispered. "I'm taking a G.S. Wagon into Poperinge."

'General Service Wagon,' Fraser muttered for Harriet's benefit, then addressed Arthur, clearly enunciating each word: 'What was he doing in Poperinge, Arthur?'

'Nobody knows,' he said with wide eyes and expanded arms.

'*When* did he take a wagon to Poperinge?' Harriet asked.

'The night before...'

'The night before he went up onto the parados to fix the...the things...the batteries?'

'That's right.'

'Was that usual for him to do that?' Harriet asked.

Arthur shook his head so hard that Harriet feared that he might fall off his chair.

'Thank you, Arthur. You've been most helpful.'

'Hmm,' Fraser added, following her out of the room.

'Is there anything off to think about Malcolm taking a wagon into Poperinge?' Harriet asked when they were upstairs in their bedroom.

Fraser took a moment to answer. 'It is *quite* odd. Soldiers with his kind of job would have to move up and down the line, and cadging a lift from a G.S. wagon wouldn't have been uncommon, but taking one into Poperinge... I don't know.'

Harriet sighed, wondering if she would ever know the full extent of Malcolm's final movements. She sat on the bed, thinking.

'It can't be because of *her*, though, can it?' Fraser said. 'Lina Peeters, I mean. She was in Woolwich at the time.'

'I had just reached the same conclusion myself,' Harriet said. 'I don't know. Come on, let's get out of this place.'

Fraser placed his bowler hat onto his head, picked up a suitcase in each hand, and headed down the stairs. Harriet followed, thanking and paying Mrs Tillens on her way out to the Sunbeam, where Joe was waiting in the driver's seat.

'Cheerio,' Fraser said to Jesus, tipping the front of his bowler hat, then climbing into the old ambulance.

Harriet scowled at him, then got in beside him, taking one final look at the condemned farmhouse.

Then, they were on their way.

The journey back to Essex Farm Cemetery somehow seemed much shorter than their journey had been in the opposite direction. Joe drew the Sunbeam to a stop just outside the entrance. 'Leave your cases in 'ere; they'll be safe enough.'

Harriet and Fraser climbed down and followed Joe across a pathway, diagonally facing the stone cross that stood at the cemetery gates. They had walked just a few paces when Joe pointed in front of them. 'So... That's the Essex Farm Advanced Dressing Station.'

'Oh,' Harriet murmured. A little way ahead of them was an ugly concrete structure cut into the mud bank of the canal. It looked nothing at all like a structure in which critically wounded men could satisfactorily be treated.

They continued across the grass towards it, then, when they had reached the first room, Joe stood back, allowing them to peer inside.

Harriet stared into the gloom but could see nothing at all inside; all that she could detect was the harsh smell of mildew and damp rising from within. How had the Duchess of Westminster described the place? Something like windowless and dreary, something of an understatement.

'This was the Officers' Mess,' Joe said.

'It's beautiful,' Fraser commented wryly.

Joe moved to the next door. 'This one was for walk-in cases, then the next was for stretcher cases.'

Harriet stepped inside the latter room to which Malcolm would have been conveyed, unexpectedly feeling a cold wetness in her shoes. She glanced down and, from the limited amount of light entering the doorway behind her, could see that she was standing in a couple of inches of water.

'Great. My shoes are now soaked,' Fraser lamented from behind her. 'Just brilliant.'

Suddenly, the room was illuminated with a burst of white light, as Joe struck a match.

'Glory,' Harriet said, observing the room. But for the cold water in which they were standing, it was empty. It probably could have housed eight, or maybe ten beds at a push. The walls were a horribly dull concrete-grey, lined with wet green streaks and the ceilings were oppressively low. As the light from the match began to flicker and fade, she hoped with all her heart that it hadn't been like this for Malcolm's last few hours of life.

'What was..?' Fraser began to say, stopping when the light died, plunging them into a horrible cold darkness.

'What was what?' Harriet said.

'On the wall,' Fraser replied. 'Have you another match, Joe?'

Joe answered by striking another.

114

'There!' Fraser said, an excitement evident in just that single word. He was pointing to the wall on the opposite side of the room.

Harriet strained her eyes but could see nothing. She stood back, allowing Joe and Fraser to approach whatever it was, which he thought he had seen.

'Look, Ma,' Fraser said, beckoning her over with a wave.

As she walked, the water crept uncomfortably higher over and into her shoes, reaching to her ankles. She leant in between the two men, staring at the wall. It was some kind of a blemish, like a large blueish birthmark. Then Joe held the light to within just a couple of inches, and she could now identify it: a single blue poppy with the letters *MMcD* marked in black below it.

'Malcolm painted it,' Fraser said needlessly.

The light died again, and Harriet wondered if this was the poppy to which Mrs Leonard had referred; the one which she had said '…would help with it all.' It certainly wasn't helping anything, right now. In fact, being here in this God-forsaken place made it worse, and, feeling a sudden wave of nausea, she hurried from the small enclosure.

Back outside in the warm sunlight, Harriet sucked in great lungfuls of air, as though she had been holding her breath underwater for some time.

'Are you alright, Ma?' Fraser asked, appearing behind her and placing his hand between her shoulder blades.

'Yes, yes,' she insisted, giving him a half-baked smile.

'So…' Joe said. 'Malcolm would have arrived here in an ambulance very similar to the old Sunbeam out there,' he said, gesturing back to the vehicle in which they had just travelled.

Harriet nodded, abhorring the very clear imagery forming in her mind, linking together what Timothy Mogridge, the Duchess of Westminster, Arthur whatever-his-name-was and Joe had told her about Malcolm's final hours. They were painful and real in her mind now, as though she had witnessed them for herself. But, in some dreadfully primordial, almost sadistic way she needed that pain and first-hand knowledge. She paused, then turned to Joe with a brighter transformed look, and asked, 'And what were the rest of the rooms used for?'

'The next was the latrines. Even one year on after the war ended, I still wouldn't suggest going in there,' he relayed with a chuckle, to which Harriet agreed. Then he continued, pointing to the next door. 'That one was the dressing room, then the kitchen, then the evacuation room, where soldiers waited, before either going back to their regiment, or being sent back to England for recuperation or further treatment and operations.'

'A room which Malcolm never got to see,' Harriet observed, unable to disguise the bitterness in her voice.

'No,' Joe mumbled.

Harriet's breathing had at last normalised. She took a step back and looked at the awful structure where her son had succumbed to the effects of the very thing, which he had meticulously studied and trained to understand. It was just like Arthur had told her in his unfiltered way: that P Company was known as The Suicide Company.

'D'you still wanna see the trenches?' Joe asked.

'If it's not too much bother,' Harriet replied. 'Fraser—will you be alright with that?'

'Provided there are no armed Bosche in them, then fine.'

'Definitely no *live* ones,' Joe answered with a snigger. 'This way.'

They walked at a thankfully leisurely pace around the Dressing Station and along behind the back of the cemetery. They continued a short distance and then crossed over a bridge to the other side of the canal.

They wandered in silence, the sounds made by their feet meeting the gravel the only noise to be heard. Harriet found the peacefulness to be contradictory in the way in which it managed to be both calming and unsettling at the same time. She somehow couldn't conceive of there having ever existed there the mania, terror and utter frenzy of war just eleven months ago.

Her eyes lazily rolled over the still water, catching the fleeting movement of some bird in the fledgling trees opposite, or a moorhen swimming hastily past them. The tranquillity soaked into her mind, and she listlessly tried to tease apart a knot of feeling inside her. Had she been correct in her assertion to Fraser that she would know when the time were right to stop her investigations? Apart from speaking with Lina Peeters, there was little else to learn; and yet, notwithstanding this, she felt inexplicably dissatisfied. Maybe she wouldn't know after all, when she should desist. Or was all of this just some enormous self-delusion, a refusal in some way to accept that Malcolm was really gone?

She touched Fraser's elbow, and he looked at her. 'Tell me. Am I really going too far with all of this?'

He thought for a moment and looked out over the canal. 'No, Ma. I don't think so. Not anymore.'

She nodded, still not convinced either way.

A few feet farther along, they followed Joe off the path through a gap in the hedgerow, which opened out onto a vast field of knee-high grassland. But for a small thicket of trees in the distance, the landscape was barren.

'Most of 'em have been ploughed over and filled in, but for some reason this bit ain't,' Joe informed them, continuing through the field. He stopped abruptly and pointed to the ground. 'Right 'ere.'

'Good gracious! Oh, my goodness,' Harriet exclaimed, suddenly finding herself teetering on the edge of a long, narrow trench. Pieces of unidentifiable wooden debris jutted from the water-logged floor and, on the other side of the trench, were half a dozen sandbags in varying stages of ruination. 'Was this a British trench?'

'Yep. The German trench was just over there,' he said, pointing to a not-too-distant cluster of saplings.

'Where? Just...*there*?' Harriet did not believe that she could have understood him correctly, as she confirmed that Joe had indeed been indicating the same spot as she was now looking at, not even a football pitch in length away.

'That's right, yeah,' he confirmed, then pointed down at the trench in front of them and added, 'It's very likely your Malcolm would have been right 'ere...'

The words, the notion, the confirmation, all cut into Harriet's heart, as she pictured him down there, preparing to release some noxious, illusorily titled substance across No-Man's-Land in the hope of killing other young men just like him but dressed in a different uniform. Of all of the complex threads unspooling in her mind at that moment, it was once again the futility of it all that most ravaged her. It must have hit Fraser, too, for he sharply turned and hurried back towards the gap in the hedgerow.

'Right,' Harriet said quietly. 'I think it's time that we moved on, don't you? Thank you ever so much, Joe...for everything.'

'You're welcome, Mrs McDougall.'

Back on the canal path, Harriet spotted Fraser on the bridge, elbows resting on the rail with his chin propped in his splayed palms.

'So, you're off to Wipers, then?' Joe asked, as they walked.

'That's right,' Harriet confirmed. 'I'm looking for a young lady, Lina Peeters who was friendly with Malcolm. I'm not overly confident of finding her, though, in such a large city. Eighteen thousand pre-war residents, apparently.'

Joe glanced sideways at her, his expression ambiguous. 'The opposite might be true, actually. The place is a wreck and there ain't much left of it, to be honest.'

'Right…'

'I don't know any official numbers, but pretty sure there ain't eighteen thousand living there.'

'Oh,' Harriet responded, unsure of the implications of what he had told her.

They had reached Fraser on the bridge, but it appeared to startle him, when Harriet touched his arm and said, 'Ready?'

'Yes,' he said, with a hint of shortness at having been drawn back to reality.

The three of them walked the short distance back to the cemetery entrance, where Joe shook Fraser's hand. 'Good luck in Wipers,' he said, turning to Harriet, taking her hand in his and giving it a rigorous jiggle.

'I cannot express enough my deep gratitude to you, Joe,' she said, pressing a small cigar-shaped bundle of two-Franc notes into his hand. 'It really is much appreciated.'

'You don't need to do that: it's my pleasure,' Joe countered, trying to pass the money back.

Harriet shook her head and said, 'I insist, absolutely.' As she did so, she noticed over Joe's shoulder that a small flower stall had appeared at the entrance to the cemetery.

With a show of reluctance, Joe pocketed the money and thanked her: 'Goodbye.'

'Fraser,' Harriet began, 'go with Joe and fetch the cases, would you? I'll be back with you in just a tick.'

She headed with a purposeful gait to the flower stall, a simple wooden table with a small selection of flowers protruding from half-a-dozen metal buckets. Working behind the stall was a girl, who could not have been more than fifteen years old, with unkempt brown hair and ill-fitting clothes, which had clearly seen much better days.

'Hallo,' Harriet greeted.

'Goeiemorgen,' the girl replied in Flemish with a wide smile. '*Kan ik je helpen?*'

Harriet scoured the bunches of flowers, quickly selecting some white roses. 'These are very beautiful, er, dank uwel,' she said, passing over a one-franc note.

The girl nodded: 'Dank uwel.'

118

'Two minutes,' Harriet called over to Fraser, who was standing beside the Sunbeam, waiting with their suitcases. She strode decisively back into the cemetery, heading directly for Malcolm's grave.

She bent down, propping the flowers against the cross, and stared at the grave, taking long breaths. Finally, she was able to speak to him: 'This might be the last time that I can come here and see you, my dear Malcolm… But you know, though, don't you, that you will always be alive inside of me, in my heart. I'll remember the short time that you were with me, my beautiful son, for ever more, and I'll cherish every sweet moment of it until I breathe my last. Dearest, darling Malcolm, I do love you so…'

Harriet sobbed into her handkerchief. She cried for all of the wonderful things that Malcolm had ever been. And she cried, more so, for all of the wonderful things that he could now never become.

Through the haze of her tears, something moved. She dabbed her eyes and, when she saw what had landed on the top of Malcolm's cross, snorted in a strange half-laugh-half-cry.

A male Ghost Swift moth was gently flexing open his silvery wings.

Harriet laughed a strong cavernous laugh, but which, when she felt her acceptance of his absence returning, morphed into weeping once again.

'Goodbye,' she breathed.

Chapter Eleven

12th September 1919, Ypres, Belgium

Harriet's mouth was agape. 'Good grief,' she muttered, drawing out the words. 'Have you ever... Did you ever...'

'Oh...my God...' Fraser said, stepping from the taxi-cab.

Before she could link its departure to the inevitable ramifications of what she was seeing around her, the taxi-cab had pulled away, leaving them standing in a cloud of fumy, hot dust.

'Wait!' Fraser called after the car, realising at the same time as she that, even though the driver had followed their instruction to drop them in the centre of Ypres city, he had ostensibly abandoned them in some accursed biblical abyss, certainly *not* the quaint, gentile place depicted on the postcards that Malcolm had sent home.

Harriet turned around slowly, unable to comprehend the scene surrounding her. The devastation was unimaginable, like nothing, which she had ever seen before. In every direction, for as far as the eye could see, were ruins—not a single complete building anywhere in sight—just the odd wall here and there, rising soberly from among great piles of wreckage.

Harriet raised her hands to her cheeks, disbelieving her sight. And the silence of the place! It was dead, devoid of any kind of life. Where were the city's people gone? Surely her mind was playing a trick on her? This *could not* possibly be Ypres. Had they mispronounced Ypres...or *Ieper*? She stared at Fraser, wanting some reassurance, but she knew from his face that he was seeing the same underworld as was she.

It was all a dream, she told herself, gazing dumbfounded at the four- or five-storey tower, smashed and barely standing, which was in front of them. Beside the tower was a single wall of gothic arches, once presumably windows, but now with nothing at all behind or around it.

Slightly panicked by her inability to grasp what was happening, she opened her raffia bag and withdrew the collection of Malcolm's postcards, quickly thumbing through them until she reached the one of the magnificent Cloth Hall, photographed in 1914. Holding the card up at arm's length, she made minor adjustments to the height and distance until she could see with her own eyes that the carcass of the building in front of her had indeed once been the Cloth Hall, built in the eleventh century: they *were* standing in the centre of the city of Ypres and she was not—as really she had feared that she knew all along—dreaming.

Harriet sighed, her resolve weakened by the shock of such unexpected desolation and destruction. Joe had been right; how much harder it would be to find one person among none, than one among a city of eighteen thousand.

'At least there's a nice selection of hotels,' Fraser quipped.

'Thank you—very helpful,' she scorned, her determination waning further still with the acquiescence to the loss of a decent meal and a hot bath, something for which they were both now desperate.

Fraser shrugged. 'Now what?'

She would not be beaten. 'Now, Fraser… We think,' she said, taking Fraser's two hands in hers and looking him in the eyes. 'You've lived in England for four or so years. The British government wants you out; so, you go home. But you find fire and brimstone have rained down and completely destroyed it. What do you do?'

'Go back to England?' Fraser suggested.

'A possibility, yes,' Harriet agreed. 'But not likely if you're not wanted and you have no money for the fare. Besides which, wouldn't you go back to somewhere you were familiar with? Back to Miss Yavuz in Woolwich?'

'Are you asking me, or telling me?'

'Thinking out loud,' Harriet answered. 'Where else might you go?'

'Family…or friends?'

'Right, yes,' she said, nodding. 'And if their houses were destroyed, too?'

'Go further afield?' he offered.

'Yes!'

'But that could mean anywhere in any part of Belgium. Or the world, for that matter,' he replied.

The enormity of the task loomed large once again, a shapeless, nebulous undertaking that bordered on sheer lunacy. What *would* they do: check every village, town and city in the country until they found Lina Peeters? Harriet couldn't think like this, or else she would be on the first train back to Calais. 'First things first,' she said. 'A hotel that serves hot meals and hot baths. There *must* be one.' She looked around her again and randomly pointed down a road: 'This way.'

The strange other-worldliness of the place continued unabated, as they walked. But for the odd crater here and there, the cobbled streets remained bizarrely intact, running alongside great open spaces, where buildings had been razed to the ground and subsequently cleared.

After several minutes of walking, Fraser asked, 'Are you sure about this, Ma? There's not one building or one person to be seen in any direction.'

Of course she wasn't sure; she hadn't a clue, but at some point they simply *had* to encounter someone. 'Yes, just keep walking,' she encouraged.

'If you say so,' he mumbled.

'What's that?' Harriet asked, whirling around to locate the cause of a low, distant murmuring.

Fraser had braced himself for a telling off but realised that she was referring to another sound. They both stopped and looked back towards the ruins of the Cloth Hall.

'A motor car!' Harriet shrieked, sounding very much as though it were the first time that she had ever clapped eyes on one. 'A motor car!' She manoeuvred herself into the centre of the road and stood star-like with her legs apart and arms stretched wide.

'What are you doing, Ma?' Fraser asked incredulously.

'What I'm *not* doing is letting this jolly fellow pass without helping us.'

The small black car drove steadily towards them. When it drew to within thirty feet, the driver began to beep his horn and wave his hands for her to get out of the road.

Harriet stood smiling but unwavering, not moving a fraction of an inch.

The car drew to a complete stop and a little man with a thin black moustache poked his head out from the car. '*Mais, qu'est-ce que vous faites? Vous êtes folle!*' he yapped.

Harriet smiled. 'Bonjour. Do excuse me, I'm English. I'm looking for accommodation.' She enunciated the words slowly and with an odd widening of her mouth around the vowels, as though they were a burden to articulate.

'*Un…hôtel,*' Fraser added, with an attempt at a French accent.

The man sniffed and held up his index finger: 'One. One hotel *seulement.*'

'Marvellous!' Harriet exclaimed. '*Et, c'est où, exactement,* Monsieur?'

The little man pointed in the direction in which they had already been walking, and Harriet nodded smugly to Fraser.

'Can you give us a lift there?' she asked, pointing to the car and mimicking holding a steering wheel. 'Drive—*conduire* us...*nous*?'

He nodded resentfully, made a vague gesture to the car and leant over to push open the passenger door.

'Oh, thank the good Lord,' Harriet said, flopping down noisily in the back seat. She felt as though she had been on her feet for months on end.

Fraser muttered his thanks in French, as he closed the passenger door.

The man pushed the car into gear and it lurched forwards.

'What is your name? *Er... Comment vous-appelez tu...vous?*' Harriet called from the back.

'Monsieur Chaput,' he replied, briefly turning around to answer.

'I'm Mrs McDougall,' she said. 'And this is my son, Fraser.'

Monsieur Chaput either didn't understand or didn't care, driving impassively onwards.

'Buildings!' Harriet gasped, poking Fraser in the arm. 'Look!' The buildings, which they were passing, had all suffered some kind of damage—some were missing their roof, others were missing windows and doors—but remarkably they were still standing. The knowledge that they were leaving the obliterated city gave rise to a new buoyancy inside Harriet, and she began to look hungrily through the windscreen at what they were approaching.

In the distance she saw people, cars, and new wooden buildings: whole rows of complete houses, shops and businesses! She couldn't help but sigh with relief at the wonderous sight just yards ahead of them: a two-storey wooden structure with *SPLENDID HOTEL* painted in large black letters on the roof.

Monsieur Chaput stopped the car directly outside the hotel and jerked his thumb sideways at the building. '*Adieu.*'

'*Au revoir,*' Harriet replied, cheerfully. She paused, one leg out of the car. 'Oh, before we go, you don't know a lady called Lina, do you? Lina Peeters?'

'*Non,*' he answered, not giving the matter much, if any consideration.

Harriet and Fraser thanked him and climbed out. The moment that they were out of the car, he sped away.

'Oh, Fraser!' Harriet said. 'You have no idea how happy I am to see this hotel.'

'Well, don't get too excited, Ma. We don't know if they've room for us, yet.'

'Nonsense!' Harriet said, marching towards the entrance with Fraser following dutifully behind with the two trunks.

She entered a small lobby lit by a dim, green-shaded lamp standing on a wooden counter. Behind the counter was a smart, suited man. He was bald-headed with harsh, crumpled facial features. Despite this, he grinned, as Harriet approached him. 'Do you speak English?' Harriet asked, loudly and slowly.

'I would certainly hope so,' he replied. 'Seeing as how I grew up in Buckinghamshire.'

'Oh, how wonderful,' Harriet said.

'Sorry, I'm being facetious. How may I help you, madam?'

'A room!' Harriet yelped with mock desperation and throwing her hands in the air. And then, calming herself somewhat, repeated, 'A…a room…please. Wait. Even better, *two* rooms. Two rooms, a hot dinner and a hot bath.'

The man grimaced slightly. 'I *can* do all of those…'

'But..?' Fraser put in, pre-empting the man's own caveat.

The man seemed suddenly uncomfortable, glancing quickly at Fraser before returning his attention to Harriet. 'But…as I am sure you've seen, Ypres is in rather a desperate state, and we have guests from *all* parts of Europe, here to work and help rebuild the city.'

Harriet frowned tetchily, not following. The man either had rooms or he didn't. Or was he implying that they would have to share a room with a foreigner? What *did* he mean? 'I'm terribly sorry, but I don't understand.'

The man glanced to the open door over his shoulder, then leant over the counter, and whispered, 'We have all kinds of nationalities here…including some young *German* men.'

'Oh!' Harriet said, understanding now, but not really knowing *how* she felt about this new information. The idea that they might meet young German men on their trip simply had not entered her mind. She hadn't much time to think about it, either, for the hotel receptionist was staring at her for an answer. She looked sideways to her son. 'Fraser?'

Fraser shrugged. 'Fine with me. They were just doing the same job, as was I—forced to take up arms against an enemy with whom I actually held no disagreement or quarrel at all. It's fine—not a problem.'

The receptionist, having wanted only to avoid embarrassment for all parties, seemed entirely satisfied by Fraser's answer: 'So, two rooms, then?'

'Yes, please,' Harriet confirmed.

'Excellent,' he said, sliding a thin ledger across the counter. 'If you could just fill in these details. Your rooms are on the first floor. The bathroom is at the end of the corridor, and dinner will be served just through the door behind me from six o'clock.' He clapped his hands together, as Harriet completed the necessary paperwork. 'May I ask the nature of your visit?'

Fraser explained that they had just come from visiting his brother's grave, and the receptionist instantly became more solemn. 'A pilgrimage of sorts, then,' he said. 'We have other guests staying here, who have come for similar reasons.'

Harriet returned the book. 'Why is there literally nobody in the city centre? We didn't see a single builder, carpenter, beggar or thief: it was really *most* queer.'

'It's a Sunday in a very religious country,' he explained, giving a light shrug of his shoulders, which either conveyed that the answer was obvious, or that he too didn't understand why a city, in such desperate need of repair, should grind to a halt because of religious observance.

'Oh, goodness. How silly of me!' Harriet said, flushing with shame for having made herself sound like a heathen. 'I'm completely all over the place.' She slapped Fraser on the arm, thereby bestowing a portion of her ignorance and culpability onto him.

The receptionist laughed politely, as he removed two keys from a bank of brass hooks hanging on the wall behind him.

'We've also come to Ypres to look for someone: a young lady—Lina Peeters—who lived here before the war.' Harriet started. 'We're reliably informed that she returned. What…where might such a person have gone?'

As he handed Harriet the two room keys, the receptionist answered: 'Almost everyone, who lived here before the war, lost their homes. The majority of people returning are in the *Plaine d'Amour* area, just north of the city.'

'Oh, right. Thank you,' Harriet said. 'That's most helpful.'

'The Belgian Ministry of Internal Affairs has provided temporary pre-fab houses for the people returning to live in. That's the most likely place you'll find her, to my mind.'

'Splendid,' Harriet said.

'That's our name,' the receptionist quipped, but Harriet didn't understand to what he was referring, so she smiled politely, tilted her head away and said, 'Come along, Fraser.'

At the top of the stairs, they found an inadequately lit narrow corridor, which fed six solid green doors. On each door was tacked a brass number.

Harriet examined the numbers burnt into a small wooden rectangle attached to each of the room keys. 'Six or seven?'

'Seven,' Fraser said, with an odd immediate decisiveness.

Harriet handed him his key. 'I'm going to bathe. What say, we meet downstairs for six o'clock, then?'

Fraser nodded. 'What say, you knock on my door at five-to-six because I'm certain to be still asleep.'

'Settled,' she agreed, plunging the key into the lock, before picking up her case and stepping inside.

Following their stay in Mrs Tillens's house, the room, into which she entered now, was positively palatial. She closed the door behind her with a contented sigh. The room was of a good size, with a clean double-bed, a narrow wardrobe, a washstand, a velveteen armchair and a dressing table. She set down the case and sat in the chair a moment. The bed looked decidedly appealing, but then the idea of taking a long hot soak in the bath was even more so. She looked at a wooden carriage clock on the dresser; it was only just gone midday.

'Goodness me,' she blurted out, standing up sharply. 'What on earth are we thinking?'

Striding over to the washstand, Harriet splashed her face with water and freshened up, then picked up her bag, marched out of the room and knocked on Fraser's door. She heard a groan of displeasure and the sound of feet shuffling heavily across the room.

'What?' he snapped, appearing in his blue-and-white-striped pyjamas with a severe scowl etched on his face.

'Have you noticed what time it is? Come on. Get dressed,' Harriet instructed. 'We've got a good few hours yet before dinner: let's go and find Lina.'

Fraser blew out a puff of exasperated air: 'No.'

'Pardon?'

'No,' he repeated more earnestly. 'Let's just do what we agreed: rest, bathe and have a meal. *Tomorrow* we go looking for Lina.'

Harriet stared at him for a moment, measuring her reply. She didn't want to waste a moment of time out here, but she saw the tiredness, the vulnerability in her son. 'Yes, quite right, too. Go back to sleep and I'll wake you, as arranged.'

Fraser closed the door, and she heard the sounds of retreating scuffing feet and the grumbling give of the bed springs, as he dropped back onto the mattress.

Harriet placed the key into her door and went through the motions of opening and closing it, all without moving from where she was standing in the corridor. Quietly, she stole down the stairs and into the lobby.

'Everything okay with the room, madam?' the receptionist asked, leaping up from reading a newspaper behind the desk.

'Oh, perfectly, thank you,' Harriet replied. 'How far away is that area you mentioned earlier – the plaine de…something-or-other?'

'Plaine d'Amour,' he corrected, putting on some sort of affected French accent, which made her wonder why it wasn't called something Flemish.

'Doesn't that mean 'plain of love' in French, or something like it?' Harriet asked.

'I believe so.'

'How very odd. Where will I find this Plaine d'Amour?'

The receptionist crouched down and reached under the counter. 'Here,' he said, placing a piece of paper down between them: a map, she realised, although one clearly made of the city before the war. She watched, as he drew a pencil circle around a building. 'We're sort of here.' He briefly flipped the map around and drew another circle, this one much larger, and then turned the map back to face Harriet. 'That's sort of the Plaine d'Amour.'

'Right,' she said, sort of understanding.

'The roads are all the same, just don't take any account of the buildings marked on the map.'

'Oh, may I keep it?'

'By all means,' he enthused. 'Good luck.'

Harriet smiled, thanked him, and left the hotel with a confident stride. When she was safely out of sight, she paused to scrutinise the map, not having the foggiest where she was going, or even if the area was within reasonable walking distance. Just in front of her was a crossroads and she searched for any indication of the names of the intersecting streets. It was all very well to say that the roads had not changed, but there was not one sign to give any indication of a name.

'Mrs McDougall!'

She recoiled slightly, knowing that the voice belonged to the hotel receptionist. She knew, also, what he was about to say, so she decided to pre-empt him. 'It's *that* way,' she said, as if to herself, and turned to see him.

'Yes, it is that way,' he said with a chuckle. 'Then the next right, then carry on straight ahead for a while, then left… I can't remember precisely after that, but you'll almost be there by then.'

'Marvellous,' she responded, trooping back past him self-assuredly.

She took the right turning and continued down a long straight road, which was cluttered with an unsightly fusion of damaged abandoned buildings and new hastily erected ones devoid of architectural style or merit. The whole area reminded her of pictures, which she had seen from the Wild West of America, where whole towns full of gold-speculators had sprung up overnight.

Looking at the map, she could see that she was making very good progress and needn't march at such an athletic pace. The sky above the motley collection of buildings was an empty lacklustre shade of grey, ostensibly reflecting the mood of the city below it.

'*Goeiedag*. Hallo. Bonjour,' she greeted the first person upon whom she clapped eyes.

The lady—an old woman—nodded with a mistrustful, suspicious air about her and continued past.

'*Ik zoek iemand, die* Lina Peeters *heet*,' Harriet called, but still the old lady walked without turning.

After a few minutes more, she reached a junction and, hammered into the ground, was a white sign with one end pointing across the street with black writing, which read *PLAINE D'AMOUR*.

She needed only to continue a short distance further before the map became purposeless: in the near-distance was a great profusion of pre-fabricated homes.

Harriet stopped and stared at the mini-city of identical homes, single-story wooden structures with low-pitched roofs. Each had one window on the back, one on the front beside the door and two on the side. Territorial divisions between each house were non-existent: dogs and small farmyard animals seemed to roam the area freely. Compacted dirt had engraved well-trodden paths through the mud upon which the estate had been erected.

Through the general stillness of the place, which Harriet now attributed to the Sabbath, she caught reassuring glimmers of life: a baby crying somewhere in the distance; the low, barely audible babble of men in conversation; a dog barking; a window closing.

Harriet began to follow the nearest path, entering the Plaine d'Amour. She intended to stop and talk to the first person that she met, but as she continued to walk, she saw nobody; just endless rows of indistinguishable pre-fab houses. A sudden wave of panic came over her, thinking that she might never be able to find her way back out again. She spotted the remnants of the Cloth Hall tower in the distance, and realised that, if she just headed in its general direction, then she should eventually get herself out of this strange maze.

She was startled by a sound to her left and whipped around to see an equally startled elderly lady standing in an open doorway. Harriet hastily composed herself and smiled. 'Hallo,' she said, before repeating the phrase, 'Ik zoek iemand, die Lina Peeters heet.'

The old lady's eyes widened. '*Ja, die ken ik wel.*'

'Ja?' Harriet repeated, quite surprised to have found someone, who knew her so quickly.

The old lady nodded. 'Ja.'

'Where does she... *Zij... woont... waar?*'

'*Naast de stallen,*' the old lady said, pointing down the path.

If her very limited Dutch was correct, then Lina Peeters was to be found next to something, but quite what *stallen* were, she had no idea. Her look of bewilderment prompted the old lady to whinny and raise her head up and down. 'Ah! A horse—stables! Yes, thank you.'

The old lady grinned a wide toothless smile, pointed down the path again, and then whinnied once more for good measure and guffawed. It lifted Harriet's spirits to see someone able to achieve such an expression of happiness in this oasis amid such utter desolation.

Harriet almost skipped down the path, so excited was she to finally meet Lina. When a stable complex came into view, her pace increased almost to a trot. It was a long wooden building painted black with a dozen stable doors, most of which were open at the top, giving a view of the horses inside.

She arrived at the stables, breathless but grinning like a fool.

'Kan ik je helpen?' a young voice asked from somewhere beside her.

She turned to see a youthful-looking man pushing a wheelbarrow of hay towards her. Harriet greeted him, then repeated her memorised phrase about looking for Lina Peeters.

The young man nodded and pointed to the pre-fab house to the right of the complex.

'Dank uwel,' Harriet said. This was it. She drew in a breath, not having the foggiest of what she was going to say, or how she was going to say it. She knocked on the door and waited.

It took just a few seconds for the door to be opened by a pretty lady, who appeared to be in her early thirties. Her hair, dark with grease for want of a good wash, was pulled back behind her head and she wore dirty, unkempt clothing. 'Hello. I'm looking for someone called Lina Peeters.'

'*Pardon? Ik begrijp u niet.*'

'Lina?'

The woman nodded but then changed to shake her head, as she continued: '*Ik spreek geen Engels.*'

Harriet was confused. She was certain that Miss Yavuz had said that Lina had had a good grasp of English by the time that she had left Woolwich. 'Lina Peeters?'

'Lina Peeters, ja.'

'Woolwich? England? Malcolm McDougall?' Harriet said, painfully slowly.

Lina shook her head. '*Ik begrijp het niet.*'

Harriet sighed, as the realisation that this woman could not be the correct person began to sink in. She pointed at Lina and, just to be absolutely certain, said, 'You, England. War. Erm…?' Then, she found herself sounding very much like Arthur Dooley, making sounds of explosions with her fingers erupting from clenched fists.

Lina shook her head firmly. She had understood.

'Malcolm McDougall?' Harriet persisted.

Lina shook her head once more, but this time not disguising her growing irritation. Without saying anything further, she retreated and closed the door.

Harriet's newfound vigour suddenly faded, and a heavy tiredness returned to consume her. For today at least, she admitted defeat and turned back on herself to retrace her steps out of the Plaine d'Amour, chin tucked to her chest.

She arrived back at the hotel, exhausted.

'How did it go, Mrs McDougall?' the receptionist asked. 'Any joy?'

'Unfortunately not, no,' Harriet answered. 'I found the place, no problems with that, thank you, but no sign of the correct Lina Peeters.'

'Oh, terribly sorry to hear that.'

Harriet shrugged, as she strode towards the staircase, trying to muster at least a light resilient indifference. 'I can but try again tomorrow.' She stopped and called back, 'Oh, I'd be awfully grateful if you could keep from mentioning this little...excursion of mine to my son, he does like to worry so and—'

'Ah,' the receptionist replied, in what could only be the commencement of a confession. 'I'm afraid he already knows. Terribly sorry. He tried knocking for you and, when you didn't answer, he came down here asking me to open up the room to check if you were alright. I rather felt I had no choice but to tell him that you had in fact left the hotel...'

'Yes, of course,' Harriet agreed, swallowing down her annoyance. 'And where is he now? He didn't go looking for me, did he?'

He indicated to the room behind him. 'No, no. I believe he may be waiting for you in the saloon, Mrs McDougall.'

'Right,' Harriet said, changing direction for the saloon, feeling oddly child-like, as though she had just been sent to the headmaster's room for misbehaving. She was expecting to see Fraser facing the door, arms folded and sporting a severe, officious expression. Instead, she found him sitting at a round table with three men of a similar age, drinking beer, smoking cigarettes and looking rather jovial indeed.

'Ma, nice of you to join us!' he called. 'Come and sit down.'

Harriet smiled and approached the table, not finding herself able to match their established jaunty mood.

'These are my friends,' Fraser said, pointing first to the chap on his left, then proceeding to introduce the other two men. 'This is Stefan, Kurt and Franz.'

Baffled, Harriet watched, as the three men each stood in turn and shook her hand. They greeted her in English but with an unmistakable lilt of German. 'Hello,' she said meekly.

'Sit down, Ma,' Fraser insisted firmly.

'Goodness,' Harriet murmured, lingering momentarily behind the one vacant seat at the table between two German men, as a whole host of questions and competing thoughts spooled into her mind, and wrestling with an ingrained prejudice.

'Did you find her?' Fraser asked. Without giving her time to answer, he turned to the German men and, in a voice lightened by alcohol, added, 'My mother went off on an errand to track down the elusive Lina Peeters, my dead brother's lover by all accounts.'

'No, unfortunately not,' Harriet answered. 'But I had a good scout around. I'm sure we can find her in the morning.' She turned and caught the waiter's attention. 'Could I trouble you for a cocoa, please?'

'What was I saying, Stefan?' Fraser asked the man beside him.

'Christmas truce...' Stefan answered, taking a long swig of beer and nearly quaffing the lot in one go.

'Ah, yes! The Christmas truce of 1914. That was it.' Fraser hung his head, eyes closed recalling what it had been like. Then, he opened his hands in incredulity. 'I was there—in No-Man's-Land—playing football against them...against *you*,' he said, his eyes indicating the three German men. 'It was actually rather fun.'

'And so *friendly*,' Kurt added.

'Yes, absolutely friendly,' Fraser continued. 'Why in God's name didn't we just *refuse* to fight? Can you imagine what might have happened if the two opposing trenches had just said 'No! We're not fighting anymore!' I mean, they couldn't have done anything about it, then.'

The three men seemed in agreement, each of them nodding with dreadful discernment, which came crashing in on the back of hindsight.

'We should have been stronger, ja,' Stefan agreed. 'What, would they have shot every one of us? Of course not.'

'Do you know, when we returned to our trenches on Christmas night,' Fraser said, 'I was actually happy. I actually felt like something considerable and powerful had shifted in the world; the men on both sides were just that: men, not soldiers. No-Man's-Land was just a football pitch. I could feel it; not one person in either trench wanted to continue fighting on.'

Franz dabbed his eyes with his sleeve. 'I felt this same thing, also, on our side...' His voice became pinched, and whatever else he had wanted to say caught and stuck in his throat. He blew out his cheeks and picked up his glass of beer.

Harriet leant across the table, placed her hand on Franz's and gently squeezed. For a few seconds he held his hand motionless, then rolled it over and squeezed hers in return. As their hands united, the vying thoughts about the morality of socialising with these men all but vanished. Only one unanswerable question remained, unshakable in her mind: What would Malcolm and Edward have thought? But she had to believe that they, too, would have longed for such a peace to reign.

'It must be difficult, being here so soon after the war,' Harriet commented to nobody and everybody.

'Yes, it is,' Kurt agreed. 'We keep low and we keep quiet, and we do our work.'

'What is it that you do, exactly?' she asked.

'Stonemasons,' Stefan answered with a scoff. 'You can imagine the—what is the word? Bad humour?—of the situation: the Germans destroy the city, then they have to come back to rebuild it because the Belgian masons are all dead. Many do not like this.'

'Irony's the word,' Harriet said. 'And yes, I do see that.' She glanced at Fraser. 'He's a civil engineer—erm, building engineer—and I'm sure the authorities here must be crying out for such a talent.'

'Yes, of course,' Kurt said. 'Here, especially. If you want me to, I can ask if there is work here for you?'

Fraser shook his head. 'No, definitely don't do that,' he said, shooting a look of contempt at his mother.

'Why not?' Stefan asked searchingly.

Fraser sipped his drink, taking his time to answer. 'Because… I just can't; I don't care enough. When I woke up on Boxing Day morning in 1914, I was still so full of hope. The world seemed full of potential and possibilities. But then we'd barely been awake for an hour and the orders came through to attack those men…those men, whose hands I'd shaken just hours before…those men, who I had shared songs with…exchanged jokes…had a football match. That hope, potential and possibility was suddenly gone, replaced with a deep anger at the bloody faceless men reigniting war from the safe confines of their warm offices in London. All, as I watched more and more friends, and then my own two brothers get slaughtered on the bloody battlefield. By the time the Armistice came, all I was left with was numb indifference. Complete…and utter…indifference.' Fraser began to sob. 'It's consumed me. It *is* me and I'm scared that it'll never leave me or change…'

Kurt put his arm over Fraser's shoulder, and Fraser leant into his side and cried more than Harriet had ever seen him cry in his entire life.

Chapter Twelve

13th September 1919, Ypres, Belgium

With a restored Fraser at her heels, Harriet strode into the saloon, certain that she, too, had not had such a good night's sleep in donkeys' years. She felt refreshed, invigorated and, after some breakfast, ready to track down Lina Peeters.

'Oh,' Harriet said, pausing at the doorway to the saloon; each of the ten tables was already occupied.

'We are rather late, Ma,' Fraser whispered behind her.

Harriet blushed at the glances noting her tardiness, which came from the eyes fixed on her around the room. She smiled pleasantly and noticed two vacant spaces at a middle-aged couple's table, whom she had overheard speaking English the night before. 'Good morning, may we join you, please?'

'Oh, please, do,' the man said. He was smartly dressed in a black suit, white shirt and black tie. He was balding, but an unsuccessful attempt had been made to drag hair from close above his right ear in order to cover the fact.

'Thank you. I'm Mrs McDougall and this is Fraser, my son,' Harriet said, sitting beside the lady and nodding courteously. Harriet stared across the table at the man's hair, fascinated. She wondered how it must look when wet. Presumably it tumbled down over his shoulders, almost to his chest. A most odd and slightly unpleasant image, she thought.

'I'm Jack and this is my wife, Daisy.' The man thrust a forkful of bacon into his mouth, as it brushed through his substantial grey moustache.

'Harriet,' she felt the need to say. Quite what the rules were regarding this growing informality, she had no idea.

Jack was quick to prevent a silence from forming: 'May I ask the purpose of your visit to Ypres?'

'My brother was killed in action not far from here,' Fraser explained. 'We came to visit his grave, and…well…just to see the area, I suppose.'

'And, importantly,' Harriet added quickly, 'to find a certain young lady involved with my son. Lina Peeters.' She looked hopefully at the couple, as if they might have encountered her on their travels, but they made no reaction upon hearing the name.

'What about yourselves?' Fraser asked them in return.

'We're trying to find out what happened to our poor Sidney,' the lady said quietly. 'Killed in the Second Battle of Ypres but his body was never found…'

'Oh, I am sorry,' Harriet said. The absence of a body, she felt, must add a further layer of anguish and uncertainty to the grief shared by every parent faced with the worst news imaginable. Cruelly, it also maintained the unlikely perennial possibility that a mistake had been made and that he was alive somewhere, perhaps confused in a foreign country, or lying seriously injured in a hospital. She herself had imagined every possible scenario, and every door-knock or postal delivery offered a glimmer of optimism for an alternative outcome.

'We're still no closer to the truth, though,' the man said. 'One minute he was there, running across No-Man's-Land under a hail of bullets, and the next he was gone. None of his comrades saw him enter the German trenches, or return to the British line, or get hit. And…to the best of our knowledge, there were no mortar explosions.'

'He just vanished,' the lady said.

'Well,' Harriet began, 'if there's one thing I will say, it's that you must persevere; the answers are out there, somewhere, you just need to persist to find them.'

The couple nodded and murmured their mutual agreement.

'Good morning!' a young male waiter said breezily, appearing beside Fraser at the table. 'Can I get you a tea or coffee?'

'Coffee, for both of us, please,' Harriet ordered.

'Lovely,' he said, scribbling on a notepad. 'And to eat we have porridge, or we have toast with bacon and egg.'

Harriet and Fraser ordered bacon and egg, then, as the waiter disappeared to the kitchen, Daisy whispered, 'You just *cannot* get a decent cup of tea *anywhere* outside of England, can you, Jack?' she said, turning to her husband.

'No, Daisy. It's a disgrace,' he concurred. 'As soon as you cross that channel of ours, you've had it. I don't know what's wrong with people but they *cannot* make a good cup of tea for toffee.'

A sudden burst of laughter from the corner of the room drew attention from tables around the dining area. It was the three German stonemasons sharing a joke.

Jack shook his head. 'They've got a bloody nerve,' he said loudly.

'Jack…' his wife said, the leaning of whose tone Harriet could not quite discern.

'Don't *Jack* me. Well, who do they think they are? Hmm? They really have some ruddy gall, I tell you,' he fumed. 'They should never be allowed to step foot in this city…or this bloody country, for that matter.'

'Jack, that's enough,' his wife said weakly.

Fraser, saying nothing, stood up and left the table.

Harriet watched, as he walked across the room to join the three Germans.

'God!' Jack blustered, his crimson head flicking incredulously between Fraser and the Germans, his wife and Harriet, disturbing his hair in the process. 'Whatever's he doing of?'

'They're all just men, who did whatever their country commanded,' Harriet appealed.

'Really? And how would you feel, knowing that one of those…those Hun over there, had killed your son? Hmm? I tell you, if I knew it…!' he continued to rant. 'If I knew it, I'd string them up by their ankles and leave them to rot. I would, you know.'

Harriet wanted to say something pious, something which elevated her onto a higher moral plain, something about forgiveness. Or perhaps say something pithy, flipping the situation, and asking him to imagine the countless poor German women currently mourning *their* sons' lives, which would have, doubtless, been taken by their son, Sidney. But the truth was infinitely more complex: she didn't know how she would feel if she really came face-to-face with the man who had taken Malcolm's life.

'There! See! See!' Jack raged. 'It's in your *eyes*, but you don't have the nerve to say that you despise them, too. Now, control your son, won't you?'

Every table around the room had fallen silent.

Everybody was listening and looking.

Harriet knitted her fingers together in front of her and cleared her throat. 'No, I shan't *control* him. And—while we are on the subject, if you must know—I don't despise them. Really, I don't. I feel nothing but compassion. My heart overflows with compassion towards them, and all the other men like them around the world, who, despite their having been asked to do *the* most arduous, horrendous and unspeakable of things to each other in the name of their country, have survived against all odds. And…at the same time…I feel nothing but compassion for you, too, for your indescribable loss.' Harriet paused and drew in a breath. 'No, the people I despise are the craven instigators of war, men who think nothing of sending thousands upon thousands to their deaths in order to maintain ill-gotten, archaic, colonial allegiances, nationalistic superiority and a dying empire's power. *These* are the men, who killed our children—*all* our children.'

The room seemed to hold its collective breath, as Harriet finished speaking.

Nobody spoke.

Nobody moved.

Time stood quite still for a while.

'Two mugs of our *delicious* Turkish coffee!' the waiter sang, prancing merrily back into the room. He placed the cups on the table, and then stopped, his index fingers still coiled around the handles, as he gradually angled his gaze up and around the saloon. 'What is it?' he breathed, slowly looking over his shoulder, as if an unseen attacker were lying in wait behind him.

'It's nothing,' Jack said calmly, his eyes moist. He dabbed his mouth with a napkin and rose from the table. 'Good day.'

'Good day to you, Jack.' Harriet replied with sincerity.

His wife looked at nobody and swiftly followed him out of the room, her face sallow and her cheeks flushed.

Harriet picked up the two coffee cups and carried them over to where Fraser was now sitting. 'Please, may I join you?'

There was a light coolness to the air in what was an otherwise sunny September morning; one of those lingering summer days, which, back home in England, was a foreshadowing of a pending change of season, when leaves' colours changed, as they prepared to fall. 'Phenology', Malcolm had told her, once: nature's response to the changing seasons. But here in the Plaine d'Amour, there were no trees or vegetation, or signs from the natural world of the approaching autumn.

'What a place,' Fraser commented.

'Quite,' Harriet agreed.

Today, the sight was very different to the one which she had visited yesterday; there was an air of busyness, of its being a normal working day: women were hanging laundry on string lines, which ran between the houses; bare-footed children were running and playing; men were employed in various labouring roles, fixing roofs, erecting even more pre-fabs, calling to one another in a blend of languages. That general

137

busyness of the area seemed to magnify the scale of the task ahead of them.

'Do you think that we ought to separate and tackle half a side each?' Harriet suggested.

'Are you sure you'll be alright by yourself?' Fraser asked.

Harriet frowned. 'Yes, thank you. Will *you*?'

'I'll yell if I need you,' he replied.

'Have you remembered the phrase?' Harriet asked, not giving him a chance to reply, before saying, 'Ik zoek iemand, die Lina Peeters heet.'

'Ja,' Fraser answered. 'Dank uwel.'

'Good. Right, then, I'll take this side,' Harriet said, pointing to the vaguely defined area on her left, in which was contained the stables that she had visited yesterday. She felt that she would be in a better position than Fraser to tackle the inevitability of being directed back towards the incorrect Lina Peeters.

Harriet walked briskly, not entirely sure how she was going to approach today's mission. Would she knock on every door and ask if they knew her, or just talk to the numerous people going about their business in the streets? She settled on the latter idea, certain that the community was close-knit enough so as to be reasonably acquainted with those living around them.

Just two houses into the make-shift street, Harriet spotted a man who was chopping wood. She approached him and asked if he knew of Lina. He looked up to the sky briefly in consideration, then shook his head. Harriet thanked him and continued towards three women dressed in filthy clothes, washing linen in a large copper bucket. She asked the same question, and the three women looked each from one to the next, doubtful, and all replying in the negative. 'Dank uwel,' Harriet said, moving on down the street.

A short distance away, Harriet spotted a young girl, sitting in the open doorway to her home. Her head was resting sulkily in her hands, her elbows propped on her knees. Harriet approached her with a wide grin. 'Hallo!' she said with an accent, followed by her standard request phrase.

The girl gawked at her, but said nothing, so Harriet repeated the question and then, for good measure, said it in French and then English. The girl shrugged.

'Rightio. Marvellous,' Harriet said, thrusting her head upwards, as she changed direction, ready to intercept a young lady who was walking towards her. She took in a breath, her face a fixed rictus, as she asked the woman politely if she knew of Lina.

The woman looked to be in her mid-twenties, tall with long blonde hair. 'Erm…are you English?' she asked in a heavily accented voice.

'Yes, is it that obvious?' Harriet replied bashfully.

The woman grinned. 'A little. Lina Peeters—yes, I know her. Well, actually I know two.'

Harriet emitted a small gasp at the news: 'Does one of them live by the stables?'

The woman's eyes lit up. 'Yes, that is right; she is my good friend.'

'Not that one,' Harriet quickly corrected. 'The *other* one. Where might I find *her*?'

'I can take you to her house, if you would like this?'

She clapped her hands together for joy and exhaled: 'That would be just wonderful! Thank you.'

'Follow me this way,' she instructed, taking a cut-through between two pre-fabs.

'Do you know if this Lina Peeters lived in England during the war?' Harriet asked, as they walked on.

'Yes, that is right. Yes.'

'She knew my son!' Harriet declared, before adding, 'He was killed in the—' she stopped herself and listened. She thought that she had heard 'Ma' being called. There it was again! Clear as day. Fraser was calling her from somewhere in the direction in which they were headed. 'Is it nearby?'

The woman pointed vaguely to the stretch of pre-fabs in front of them. 'Just there.'

The houses to which she pointed were notably grubbier than the rest, perhaps the first ones to have been built. They stood on the extremity of the Plaine d'Amour boundary, in stark contrast to the ruins of the old city visible behind them. The crumbling towers of the historic Cloth Hall and the cathedral seemed all the more doleful and tragic when viewed against the vulgar, gaudy pre-fabs.

The woman stopped in front of one of the houses, just as Fraser appeared from behind it. They both pointed simultaneously to the same pre-fab.

'Thank you so much,' Harriet said to the woman, before rushing to knock on the door. This was it; she was certain.

The door was opened a few seconds later by an elderly man, with dirty skin and dirty clothing, stooped over a cane.

'Ik zoek iemand, die Lina Peeters heet,' Harriet said, trying her best not to sound trite, having said the same thing for the umpteenth time.

Through narrowed eyes, which looked painful, he muttered something, which she doubted that she ever would have understood, even if she had been fluent in Flemish.

'Lina Peeters?' Harriet said, more loudly and clearly. 'I'm from England and I would like to meet her.'

From somewhere in the house, a female voice called out, 'Lina is working. British Tavern. Grand Place.'

Harriet craned her neck around the bent figure before her, searching the dull room from where the voice had emanated. Every inch of floorspace was taken with grubby mattresses and bedding. The windows were inexplicably covered with dark baize material, but despite this, she could make out the shapes of several people. 'Thank you,' Harriet called openly into the dimness.

With some difficulty, the old man turned and closed the door.

'Well?' Fraser asked.

'Apparently she's at work: the British Tavern in Grand Place, wherever that may be.'

'Isn't it the square in front of what was the Cloth Hall?' Fraser turned and pointed towards the historic ruins. 'Just over there. We can walk that in five minutes, no trouble.'

'Let's go.'

As they walked, Harriet told Fraser of the awful conditions, which she had just witnessed inside the pre-fab. 'Poor Lina,' she said. 'Whether she's *our* Lina or not, poor girl, living like that. What these people have been through.' 'I mean, just look at that,' she said, drawing to a stop a short distance before the ghostly skeleton of the Cloth Hall. 'Seven hundred years that's managed to stand there. Now look at it.'

'Personally, I don't think I would have come back, if I were her,' Fraser commented. 'Too depressing.'

'Yes,' she agreed absent-mindedly, as she read a white sign, written in English, beside what was once an entrance to the Cloth Hall: *Notice. This is Holy Ground. No stone of this fabric may be taken away. It is a Heritage for all Civilised Peoples.* The declaration was signed in the bottom right corner by the Town Mayor of Ypres.

'Come on. Let's find this jolly tavern,' Fraser said, turning to face the run of newly built wooden premises on the opposite side of the square. 'I'm in need of a coffee, if nothing else.'

'There it is!' she pointed. 'Can't really miss that, can you?'

The building, standing among several other new structures lining the Grand Place, was painted bright blue and the words *CAFÉ RESTAURANT* were written in large letters above the door. Arching around a central window on the first floor were the words *BRITISH TAVERN*. To think that yesterday they had been dropped off by the taxi-cab just yards away on the other side of the Cloth Hall, where the rebuilding of the city centre had yet to begin.

Harriet grabbed Fraser's arm, and hurried across the square towards it, a sudden niggle of nervousness rising in her stomach. Uncertainty snuck into her mind and began posing unhelpful questions. What if she wasn't the correct Lina Peeters? What if she didn't want to answer her questions? What if she had something terrible to say about Malcolm?

'Ma? What's up?' Fraser asked.

'Nothing. Let's get inside.' She pulled open the front door and entered the tavern. It was a large space, filled with a motley mixture of tables and chairs, at which were sat an eclectic mixture of people: soldiers, builders, well-dressed men and working women.

Fraser headed to a small, vacant, square table with two chairs nearby, and sat down. Harriet sat opposite, and immediately began scanning the room for waitresses, who might have been Lina. There were three women, each dressed in a plain white blouse and a black skirt, scurrying between the tables and an unseen kitchen through a door behind the counter. She judged all three to be within an acceptable age-range of Malcolm. She reasoned that there was only one expedient way to find out. 'Lina?' she called across the restaurant.

'Ma!' Fraser whispered harshly, as half the restaurant turned to look in their direction.

All three waitresses glanced over, but then two of them took a sideways glimpse at the third, presumably wondering if she was acquainted with the woman, who had called out her name.

Harriet smiled at the waitress and beckoned her over.

'Well, that was mightily embarrassing, Ma,' Fraser scorned under his breath. 'Would it have been too much to expect you to have just gone over, and asked politely which one she was?'

'Poppycock,' Harriet dismissed.

The waitress approached their table, a polite but reticent look on her face. She was a slight, young thing with long brown hair tied back in a bun behind her head. She had dark eyes and beautiful long eyelashes and a soft, warm smile.

Harriet stood up, thrust her hand forward, and said, 'Hello! I'm very much hoping that you are one Lina Peeters, who lived in Woolwich, England during the war?'

Lina's face contorted into astonished confusion, as she hesitantly shook Harriet's outstretched hand. 'Yes, that is correct. Do I know you? From England?'

'No, you knew my son, Malcolm McDougall.'

Lina inhaled sharply, and her eyes circled, settling briefly on Fraser, then returning to Harriet. 'I see,' she muttered.

'I understand you were a good companion of his? Could we talk?'

Lina nodded. 'Yes, of course. I will get you something to drink, and then we will talk, yes?'

'Marvellous,' Harriet said. 'Two coffees, thank you so much.'

Harriet returned to her seat, watching as Lina walked over to one of the other waitresses. From the surreptitious backward glances, their hushed conversation undoubtedly involved Harriet's and Fraser's visit.

'Now we've actually found her, what exactly do you want to find out?' Fraser asked, drawing Harriet's attention away from the waitresses.

'Just to know who she is, that's all, and to let her talk about Malcolm a bit,' Harriet said. 'He did use his *one* annual pass to visit a woman about whom he'd never uttered a word to us: she must have meant something to him.'

'Well, don't blame *her* that he didn't mention it; it's not her fault.'

'Thank you for that piece of advice, Fraser McDougall,' she said, folding her arms. She looked across to see that Lina was on her way back over, carrying a tray of three drinks, which she placed down on the table.

'Here are our drinks. I can have a fifteen-minute break, so I will talk with you,' she said, reaching for a chair from the neighbouring table and sitting between the two of them. 'So you are Malcolm's mother, yes? You are exactly like he described.'

Harriet's eyes widened, not sure of the implications of her words. 'Right...'

Lina laughed, and placed her hand on Harriet's forearm. 'No, it is always good things he said about you.'

'Really?' Harriet said, disbelievingly.

'Really,' she insisted. 'He spoke a great deal about his family in Sedlescombe—is that the name?' Harriet nodded, ignoring the clumsy mispronunciation, and then she continued. 'And you are Malcolm's brother, yes?'

Fraser nodded and offered her his hand. 'Fraser.'

'Ah, the *older* one,' she said.

'That's me,' he confirmed.

'Are you here in Ypres to find me?' she asked, sounding both intrigued and surprised.

'That's right, yes,' Harriet answered. 'It's all a rather long and complicated tale, but the gist of it is that I wanted to know what happened to Malcolm before he died, and when your name came up, I knew that I just had to find you.'

'I see,' Lina said with a smile. 'And did you know that I would be here, in this place?'

'Your old landlady, Miss Yavuz said that you'd—'

'Miss Yavuz?' Lina interrupted with a laugh. 'My goodness!'

'Yes,' Harriet said, realising that she perhaps sounded a little unbalanced in the evident doggedness of her pursuit and that her explanation required simplifying somewhat. 'Miss Yavuz led us to Ypres, and a chap at the hotel suggested going to the Plaine d'Amour.'

'And the Van de Veldes sent you here?' Lina guessed.

'That's right.'

Lina sat back with a sigh, which appeared to represent a shift towards guardedness. 'But what is it that you think I can help you with? You've come all this way and what for?'

'You don't need to be nervous of us,' Fraser said, corroborating what Harriet herself felt that she was witnessing in the young girl.

'It was really just to talk to you,' Harriet said. 'You were clearly important to him; he returned to England to see you, and you alone...'

Lina clutched her cup, her eyes shifting from Fraser to Harriet. 'He said that you would not be happy if you found out that he was in England without telling you that.'

'Well,' Harriet began, sensing a sharp glance from Fraser in her peripheral vision, 'it certainly was a little *odd* to discover that he had visited England in June 1917.'

'Yes, I am sure. We had a week together doing our best to forget the war, just for one moment. We went to the theatre and music hall, and we took walks in the park. One day we went into London, and we saw Buckingham Palace and Big Ben...' Her face lit up at the recollections. 'We made plans to come—together, I mean—to visit with you at the end of that week. A surprise. Malcolm bought the train tickets and knew the train we should take, everything. But the night before we would have come, I fell over in the…in the blackness, you know, no street lights, and cracked my head.' She tilted her head and pointed to an inch-long scar just above her right temple. 'I went to hospital, and there was no way I could go to Sedlescombe now. I said to Malcolm he must go, but he stayed with me, and then he went back to his army…his regiment.' She shrugged forlornly and Harriet placed her hand on hers, as she was gripped by the deepest sadness over what could have been.

The gravity of the fact that Malcolm had wanted to bring home a girl for the first time struck her heart; that he had stayed by her bedside instead of coming home provided even greater evidence of the seriousness of their relationship. She knew it could have meant only one thing. 'You were to marry, weren't you?' Harriet asked.

Lina nodded, but did not look up.

'Oh, goodness…'

'He asked me to marry him when we were in London. We had dinner in the Waldorf Hotel with an orchestra playing; it was just wonderful. Then we walked along the Thames, and he got down on his knee and asked me to marry him, and I said yes. It was that night, getting back late in the dark to Woolwich, when I fell over.'

Harriet breathed heavily, tears welling in her eyes, as flickers of scenes from their unlived, long, happily married life, which they should have led together, momentarily reeled over her mind's eye. But it was a life destined not to be.

Fraser cleared his throat and punctured the thick silence: 'I presume you met Malcolm when he came over in 1916 to the gas labs at Woolwich?'

'No, actually,' Lina corrected. 'That was a happy chance. We met here, in Ypres in May 1915.'

'Oh, right,' Fraser said.

'Yes. From the end of 1914, the German artillery began to attack the city. On November the twenty-second, the beautiful Cloth Hall and cathedral were destroyed, and the people here left in lots of great groups. I lived just behind here with my family and our house was hit by a shell. My mother was killed, but my sister and I were lucky to be pulled from the wreckage by a group of British soldiers. One of them was Malcolm, and he looked after me when it was a very dangerous place, here. He and his friend carried me out on a stretcher and got me medical help.'

'Goodness me,' Harriet said.

'Malcolm saved my life, but I did not get to thank him. The city was completely destroyed: not one house or tree was left standed up at the end of 1917. Not one. Our neighbours, the Van de Veldes looked after me and took me with them to England.'

'What about your sister and the rest of your family?' Harriet asked.

'By then, I had no other family; just my sister. She fell in with some bad girls and she stayed in Belgium with them.'

'What about your dad... No other brothers or sisters?'

'Many Belgian people were punished for any delay in the German advance. Houses were raided and put on fire, and thousands of normal peoples were killed. My father was one of these. My brother, as the only male child, was called up to fight. He was taken prisoner and put in Soltau Camp in Germany, where he died from tuberculous two weeks before the end of the war.'

'My dear girl,' Harriet said, shuffling her chair closer to Lina, and placing her arm over her shoulder. 'And now you live in that place...'

'Yes, we are lucky,' Lina said. 'Many have nothing.'

Harriet hadn't considered Lina lucky to this point, but, given the high numbers of those destitute, whom she had had cause and the misfortune to notice recently, maybe she was indeed one of the more privileged ones. But she couldn't help thinking that she would have had a better life remaining in Woolwich. 'Did you actually *want* to leave England?' Harriet asked.

'No, but the Van de Veldes... They do so much for me, and they wanted to come back, and so I went with them and live in their house. I have no choice.'

A short but meaningful quietness wrapped around them, as they drank their coffees. Harriet's thoughts were clogged with the new information, which she had just learned. By all accounts, in the closing weeks of his life, Malcolm had been happy, and the reason had been Lina, a woman whom she would likely never see again after they left this restaurant.

'Did you visit his grave already?' Lina asked.

Harriet nodded.

'I put on the ground the seeds of a flower, which he liked a lot: the blue poppy. Were there flowers when you visited?'

'Ah, that explains it,' Harriet said. 'Yes and beautiful they were, too.'

Lina smiled, as she placed her empty cup onto the table. 'Unfortunately, I must go back to work. It was very nice to meet you both, and, who knows, maybe one day I will come to England and see you.' She rose from her chair, offering them her hand to shake.

Harriet stood up and sandwiched Lina's hand between both of hers, unable to deal with the thought of never again seeing somebody, who had meant so much to her son. Marriage and children would undoubtedly have conferred upon Harriet and Lina a life-long bond, which the war and Malcolm's death had now decisively denied them. All she could think to say, in order to surmount this crushing sense of loss, was, 'May I write to you?'

'I would like that very much,' Lina answered.

'Splendid,' Harriet said, rummaging in her bag. She placed a piece of paper on the table, and then wrote out in block capitals her name and address. 'Here you go.'

Lina tucked the piece of paper into a pouch in the front of her apron, then shook her hand once more. 'Goodbye.'

'Wait,' Harriet said, opening her purse. She poured out the few francs, which she had on her person, and handed them to Lina.

'But this is much more than two coffees,' Lina protested.

'Call it…a tip,' Harriet said.

Lina hesitantly slipped the money into her apron. 'That is very kind, thank you.'

'It's the least I can do in return for the happiness you brought my son in his last weeks.'

'Goodbye,' Lina said affectionately, before turning back towards the counter.

'Bye,' Fraser said.

'Cheerio,' Harriet said. Then, facing Fraser, 'Come on, I need some fresh air.'

'Well, I wasn't expecting a fiancée,' Fraser commented, when they were back out in the square. 'Were you?'

'Not for a second, no,' Harriet answered. 'I began to suspect it, when she said they had both planned to come down to Sedlescombe. She seems very nice, I can see why Malcolm liked her.'

'Hmm,' Fraser agreed.

Harriet threaded her arm through Fraser's and they walked at a leisurely pace with the Cloth Hall behind them. She watched the life of the city going on obliviously around them: horses and carts came and went in the square; the odd motorcar lumbered across the cobbles;

tradesmen trod past grieving women, dressed in black; cheerful youngsters cycled through on bicycles. Each of them endeavouring to forge a new life out of the ruins of material and personal devastation.

'The Menin Gate,' Fraser said, nodding his head forwards.

'What is?' she asked, not seeing anything resembling a gate.

'There, where the ramparts of the city walls taper down to admit the road.'

She had heard of the Menin Gate from the newspapers back home. It was one of the entry- and exit-points most-used by the troops fighting on the Ypres Salient. Malcolm would unquestionably have passed along this very spot.

They stood side by side at the gate. Piles of debris littered the place, and, rising from the top of the ramparts, were tall tree trunks, eerily devoid of branches or leaves, jutting up from the ground, as though poking up from an underworld, reminding all of the city's previous diabolical incarnation.

Harriet shuddered: 'Let's get out of here. I think our work is done in Belgium, don't you?'

'Yes,' Fraser agreed.

Turning around, they walked arm in arm away from the Menin Gate.

Chapter Thirteen

14th September 1919, Ypres, Belgium

Harriet woke with a breathless gasp, panicked. She sat bolt upright, struggling for air, and swung her feet down to meet the rug beside the bed. Beneath the net, her damp hair was sticking in patches to her scalp. She stood up too quickly and felt the rush of blood from her head, and she tumbled backwards onto her bed. 'Oh!' she squealed, immediately grimacing more at her own fuss than at her malaise.

She sat up again, slowly this time, and took some long, steady breaths.

The faintest nascent rays of daylight were struggling to illuminate the bedroom, as Harriet's thoughts began to re-collect, and she realised that, having slept so very badly, she had just woken from a nightmare. It had been about Malcolm, of course. The level of detail, which she had garnered in her investigations, had infused the dream with such awfully vivid imagery, for which she only had herself to blame. The nightmare had crept into her semi-conscious thoughts after having spent much of the night awake, fretting over Lina Peeters and her terrible living conditions.

With a tight grip on the iron bedstead frame, Harriet hesitantly rose from the bed, walked over to near the door and switched on the light.

She placed her bag onto the bed, removed her purse and counted out her remaining Belgian francs. She satisfied herself that there was more than enough to last until their return home later on that day. Taking a second-class train carriage would save money, too. She set aside a nominal amount, with which she would have to make do, and put it into her purse. The rest she tucked into an inside pocket in her bag, and then she sat back down on the bed. Only now had her heart rate and thoughts returned to something close to normal.

Harriet glanced up at the clock. It was just approaching half past five in the morning: too early to leave the hotel and too early for breakfast. A leisurely bath; that's what was needed, she decided. Time just to relax and think—or not think. Gathering up her toothbrush, Pomeroy toothpaste, Oatline shampoo powder and bar of soap, Harriet quietly stole from the room, down the corridor to the bathroom.

148

Harriet knocked for Fraser at seven o'clock sharp. The long soak in the bath had done the trick, restoring her usual verve and zeal. She had washed her hair and was wearing a fresh black ankle-length dress.

'Morning, Ma,' Fraser mumbled, opening the door. 'Sleep well?'

'Wonderfully, thank you,' she lied. 'And how did you sleep?'

'Wonderfully,' he echoed, a strong note of sarcasm alluding to his own frequent private night terrors, where, like last night, he would wake at intervals with a murderous scream.

Harriet nodded, joining the pretension with a smile. 'Let's go and get some breakfast.'

As they entered the saloon, the waiter took their breakfast and drinks order, and then, under the cold reproachful stare of Jack and his wife, Daisy, they joined their three German friends at their table at the far end of the room, away from the other guests.

'Are you certain that you want to join the—how do you say—quarantine table?' Kurt asked with a sly grin.

'Oh, just ignore them,' Harriet said, with an indifferent wave in the direction of the other guests.

'So, this here is your last day, yes?' Stefan asked.

'Yes, time to go back to old Blighty,' Fraser replied. 'I can't say I won't be glad to sleep in my own bed again.'

'Yes, this is true,' Kurt agreed. 'But it will be a long time until we return to our home, so I don't try to think of it.'

'Has it been a successful trip?' Stefan asked, addressing Harriet, next to whom he was sitting.

That very question had occupied most of Harriet's thoughts in the bath. In little over one month, her investigations had gone a long way to filling in the gaps in her mind about Malcolm's last few weeks. Not every query had an answer, but then maybe she had been expecting too much to know every detail. 'Yes,' she eventually answered. 'I should say it has been very successful.'

'And will you do this for your other boy, also?' Kurt asked.

'Oh, goodness,' Harriet said, taking in a deep breath.

'Edward died in Salonika in Greece,' Fraser chipped in. 'So…no.'

Harriet squinted at Fraser curiously, then faced Kurt with her considered answer: 'Yes, I probably shall.' In her peripheral vision, she saw Fraser's mouth fall open, halt and then close again, before he rolled his eyes and lightly shook his head.

'Fair shares for all,' he quipped, quoting a clichéd family phrase, frequently used on the three brothers growing up.

Harriet was about to counter his statement, when the waiter arrived with their coffees and a plate of bread, ham and cheese each.

'Thank you,' she said pleasantly to the waiter. The interruption in their conversation drew a neat line under Fraser's statement, and Harriet briefly toyed with leaving it there, but ultimately settled on the need to clarify: 'It's not about fairness, Fraser,' she said. 'It's simply that the not knowing is more unbearable and more unpalatable than resigning oneself to live one's life in ignorance or denial.'

'I understand this,' Franz said, having been quiet since their arrival. 'My mother did so, also, for my brother. She had to go and find where he died on the Somme. She had to.'

'Exactly. You'll understand when you have children,' Harriet commented to nobody in particular.

Fraser scoffed, assuming that the statement had been intended for him personally: 'I'm *never* having children.'

The force of his words took Harriet by surprise: the certitude of having grandchildren from at least one of her three boys had taken root at some undefinable point during their childhood. That conviction had wordlessly been bestowed entirely onto Fraser, now, following Malcolm's and Edward's deaths. 'Whatever can you mean?'

'Just that. I do *not* want children,' he said, as though he were refusing some heinous and monstrous proposal.

'But...' Harriet began, trying not to become upset. The news had wounded her heart much more deeply than she could explain or even understand.

'Look around you, Ma. Look at the state of the world. What kind of a person would willingly bring another life into a world such as *this*?'

These were the scars of hopelessness and despair speaking, she told herself, stifling her tears. He would change his mind, in time. He just needed to meet the right girl, settle down and let nature take its course.

The conversation continued to ramble between the four men about their thoughts on child-rearing, but Harriet had stopped listening. She no longer had an appetite. She set down her knife and fork and stood with a fixed smile. 'I'm going to go out and get some fresh air, then return to pack up and leave. I don't expect I'll see you boys again, so goodbye and God bless,' she said, offering them her hand to shake.

Each of the men stood in turn and, with heartfelt civility, each said goodbye.

'Do you want me to come with you, Ma?' Fraser asked, visibly perplexed by her sudden keenness to leave without having eaten.

'No, no,' she reassured. 'Absolutely not. I've got a short errand to run, then I'll be back to pack. Finish your breakfast. Relax. I'll see you later.'

Harriet returned to her room, collected her bag and strode from the hotel, drawing in long, deep mouthfuls of Belgian air. It was another cool day, where the sun was failing to penetrate through a solid grey stratum of cloud, as if signalling its surrender to the looming, vanquishing autumn.

She walked purposefully through the Plaine d'Amour, nodding her greetings to those whom she passed. It was still early in the morning, but already the place was bustling with life and activity, as it had been before. She reached Lina's house and tapped lightly on the front door.

Lina answered almost instantly, as though she had been expecting someone. Her face, smiling and warm, changed to mild panic.

'Hello,' Harriet said. 'Sorry to just drop by like this. I just wanted to give you something.' She opened her bag, unclipped the internal pocket, and pulled out the folded bundle of francs. 'Here.'

'What? What is this for?' Lina said, not taking the money.

'It's something, not much, but something in lieu of what Malcolm would have provided you with,' she said, pushing the money closer. 'Please, take it. I will feel so much happier.'

'Really, Mrs McDougall, there's no need,' Lina insisted. 'I make it work. There are many people who don't have a home or a job, please, give it to them. I must go now and get ready. Goodbye.'

The door closed on Harriet, and she was left with the money in her outstretched hand and a curiosity about Lina's curtness. Something didn't feel quite right somehow. She went to knock on the door again but, as she did so, caught the sound of a single word from inside, which startled her to her core. The word, which she thought that she had heard, *Mumma*, had been spoken by a very young child and made Harriet press her head to the door. The response, when it came in Flemish, was undoubtedly from Lina.

Harriet gasped, as conflicting and confusing thoughts collided in her mind, and she felt the same rush of blood leaving her head, as had happened first thing this morning. She reached for the doorframe to steady herself, but, finding nothing to grip, her fingers slid across the wooden surface, and instead she toppled towards the door.

It was the smell that brought her out of the darkness. A musty odour with a sharp edge of mildew, which was distinctly reminiscent of the inside of the Essex Farm Advanced Dressing Station. Harriet opened her eyes and saw nothing familiar by which to recognise her surroundings. A low beamed ceiling. Strange dimness. She turned her head to the side, noticing only then the dull pain above her right eye. Familiarity began to arrive, as the room itself began to reassemble in her vision: she was inside the pre-fab; then came the memory of knocking on the door; lastly, as she took a good look at the small gathering of people in the room, she recalled what she had understood moments before fainting and banging her head. She saw Lina and smiled feebly.

'How do you feel, Mrs McDougall?' she asked, taking her hand in hers.

'Bit of a headache, but…other than that…' she said, trying to sit up, but falling straight back onto the mattress.

'I wouldn't try to move too much just yet,' Lina advised.

'Where's the child? Harriet asked, scanning the outlines of the dim figures on the other side of the room.

'What child?' Lina said.

'I heard a child in here. It said 'Mumma', and you answered it,' Harriet said.

'No, I think the bump to your head is making you imagine things,' Lina asserted.

'Oh, tommyrot!' Harriet said, this time forcing herself upright. 'I heard a child as plain as day, now where is it and, more importantly, whose is it?'

Lina sighed.

'He's yours and Malcolm's, isn't he?' Harriet probed, seeing Lina's pretensions falling.

Lina nodded. 'She. Poppy.'

'Oh! But why didn't you tell me?' Harriet gasped. 'I was on the verge of leaving—never to see you again!'

Lina stared at the floor. 'Because I thought you would take her away from me…from all of this.'

'Take her away from you?' Harriet stammered. 'Goodness me, Lina. After all you've been through, not a thought could possibly be further from my mind. I've lost two of my own children, remember…' Her words faltered, as she welled up.

'I'm sorry,' Lina muttered, taking Harriet's hand.

'Poppy,' Harriet breathed, as Mrs Leonard's words came back to her: 'Find the poppy and it will help you…' 'What a beautiful name. How old is she?'

'Fifteen months.'

'I'm lost for words, Lina, really I am. Where is she now?'

'My friend next door has her.'

'Lina, I promise you I'm not going to take her away from you. Goodness, what unimaginable grief I would leave you suffering with. What type of a woman—type of a mother…*grandmother*—do you take me for?'

Lina stared at her, unblinking for some time.

'Can I meet her before I go back to England, Lina?' Harriet asked.

After a few seconds, Lina nodded but didn't move.

'Please,' Harriet pleaded.

Lina bit her lip, then headed across the room and out of the front door. She left the door ajar, and Harriet gaped at it, unable to believe what she had just discovered. And she considered the irony of their conversations at the breakfast table this morning, where she had been forced to face an assumed, stark truth that she might never have grandchildren.

Two silhouetted figures appeared at the door, and Harriet, still dazed, strained her eyes to see the small child, to bring her features into focus, as she tottered across the room towards Harriet, tightly holding Lina's hand.

At last, Harriet could discern the little creature. She saw past the grubby, torn clothes, seeing only her dazzling face, her happy grin and, unmistakably, Malcolm's beautiful sparkling blue eyes.

'This is Poppy,' Lina introduced. 'Your granddaughter.'

Harriet threw open her arms and scooped her up, holding her emotions firmly in check so as not to frighten this new acquaintance at their very first encounter. She squeezed her tightly, finding the little mite so thin and fragile that she could feel her bones alarmingly close to the skin. Sensing Poppy begin to wriggle, Harriet released her, sitting her down on her knee.

Lina said something in Flemish, followed by the word, 'Grandma'.

'Grandma,' Poppy repeated with a giggle. She jumped down and tottered off into the murky depths of the room.

'What a treasure,' Harriet exclaimed. 'I can't believe it. She looks the mirror of Malcolm at that age, I can't tell you.'

Lina smiled. 'Would you like a water?'

'Yes, please,' Harriet said, suddenly noticing how parched she felt. She watched, as Lina moved to the kitchen area of the house, but which was really just a wash basin, a table and a small stove. Lina took a glass and plunged it into a metal bucket on the table.

'Here,' she said, offering it to Harriet. 'Are you hungry? We don't have much, but—'

'No, no, not hungry at all,' Harriet interrupted. 'Do you manage for food? For yourselves, I mean?'

Lina shrugged. 'Just about. There are no shops, yet. We must get our food from warehouses in the city, and on Saturdays there is a market in the Grand Place, where we get eggs and vegetables, perhaps some meat, if we are lucky.'

'It's no way of life for the two of you,' Harriet said.

'Perhaps not, but we manage,' Lina insisted.

'Well, one thing's for certain. You *are* having that money I offered you earlier: no argument,' Harriet said, delving into her bag and withdrawing the cash, which, she correctly assumed, they had placed back in her bag, when she had fallen.

'Thank you,' Lina said, now accepting it graciously. 'I will get Poppy some new clothes.'

'And fatten her up a bit.'

'I will do my best. Do you want me to get Fraser and tell him what has happened?'

'Oh, glory, no,' Harriet rebutted. 'I'll be right as rain in a minute.' Harriet sipped her water, feeling better but still drowsy, and the pain was increasing above her eye. 'He didn't get to know about the baby, did he? Malcolm, I mean,' she said, judging Poppy's age against the date at which he had died.

'Yes, he knew,' Lina answered. 'It was very early days in the pregnancy, but I wrote to my sister in Poperinge to tell her that I thought I was...pregnant. By chance, Malcolm arrived when she was opening the letter and so he found out. Apparently, he was...erm...'over the moon'.'

'When would this have been?' Harriet asked.

'It was the night before he was killed.'

The night when he had taken a General Service Wagon into Poperinge. Now it made some sort of sense, although it seemed a strange risk to take for a social call. 'Why was he visiting your sister?'

'Because he was kind,' she explained. 'And he knew that I was worried about her. She was resorting to...awful things to make money

154

to feed herself. When he could, Malcolm would take her provisions: tins of beef, biscuits, Maconchie—this horrible fatty thing in gravy—whatever he could get his hands on. Anything to stop her from doing what she had been doing. He went to see her that night in Poperinge, and she had that letter from me, unopened.'

'So, he was told that night that he was going to be a father and then died the next day.' Harriet stared at Poppy, unsure of whether knowing that he would have a child, whom he would never meet, was a comfort or cause for even greater pain.

'Yes. It was my sister who told me that he'd been killed a couple of weeks later, when some of his regiment were at Talbot House in Poperinge. She wrote to me, giving me the news, and telling me that she had seen him the night before, and that he had brought her some condensed milk, tea and jam.'

'Grandma!' Poppy suddenly declared, strolling up to Harriet and handing her an eyeless teddy bear, which had seen much better days. Harriet took the teddy, resolving to go out and buy the little girl some new clothes and toys as soon as she got home. And for Lina, too, for that matter.

'Do you know what the time is?' Harriet asked, suddenly aware that she had no concept of how long she had been out for.

'Nearly midday,' Lina answered.

'Oh, my godfathers! Fraser will have sent out a search party by now. Heavens, I need to run.'

'You must not *run* anywhere, Mrs McDougall. You've just had a nasty bang to the head.'

'Poppycock, I'll be alright,' Harriet retorted, standing up just fine. But for the little pain in her head, she did indeed feel right as rain. 'Why is it so jolly dark in here?'

Lina laughed. 'It's Mr Van de Velde, he's got very sensitive eyes, or at least that's what he tells everyone. Personally, I just think it allows him to sleep without anyone noticing. You get used to it in the end.'

'Do you?' Harriet questioned, placing her hands on her hips. 'There's an awful lot that you both are having to put up with.'

Lina shrugged.

'Listen, can we go for a walk somewhere? You, me and Poppy?' Harriet asked. 'Get out of this dark dungeon!'

'Don't you have to get back?'

'Fraser can wait a little bit longer, I think. Come on.'

'Ma!' Fraser called, as she entered the hotel saloon, leaping up from a chair. 'Where the devil have you been? I've been worrying myself sick!'

'I fell over and banged my head,' Harriet explained, pointing to the bruise above her right eye. As much as she didn't want the fuss, there was no way of disguising it, so it was easier just to come right out and tell the truth.

'Do you need to see a doctor?' he asked, rushing towards her and scrutinizing her injury.

'No, no, I'm absolutely fine,' she insisted, flapping her hand in his face, as though she were being pestered by some maddening insect or other.

'Well, we need to jolly well hurry, if we're going to make that last train. Come on. I'll help you pack. I'm all ready.'

Harriet held out her hand to stop him. 'Hang on. *Slight* change of plan.'

'Oh, glory…' he said, rolling his eyes, then folding his arms, as he awaited some grand revelation.

'Yes. We're going back home tomorrow, now,' she said.

Fraser's face lightened, and he unclamped his arms. 'Oh, that's fine. Have you checked we can stay an extra night?'

'Yes, it's all arranged.'

'Good. I thought for a moment you were going to announce another fanciful expedition somewhere,' he laughed. 'Well, I might go and take a walk, then bathe before dinner.'

'Before you go,' Harriet said, catching his elbow. 'There is a *little* more to explain about this change of plan of ours.' Harriet turned to the doorway. 'In you come.'

Lina entered the room, her head shyly tilted downwards, with a clinging Poppy propped on her hip.

Fraser flicked his eyes between Harriet, Lina and the little girl. 'My God, she looks the very spit of him.'

Harriet nodded, then grinned. 'Doesn't she just!'

'This is Poppy,' Lina said. She spoke in a soft voice to the little girl. Most of the words were in Flemish, except for 'hello' in English.

Poppy smirked and pulled herself tighter to Lina.

'Sorry. She's shy,' Lina said. 'She will not leave you alone once she knows you better.'

'Let's sit down and we can talk about the arrangements,' Harriet said, leading the way to the closest table.

'Arrangements?' Fraser asked.

156

'Yes, Lina and Poppy are coming to live with us,' Harriet replied with a broad smile.

Chapter Fourteen

16th September 1919, Sedlescombe, Sussex

'So, this is the famous Sedlescombe?' Lina asked, pronouncing it correctly now from hearing its constant mention. She was standing at the apex of the village green, still and quiet under a low autumnal morning sunshine.

'Oh, yes. World-famous!' Harriet chuckled, before sighing contentedly.

'What a lovely little place. So green and so *very* different to Ypres.'

'Yes,' she agreed, taking her time to absorb her surroundings with a renewed appreciation. The disparities between the two places—separated by little more than one hundred miles—was so extraordinarily glaring as to be preposterous. 'Nearly home,' she said, as Poppy took her by the hand and tottered the short distance to Linton House.

'Is this it?' Lina said, placing her hand on the property's low iron gate and staring open-mouthed at the house. When Harriet nodded, Lina declared, 'Wow! It's like a palace.'

'Oh, nonsense,' Harriet rejected.

'Well, we'll have to see what the inside's like,' Fraser muttered.

'What do you mean?' Lina asked.

'What he's trying to say is that we've got a rather lovely house guest by the name of Timothy Mogridge. Lovely, lovely boy.'

'And you want *more* people staying?' Lina said.

'Absolutely,' Harriet insisted, pushing the gate open. 'Come on, let's go inside.'

Harriet walked up the garden path, taking surreptitious glances at the windows, trying not to let Fraser see that she, too, was wondering if she might have been too generous in entrusting her whole home and worldly possessions to a virtual stranger.

She placed the key in the lock. The pleasantly indescribable, yet familiar smell of the old place greeted her, as she pushed open the door. Such a welcome relief to be home. 'Hello? Timothy?' she called into the house, compensating for her trepidation, as she overconfidently stepped inside.

A light, barely discernible scrape came from the back of the house, which Harriet recognised instantly as being the slide of a chair against the stone kitchen floor. She tittered upon seeing Timothy shuffling towards them; she couldn't be sure why, perhaps it was just relief at the elimination of the niggling mistrusting doubts, which Fraser had instilled in her.

Fraser, then Lina and finally Poppy entered the hallway behind Harriet.

'Welcome home, Mrs McDougall!' Timothy said cheerfully, shaking Harriet's hand warmly. He was wearing a pair of John's old trousers and one of his olive shirts with a maroon tie. 'Oh, and visitors! Hello.'

'Yes,' Harriet said. 'Timothy, this is Lina and her daughter, Poppy. I'll explain everything later, but they've come to stay here.'

'Splendid,' Timothy said, leaning past to shake Lina's hand. 'Nice to meet you.'

'You, too.'

'Well, you've picked a good time for a holiday,' Timothy said. 'Apparently we're due a return to clement temperatures for a week, before Autumn digs her heels in more firmly: an Indian summer, so they're saying.'

Harriet went to correct him and to say something to the effect that they weren't here for a holiday, when, out of the blue, Poppy began to scream, taking immediate shelter in the folds of Lina's pleated skirt.

'What on earth's the matter?' Harriet asked, glancing back and forth between Fraser and Lina, wondering what she could have missed. She understood when Timothy mumbled his apologies and turned sharply back towards the kitchen.

'Sorry,' Lina said. 'She's just nervous around new people.'

'It's fine; I even have that effect on my own daughter,' he muttered, striding away.

Lina bent down, stroking Poppy's hair and comforting her in Flemish.

'Right,' Harriet began, trying to break the mounting sense of disquiet, 'Fraser, take Lina and Poppy into the sitting-room, whilst Timothy and I get a pot of tea going. I'm absolutely gasping! If there's one thing that that wretched Jack fellow from the hotel and I do agree on, it's that you cannot get a decent cup of tea outside of England.'

'Probably a slight exaggeration, Ma,' Fraser said, leading Lina and Poppy off into the sitting room.

'Oh, and put some Vivaldi on! I've missed the old Italian maestro,' Harriet called, dashing into the kitchen to catch up with Timothy.

When she reached him, she felt the need to touch his arm for human reassurance. 'How have you been?'

'You know…' he answered, not meeting her gaze, as he loaded cups and saucers onto a tray.

'Thank you for looking after the place so well,' Harriet praised, noticing that the kitchen was spotless. There was even a cake of some kind, proudly sitting under the glass cloche on the table.

Timothy shrugged. 'I needed to keep myself busy, you know.'

'Have you heard anything from Nell?' Harriet asked softly.

Timothy filled the kettle with water and placed it on the range, keeping his back to Harriet. 'Her father wrote to me and asked me to return—'

'Oh, that *is* positive,' Harriet interrupted.

'—to collect the rest of my belongings,' Timothy finished.

'Oh. Sorry.'

'And he's looking at the logistics of…' he lowered his voice and hung his head in shame, '…*legalising* the separation.'

It might well have been overestimating their friendship, but Harriet placed her two hands on his shoulders and rested her head onto his. 'It's an awful time, Timothy, really it is. But…but perhaps a fresh start is what you both need?'

'And what about Anna? Do I just forget that I have a four-year-old daughter…just pretend that she doesn't exist and never see her again?'

'No, of course not. There'll be a way to see her; I'm sure of it. Let me think on it a while. Just don't give up, alright?'

Making his lack of conviction clear, Timothy shrugged.

Harriet rubbed his arm. 'Good lad,' she found herself saying. 'Milk…' she quickly added, to distance herself from her own poor choice of words, realising that she had sounded rather as though she had been fawning over a puppy. She picked up the jug of milk from the thick slab of marble in the larder and set it down on the tray.

'How was the trip?' Timothy asked, seeming not to have taken any offence.

'Sad, interesting, illuminating, tragic, revealing, rewarding, surprising,' Harriet answered, thinking but withholding all manner of other similar or conflicting adjectives to describe the trip. 'In short: very worthwhile.'

'Good, I'm pleased,' Timothy said, his voice almost lost to the histrionic scream of the boiling kettle.

160

'I think I know as much as I'm ever going to about Malcolm's last weeks… Oh, and the biggest shocks of course are in the sitting room.'

Timothy paused, mid-way through lifting the glass cake cloche. 'Oh?'

'Poppy, that little girl,' Harriet said, finding that she was pointlessly lowering her voice, 'she's Lina and Malcolm's daughter.'

Timothy's eyes widened, as he processed the information. 'Astonishing.'

'It is, rather. Goodness only knows what the Reverend Percival is going to have to say on the matter. Or the neighbours. Or the village. Gosh, I'd not even thought of that. And Hannah!'

Timothy lifted the cake over to the tray, poured the boiling water into the teapot, then faced Harriet. 'Perhaps Malcolm and Lina had married—in secret?'

Harriet shook her head vehemently. 'No, unfortunately…' she stopped herself short, as his intonation sunk in. 'Oh. Oh! I see. Yes, *perhaps* they did.' She gazed momentarily out of the window, thinking. 'A secret wedding in Woolwich in 1916, when Malcolm came over on hush-hush war work. John, being John, would never have approved of Malcolm's marrying a *foreign charwoman*, so the poor fellow had little choice but to keep it all hidden from us.' Harriet beamed. 'That's right! Well done, Timothy!'

'Pleasure, Mrs McDougall,' he said flatly.

'I think perhaps it's time you started calling me Harriet, don't you?' she said.

'Oh, right. That might take some getting used to,' he grimaced.

'Try it. That cake looks glorious, Timothy,' she enthused.

'Thank you…Harriet,' Timothy said. 'Genoa, freshly baked today.'

'There! You did it,' Harriet said with a laugh. 'I suppose I must also tell Lina to do the same. Harriet—a bit less stiff and stuffy than Mrs McDougall, isn't it?'

'Yes, I suppose so,' Timothy agreed.

'You are a good man. You know that, don't you?'

Timothy blushed, avoiding her eye, and said, 'I think there's a little lemonade powder left in the packet; ought I make some up for the little one?'

'Fabulous idea!' Harriet replied, picking up one of the trays and moving out of the kitchen. A long-forgotten sound, overwhelming the mawkish Vivaldi composition, drew her along the hallway towards the sitting room: relaxed laughter and unguarded joy, so bold and

161

pronounced that it brought tears to her eyes. How she would have liked to stand still and immerse herself in that unfamiliar joviality. She loitered for a time and then continued into the room and into its heart-soothing embrace.

'Tea!' Harriet sang, placing the tray down on the table. 'And..!' she said, placing dramatic emphasis on the word, 'Genoa cake…made by the lovely Timothy.'

Fraser clapped somewhat dismally, and Harriet glowered at him, hoping that Timothy hadn't heard it from the kitchen, as she set out the cups and saucers and began to pour the tea.

Timothy stepped into the sitting room, awkwardly handing the glass of lemonade to Lina, holding the injured part of his face away from the little girl. 'For Poppy.'

'Thank you very much,' Lina said, taking the glass and offering it to Poppy with some words in Flemish.

As Timothy cut neat rectangles from the cake, Harriet watched as Poppy drank the entire glass of lemonade in one go, handed the cup back to Lina, then turned to the mantel piece, reaching up for one of the ornamental wooden elephants, which Fraser had sent back from Constantinople.

Lina reached out to pull Poppy's hand away, saying something with a reprimanding edge in her tone.

'No, let her play with them,' Harriet said, 'by all means.'

'Are you sure?'

'Absolutely. What else is the poor thing to play with? I'll have a hunt later for some of the boys' old toys, and we'll make the bedroom up for you both.'

'Which bedroom?' Fraser asked.

'Malcolm and Edward's,' she replied, not wishing to discuss the matter, lest she should get upset.

Fraser nodded solemnly, appreciating the gravity of this moment for his mother and also the necessity driving the decision. 'I'll help, if you like.'

'I'd rather do it alone…if that's alright. I thought after lunch, perhaps you could take Lina and Poppy on a short walk and show her all this village of ours has to offer.'

'Well that will be a very short walk, then, won't it,' he commented.

'That will be lovely,' Lina said. 'Is there a wood near here that she can play in?'

'We are literally surrounded by woodland,' Fraser said. 'And they start right here at the bottom of the garden, just over a small meadow, and run all the way to the next village.'

Lina gasped. 'Poppy's never been to a wood before. She's never really seen proper trees up-close, either.'

'Well, we'll soon change that,' Fraser said.

Harriet handed out the cups of tea, then taking one for herself, sat down with a noisy sigh: 'Home sweet home.'

Harriet was sitting on Edward's bed, stroking the bedroom wall with appreciation for how the house had listened and understood her family's needs so far in their custodianship. It was still and quiet throughout just at that moment, but it was a pleasant warm stillness, filled with promise and hope; the endless dreadful solemnity, which had woven itself into the very fabric of the walls for so long, had gone. The house was changing, responding to its new future, the next chapter in its story, and its new meaning. And she, Harriet understood that it was time, now, for her to do the same.

She stood up from the bed and backed slowly towards the door, seeing the room objectively for the first time in as long a period as she could recall. The wardrobe would need to be emptied of their clothes, the bookshelves cleared, their ablutions-paraphernalia removed from below the washstand and under their beds cleared out.

Harriet picked up Malcolm's and then Edward's pyjamas and briefly touched them to her face, attempting to evoke a firm memory of their wearing them, something tangible and certain; but her mind refused, providing her instead with a thin and feathery recollection, which might well have actually been her imagination or a splicing of several such instances from over the years. Perhaps, if she had known what their fate was to be, she would have consciously tried to retain such moments of seeming inconsequence. She carried the nightwear to her room and placed them onto her bed. Returning to their bedroom, she pulled open the wardrobe and glanced over the pitiable quantity of clothing hanging there. A set of Sunday best each, two mackintoshes, four cotton shirts, four pairs of flannel trousers, two pairs of working boots and, at the bottom of the wardrobe, a few pairs of socks, lambswool vests and pants. She gathered it all up into her arms and carried it through to her bedroom. Her plans for the clothing—and for anything else, for that matter—did not extend further than putting them onto her own bed for the time being.

163

Next, she carefully picked down the display cases of moths and butterflies above Malcolm's bed; they were certainly enough to terrify a young toddler. The thought of Poppy catching a glimpse of the morbid collection, as she was trying to go to sleep, actually made Harriet chuckle. Where a suitable location to hang them might be, she had no idea. She unstuck Malcolm's hand-drawn sketches of moths and butterflies, intending to put them up on her bedroom walls. And then there were the books, two whole shelves of them. What was she to do with those? She certainly could never bring herself to discard them, she thought, casting her eyes over the variety of titles, each demonstrating one of the boys' interests: Edward's astronomy and painting books; Malcolm's nature and chemistry books, annotated in his own hand with various comments and drawings.

It took eight trips to transfer the books through to her bedroom. Next, she crouched down beside Edward's bed and pulled out two wooden crates, containing his few belongings. 'Aha!' she said, pulling out a painting set, something which Poppy could use. 'And…perhaps not,' she mumbled, upon seeing that the paints by now resembled some cracked Saharan desert. At least she had found something which could be discarded without offending her otherwise still-raw and very intact sense of sentimentality. Below the painting set was a pile of *The Captain* magazine books, the most recent edition being *April to September 1915*. She picked up the book, glancing briefly at the articles on Australian cricket, short stories by P.G. Wodehouse and black-and-white images of a boxing match. As she flicked through, she felt the spine making the light creak and groan of a fresh volume, unread. She sighed, repacked the box, and turned to the second. This one contained all of Edward's astronomy equipment, including his brass telescope. Harriet withdrew it from the box and carried it over to the window, where she extended the tripod legs and, squinting through the eyepiece, turned the cylindrical tubes to their fullest extent.

'Ah!' she cried with delight, as the back-garden fence appeared with sudden and alarming clarity. Freshly painted by Timothy, she noticed amiably.

Time forgot her for a while, as she moved the telescope to the woods behind Linton House and contentedly searched the trees for signs of life: she watched an acrobatic squirrel gambolling along perilously thin branches, before leaping to a large trunk and running down its length, as though such a thing were no effort at all for it; she studied a solitary male blackbird, singing his heart out without a single care in the world; she spotted rabbits, nibbling tufts of tussocky grass, close to the garden gate; she observed a pair of blackcaps, flitting in the elder trees; and she saw Lina, Fraser and Timothy, standing in a clearing, talking away animatedly. She shifted the telescope to where their eyelines converged on Poppy, who was squatting down to study closely a tangle of tree roots from a fallen oak. She felt a contentment at this reminder of having watched the boys at their games, playing together in those same woods, as time finally caught up with her.

Leaving the telescope in position, she knelt down and slid out the two crates from underneath Malcolm's bed. The first was filled with his prized chemistry sets, boxes chock-full with all manner of odd-looking equipment and glass tubes of vulgar putrefied liquids. Something else, which could be thrown out, she reasoned. She set the box to one side and began with the second, which was topped with small boxes of *Cretonne Chocolates*. Harriet tentatively prodded off the lid of the first box, not knowing what kinds of decaying creatures might be contained inside. One thing that she did know; they certainly were *not* full of the chocolates promised on the outside. Four delicate, white, bird eggs with brown speckles, and all nestled in cotton wool, was what she discovered in the first box. Now that she saw them, she could recall the very day when Malcolm had discovered a female robin at the foot of a tree, dead. Then he had found the nest with four long-cold eggs inside. His father had shown him how to make a pin-prick in the top and bottom of each egg and blow out the contents so that the egg shell could be preserved and studied. The enduring hobby, which this single event had created, was evidenced in the five other boxes of *Cretonne Chocolates*, which Harriet carefully lifted out and set down beside her. Turning back to the crate, she smiled, as her eyes came to rest upon a black leather book, which she recognised but had well-forgotten. Opening it to the first page, she read the handwritten title: '*Malcolm's Nature Book!*' She and John had bought the book for him for his fourteenth birthday. Soon, the blank pages were filled with bird feathers, rudimentary sketches, pressed flowers and comments on the natural world that he discovered around him. Harriet flicked through the familiar pages, pausing when she spotted a version of the blue poppies, which he had drawn onto the walls of the Essex Farm Advanced Dressing Station. She ran her forefinger lightly across the watercolour painting, as she read his handwritten caption: '*My beautiful poppy.*' The poignant bitter-sweet significance of this discovery wrapped itself around her heart, and she smiled.

Harriet stared at the image for some time and then closed the journal. That was it; she had reached the bottom of the final crate. The task had been far less painful and far more cathartic than she had envisaged its being.

She placed the crates under her bed, then returned to the boys' bedroom. Except, it was no longer theirs; the final physical reminders of them were gone, and the room now belonged to Lina and Poppy.

She made her way downstairs, realising how drained she felt. A strong cup of tea was definitely in order. As she reached the kitchen, she spotted Poppy's grubby little teddy bear lying on the floor. She picked the ghastly thing up, thinking that it really needed throwing away. 'Drat it!' she said, having not found a single toy for her to play with among the boys' things. Then she remembered the small toy shop on Battle High Street. She looked at the wall clock: if she left now, and forwent a cup of tea, she could catch the afternoon charabanc into Battle and get back in time to make supper. If she remembered rightly, the shop had quite a range of wooden toys and dolls for young children.

Her lethargy seemed to dissipate with the resolution to go and purchase some new toys for Poppy. She dropped the teddy bear onto the kitchen table and strode into the hallway to get ready. She put on her black coat, black ostrich-feather hat and black suede Oxford shoes and hurried out of the door, down the path onto the street. She walked quickly with her head down, not wishing to get caught by one of her neighbours and end up missing the charabanc.

As she paced along the village green, she mulled over poor Timothy's situation. What could she do for him? Pay for him to have his own legal advice, perhaps? She resolved to call into **Raper and Fovargue** solicitors' office in Battle and see what they suggested. But it was part of a wider problem, the one shared by Fraser and all the other aimless men, who had returned to find that the war had changed them irrevocably and that their former place in the world simply no longer existed. And then there were people like her, left with nothing but memories and useless belongings.

A grumbling sound from behind brought her back from her introspection. She turned to see the Battle charabanc lumbering slowly through the village towards her. She was about to continue the last few yards to the stop, when she paused, glancing to her right. The sight of the village hall brought her to a standstill. She stared at the locked door of the old wooden building, as an idea suddenly took hold of her.

The charabanc drove past, pulling over at the stop just in front of her. Harriet briefly looked in its direction, then turned on her heels back the way that she had just come, but walking past Linton House, crossing the street and banging on the door to River Cottage. 'Come on,' Harriet said.

Mrs Selmes opened the door with a look of great surprise. 'Mrs McDougall... How unusual.'

'Mrs Selmes,' Harriet said with a wintry smile. 'I've come about the village hall.'

Mrs Selmes shot a worried look in its general direction. 'Whatever's the matter with it?'

'Oh, nothing at all. It's locked, and I wondered if I might hire it out.'

'What...now?' Mrs Selmes begged, folding her arms.

'Well, no. Not *now*,' Harriet replied, thinking quickly. 'I was thinking perhaps from the week after next: a sort of weekly feature.'

'And what, may I ask, would be going on inside on a *weekly* basis?'

'Some kind of war benevolence thing,' Harriet said, not yet fully understanding her own explanation and trying to clarify: 'A place for former soldiers to go and have a cup of tea and talk and—' A terse mocking laugh from Mrs Selmes interrupted this clarification, but Harriet continued regardless, '—speak to people...people who might help them or offer them work opportunities or legal advice. And a place where they can go to buy cheap or *free* clothing or things they might have use for that others—others such as myself—no longer have uses for. Clothes and the like, for instance.'

Mrs Selmes had visibly softened by the time that Harriet had finished speaking. 'I see. Well, I shall have to put it to the Parish Council, of course. Although I *am* the entrusted key-holder, it isn't actually my decision alone.'

'But you think it a good idea?' Harriet pushed.

'I suppose so, yes.'

'Marvellous!' Harriet sang, moving down the garden path.

'And how was your trip to the continent?' Mrs Selmes called after her. 'I thought I saw you arrive with a woman and child in tow this morning!'

Harriet continued walking, turned her head and said, 'Oh, yes— that's my daughter-in-law and granddaughter. Good day to you.'

'Pardon?' Mrs Selmes yapped after her.

Harriet waltzed back to Linton House with a spring in her step. Suddenly, the clouds of darkness had cleared. Everything made sense, now. She swung her gate wide and marched up the path to the house.

'Harriet! Harriet!' came a familiar but unwelcome voice, which sliced away the lightness of her mood and the spring of her step. She spun around to see her sister-in-law, Hannah.

'Hannah, how lovely. How have you been?'

Hannah was red-faced and slightly out-of-breath. Taking quick furtive glances around her, she whispered, 'Is it true?'

'Is what true?' Harriet asked, feigning ignorance.

'That…that you have a *woman* and a *girl* living here now? *Foreigners?*' she gasped.

'Oh, that. Goodness, news does travel fast. Yes, perfectly true.'

'But… *What on earth*, Harriet?'

'Well, it's quite a story, which I don't have the time to tell the full version of right now, so you will have to make do with a short summary: Malcolm…tied the knot…with a Belgian girl secretly in 1916, and in 1917 she had his baby,' Harriet said, surprised at the ease with which the lie had rolled from her tongue. 'That's it.'

'Oh, my godfathers! So—this little girl—she's *foreign?*'

'That's right, yes.'

'But how are you to communicate with her?'

'I shall speak to her in English; children are terribly intuitive, you know, Hannah. She'll be speaking English in no time at all, mark my words.'

'So, they're going to be *staying* here?' she asked. 'As in…*permanently?*'

'That's right, yes,' Harriet confirmed. 'Now, Hannah, you really must excuse me. I need to prepare the supper. Goodbye.'

Harriet smiled dryly to herself, as she stepped inside the house and closed the door, aware that her sister-in-law was still standing, flabbergasted, at the gate. The news—believed or otherwise about Malcolm and Lina's knot-tying—would soon be circulating the village with greater vigour than that which she could have paid an advertiser to achieve. She kicked off her shoes, hung up her hat and coat, put Vivaldi's *L'autunno* on the gramophone and, once in the kitchen, she made herself a very strong cup of English tea, which she carried into the parlour.

Placing the tea down on the table, she took stock of the room, realising that there was something unsettling about the place, but quite what that was, she could not put her finger on. Yes, being north-facing it was much cooler and certainly dimmer than the rest of the house; but that wasn't it. Her eyes settled on the three austere portraits of the boys, before shifting slowly around the room. Still she couldn't place the problem. Did it need redecorating? Yes, it could do with freshening up, and that could give Timothy something to do, but that *still* wasn't the issue. Perhaps, she wondered, it was the parlour's seldom-used, archaic, formal air, being reserved for high days and holidays alone. Such a Victorian custom no longer seemed aligned with the house's current occupants. Yes, that might well be it; it needed a new function and purpose, but what that was, she didn't rightly know. The first step, though, would be to strip away the trappings and shackles of the past. She gathered up the assortment of Malcolm's letters and postcards, arranging them in a neat pile on the edge of the table. Then, she picked up his washbag, snuff box, brush kit, trench mirror and his returned uniform. Opening out the blood-stained tunic, she had a flash of her visit to see Mrs Leonard. All that she had been told replayed in her mind, and Harriet suddenly knew what she had to do.

From the hallway came the sound of the front door opening and the clatter and babble of conversation and laughter. 'Welcome home!' she greeted, passing them at the front door.

'Where are you off to?' Fraser asked.

'Post Office to send an urgent telegram,' she replied.

As she strode down the path, she heard Fraser murmur, 'Oh, goodness me, whatever now…'

Chapter Fifteen

19th September 1919, Bermondsey, London

She felt a good deal calmer, this time, as she followed Mrs Leonard's heavy shuffle through the brown hallway from the front door.

'Didn't for a moment think *you'd* be coming back, Mrs Catt,' Mrs Leonard commented.

'It was all just a little…overwhelming last time,' Harriet answered, having continued under her grandmother's name for this appointment, for no good reason. They entered the back room, and just as before, it was dark and lit only by the fragments of light puncturing the holes in the curtains and a single candle placed in the centre of the table.

'Same chap, is it?' Mrs Leonard asked, in a strangely quiet voice, as though she didn't want anybody else in the spiritual world to overhear.

'That's right,' Harriet confirmed, passing her Malcolm's khaki tunic.

'Well, sit down, and I'll see if Kaifa can unearth him, again.'

Mrs Leonard's choice of verb unsettled Harriet, chiming in as it did with her considerable qualms concerning spiritualism and communicating with the deceased, widening the chasm of doubt between her recent behaviours and her faith. She had yet to return to church since being back from Belgium, having made what she now realised were a series of excuses to cover her absence; she just needed time to try and reconcile the many conflicts in her mind.

Mrs Leonard, with her hands clutching at the edges of the tunic, closed her eyes, leant backwards and breathed deeply, her exhalation pushing the candle flicker almost to extinction. Suddenly she jolted and, in the same high-pitched voice as previously, blurted out, 'He's here.'

Harriet fought the urge to speak to him, remembering from the earlier visit that direct communication was not possible, or was prohibited, she wasn't sure which.

'He said you found the poppy and that you will be very happy because of it.'

Harriet smiled, as she thought of her little granddaughter, waiting for her back home at Linton House.

'Now he's happy. But his friends here aren't happy! Oh, no.'

'Oh,' Harriet muttered, shifting in her chair at this odd revelation. Quite what Malcolm's spirit-friends' happiness had to do with her, she couldn't for the life of her fathom.

'They're ravaged with jealousy and he says you can stop it. They're plaguing him!'

'What? How?'

'And he says to let go of the past... He's not there anymore. He's all around you.' Mrs Leonard slumped forward momentarily, then back upright and said in her normal voice, 'He's gone.'

Harriet had thought that she had been more prepared in her mind for this visit than the last, but actually she was just as confused and just as eager to run from the house as before. Only this time, she didn't. She knitted her trembling fingers together under the table, trying to compose herself.

'Did any of that make sense, Mrs Catt?' Mrs Leonard asked.

'Some of it, perhaps; there was certainly little ambiguity in telling me to let go of the past,' she said. 'The bit about his friends' being jealous—what could that *possibly* have meant?'

Mrs Leonard shrugged. 'I'm just a *conduit*, Mrs Catt; a channel, that means. My place ain't to question, my place is but to *deliver* the messages from the other side, you see.'

'Are they always so brief and so cryptic, I wonder?' Harriet commented.

'Sometimes they talk for *hours*,' Mrs Leonard complained. 'And sometimes they don't come at all. Ten shillings, please.'

Setting aside her misgivings about the whole nature of communicating with the dead, Harriet spent most of the train journey back to Battle dissecting the brief information, which she had just been told. The purpose of her visit had ostensibly been to seek Malcolm's permission to make better use of his clothing and belongings, a consent which, she felt, had loosely been received. But what of his friends' being unhappy? Mrs Leonard had clearly said his friends *here* were unhappy, implying that they too were deceased.

The train jolted to a halt at Battle Station, startling Harriet somewhat. 'Oh, good Lord!' she muttered, jumping up from her seat, grabbing the paper packet containing Malcolm's tunic and stepping down onto the platform.

She looked up at the station clock: twenty-one minutes after two. If she didn't dawdle, then there would be just enough time to purchase

171

some new clothes and toys for Poppy, before catching the last charabanc back to Sedlescombe. Perfect.

Harriet walked along the High Street with a contented stride towards the magnificent Abbey, which dated back to William the Conqueror's times. She loved coming into the little market town at any time but today, with the opportunity of buying some things for her granddaughter, she was delighted.

First, she called in at *Robert's Brothers*. 'Ah, good morning, Mrs McDougall,' one of the middle-aged brothers greeted her after the tinkling bell above the door fetched him from the back.

'Good morning, Mr Roberts,' she replied, not having the first clue as to with which of the brothers she was now speaking. They were twins—identical—and, despite several visits over many years, Harriet could still not distinguish the one from the other. It didn't help matters that they insisted on *trying* to look identical. Same salt-and-pepper hair, greased from a side-parting. Same moustache, twisted and twiddled to sharp, curled points. Same shirt, tie and trousers.

'What are we looking for today?' he asked. 'We've a new selection for winter: ladies' raincoats, twenty-one shillings; fur collar coats, eighty shillings. We've some lovely new winter boots—'

'Children's clothes, actually,' she interrupted. 'A small, under-sized fifteen-month-old girl, to be precise.'

'Oh!' Mr Robert's said, a raft of questions arising from that single exclamation.

'Yes,' Harriet said, wandering over to a rack of small outfits. 'My granddaughter, Poppy.'

'Oh!'

'These are rather lovely,' Harriet said, holding up a pretty frock.

'Sale price: four and six,' Mr Roberts called over.

Harriet took two of the garments in different colours, then chose two petticoats, two woolly vests, some socks, a poplin dress, a winter coat, some napkins and a pair of dainty boots. 'This will make a good start,' she said to Mr Roberts, as she paid for the items.

'I don't believe you've ever mentioned a granddaughter before, Mrs McDougall,' he said, placing the clothes onto brown paper wrapping and deftly tying the parcel with string.

'Oh, surely I must have done?' Harriet countered.

'Ah, perhaps you told my brother!' he said with a wide grin.

'That will be it!' Harriet agreed, taking the paper parcel from the counter. 'Much obliged to you. Good day, Mr Roberts.'

'Good day to you, Mrs McDougall—bring your granddaughter in next time!' he called, as she left the shop.

'Yes, shall do. Good day.'

The toy shop, *W.B. Suter's* was just four doors along the street. Harriet paused at the window, admiring the selection of toys on display there. A clockwork train chugged an oval circuit, looping endlessly around an army of lead soldiers from the African Wars, by the looks of them. Sitting at the edge of the track was a collection of stuffed animals and, to Harriet's glee, a pair of handsome porcelain dolls.

Entering the shop was a curious moment for her, being one of the few on the High Street of which she had never had the cause to venture inside. She pushed the door open and peeped around the little room, somewhat surprised by the vast selection of toys on offer.

'My goodness—what a choice!' she mumbled.

'Everything a child could wish for,' a diminutive lady behind the counter said cheerfully in a thick Sussex accent. 'Is there anything in particular you're looking for?'

'No,' Harriet answered. 'Well, *yes*. I've a granddaughter who's fifteen months old and she's rather, well, rather lacking in the entertainment and amusement department.'

'Over there,' the lady said, pointing to one corner.

'Ah, yes!' Harriet said, running her eyes keenly over the selection of toys presented there. A doll was an absolute must, she thought. And a replacement for that dreadful teddy bear. And, oh! Harriet spotted a box of splendid, little, wooden zoo animals.

Hastily gathering up several items in her hands, she carried them to the counter to pay.

'Did you want this?' the woman said, holding up a metal train.

'Yes, whyever not?' Harriet asked.

'It's a boy's toy,' the woman clarified.

'Is it?'

'Oh, yes,' the woman asserted. '*Absolutely.*'

'But, heavens, *women* were running the railways not so long ago,' Harriet replied.

The woman raised her eyebrows, as if she had been told something so fanciful as to defy belief. 'Dangerous business, is all.' She leant over the counter and whispered, 'I've seen *things* in London what you would not believe. Ungodly *things*.'

'Right,' Harriet said, not having the first inkling to what the woman was referring. 'Like what, exactly?'

173

The woman leant closer. 'Women, *wearing men's clothes*!'

'Right,' Harriet said. 'And are you going to sell me this train, or not? Only, I am rather pressed for time.'

The woman shrugged. 'If you're certain you'd like it…'

'Yes, I am. I'm not terribly convinced that playing with a clockwork train will send my fifteen-month-old granddaughter to London in men's clothing…but thank you kindly for the warning.'

'On your head be it,' the woman cautioned, placing all the toys into a paper bag and taking Harriet's money.

'Good day to you,' Harriet said half-heartedly, as she left the shop.

'Yes,' the woman answered.

What a peculiar person, Harriet thought, marching to the charabanc stop, where two women in black, of around her age, in mid-conversation, were stood waiting at the stop.

Harriet placed her bags down on the ground and sighed, overjoyed with her purchases. As she thought of Poppy's little face lighting up, when she would see her new toys, fragments of the two women's conversation drew her ear.

'…and well, you'll never get to know, will you?' one of them said.

'Tragically, I don't suppose so, no,' the other agreed.

'The pair of them, lost forever to the Somme.'

'That's something I take comfort in, at least: that they were together at the end…'

On that agonising note, their discussion came to an end, and Harriet's gaze shifted over to the Abbey. She traced the lines of the great stone battlements, as a possible idea dawned on her, which, within the given shaky framework of Malcolm's dead comrades' being somehow envious of him, held some odd degree of logic.

As soon as Harriet returned to Linton House, she hurried into the parlour and removed an envelope from the bureau. She examined the front: her name and address scribed by an unsteady, skittish hand. She slowly withdrew the letter and re-read its contents: a short request from a lady, who had somehow heard of her investigations into Malcolm's death, asking that Harriet undertake an enquiry into what had happened to her only son, killed in the Great War. Harriet's reply, politely declining the case was on the kitchen table, ready to be stamped at the Post Office. Could this be what Mrs Leonard had meant about Malcolm's friends' being envious?

Under the sombre gaze of her three sons' portraits, Harriet thought for some time. Then, she walked into the kitchen and picked up her reply.

'Shall I post that for you, Harriet?'

'Oh, my godfathers!' Harriet shrieked, leaping around to see Timothy standing in the doorway, smoking.

'Sorry!' he laughed, 'I didn't mean to startle you. I'm just going over to the Post Office now myself—another letter to Nell.'

'It's alright,' Harriet said, her heart thumping. 'I was in my own little world as usual.' She paused and stared at him. 'Do I want you to post it...do I?'

Timothy shrugged, drawing on the cigarette. 'That's what I just asked you.'

'I don't know...'

'Isn't that your reply to the woman asking for help finding what happened to her son?'

'Yes, it is.'

'Changing your mind?'

'I rather think that I might be,' she stated, holding up the letter. 'The problem is, she doesn't provide a jot of information about her boy, other than that he died in awful circumstances. Didn't they all? So, it's all rather like shooting in the dark to accept such a request.' She heard her own words, as if spoken by someone else. Then she heard Mrs Leonard's—or *Kaifa's*—absurd voice, telling her of Malcolm's unhappy friends.

'That's it,' she said to herself, ripping her reply into four pieces and glancing heavenward. 'I'll do it for you, too.'

At that, Harriet scuttled off into the parlour to write out a new response to the enquiry.

'Cup of tea?' Timothy called from the kitchen.

'Oh, that would be just marvellous,' she returned.

175

Chapter Sixteen

Harriet was standing apprehensively in a puddle of warm autumnal sunshine, just outside the village hall. She gazed cautiously up at the building, nervous about what was about to happen.

'Terribly sorry, Mrs McDougall,' Mrs Selmes called, striding breathlessly towards her. '*Parish* business—I wouldn't be permitted to go into details, you understand—but I'm here now at any rate. Here you go,' she said, hastily thrusting a large key at Harriet, then heading back in the direction from which she had come. 'Best of luck.'

'Thank you,' Harriet called. 'I shall return it this afternoon.'

'Oh, no, you shan't. It's yours,' Mrs Selmes answered.

'My own key?' Harriet exclaimed.

Mrs Selmes stopped and turned around. 'Well, yes,' she replied, slightly taken aback at the question. 'This is to be a *weekly* fixture, is it not?'

'Yes,' Harriet answered. 'Well, I mean to say that I hope so, yes.'

'Splendid. Good day to you, then, Mrs McDougall.'

'Yes. Good day to you, Mrs Selmes,' Harriet muttered, holding the key between thumb and forefinger, the way in which she might a few times have held an unfortunate bird or beast, which had met its end in her garden.

A striking sense of responsibility entwined with a dawning reality, filling her brain with a swarm of unhelpful and oppressive thoughts about this new venture.

She smiled, as Lina and Poppy came into view.

'Grandma!' Poppy declared, doddering up the short path from the road and hugging Harriet's leg.

Harriet grinned and patted her on the head. 'Hello, my little girl! Don't you look a pretty thing?' She was pleased to see that Poppy was wearing the mauve, mercerised poplin dress, which she had purchased for her in Battle the previous day. 'And you've brought your new dolly along, too!'

'You spoiled her, Harriet,' Lina said with a laugh.

'That, my dear, is the sole purpose of a grandmother, I think you will find. Ask anyone.' She turned and unlocked the heavy-set door, hooking it open. 'Come on in.'

The inside was just how they had left it the night before. She, Fraser and Timothy had spent several hours preparing the room. A horseshoe of six plain wooden trestle tables was arranged with a sparse collection of oddments of clothing and other unwanted items, all purloined from Linton House. On several pieces of card, which were dotted around the room, were written the words: *FREE for ex-Servicemen. Donations from everyone else.* Another table with a fancy white cloth was set at the far end of the hall, with two Windsor chairs facing one another, reserved for the solicitor, whom Harriet had procured by telegram from *Raper and Fovargue* in Battle.

'Shall I set up the tea things?' Lina asked.

'Yes, please do,' Harriet replied. 'Perhaps on a table over there?' She pointed to the area in front of the serving hatch. 'There's a copper tea urn in the kitchen and a selection of mismatched cups, saucers and side plates.'

Harriet, with her hands on her hips, stood back and looked around her. In such a large space, her few knickknacks spread thinly across the tables looked paltry to say the least. She hoped that others would come, bringing with them their own donations. She glanced tentatively at the door, questioning if anyone would show up at all. She had done what she felt to be best, and now she needed to relax and wait, which was much more easily said than done, she thought, as she needlessly titivated a selection of John's old, knitted broad-end ties. She'd offered them to Fraser and Timothy, but both had declined, of course. Fashions were changing, by all accounts.

For some time, with the background bustle of rattling crockery and Lina's softly humming a tune that Harriet didn't recognise, she watched Poppy half-crawling and half-tottering about the place, exploring, dragging the poor doll around with her by its hair. The child's language amused Harriet, being a peculiar concoction of unintelligible babble, Flemish and the odd English word thrown in for good measure.

'Hello?' a thick, gravelly voice called.

Harriet twisted around to see Mr Wynn from *Raper and Fovargue* solicitors, grinning at the door, as he removed his bowler hat. He was a small middle-aged chap with mole-like features and a permanent squint. He was wearing a smart suit and carried a cane in one hand and, in the other, a brown leather portmanteau.

'Good morning, Mr Wynn. Do come in,' Harriet greeted.

Mr Wynn strode towards her with his hand outstretched, long before he neared her. His handshake was firm whilst simultaneously hot and clammy. 'Lovely to see you, Mrs McDougall.' He cast his squinty eyes around the room. 'Well, this is…'

'Yes,' Harriet agreed, saving him the embarrassment of struggling with a choice of underwhelming adjectives. 'Can I offer you a cup of tea and some home-made cake? We've got fruit cake, shortbread, rice cake or tea biscuits.'

'Oh, splendid. A cup of tea and a piece of fruit cake would be smashing.'

'Lina!' Harriet called. 'Cup of tea and a slice of fruit cake for Mr Wynn, please.'

'Alright,' Lina replied.

'Now, I've put you over there in a *discreet* position,' Harriet said, indicating to the table in the far corner.

'Most suitable, most suitable,' Mr Wynn agreed, heading towards it.

'Harriet!' came another call from the entrance.

'Timothy!' Harriet said with a smile. 'Come and meet Mr Wynn. He's here to dispense legal advice to former servicemen. He can advise you on your…your situation.'

'Thank you,' Timothy said. 'Before I do, though, could you come outside a moment. There's something I think you need to see.'

Harriet nodded and followed him outside, wondering what this ominous-sounding *something* might be.

'There,' he said, pointing.

Harriet gasped. Fixed into the ground beside the path was a sign—perhaps five feet in length and three feet in height—painted royal blue with words in white, drawn so carefully as to appear professionally made.

'Well, I'll be jiggered!' Harriet declared. '*Mrs McDougall's Benevolence & Investigation Society.*' She glanced from Timothy to the sign, her hand over her mouth. 'Did you make this?'

'Yes,' Timothy admitted.

'What a truly wonderful thing you've done!'

'No, Harriet,' Timothy countered. 'What a truly wonderful thing *you've* done—look.'

Behind her, people were walking towards the village hall. There was Mrs Morris in black, ambling along with an armful of clothing, which Harriet guessed had once belonged to her son, Percy. Behind her was young Mrs Crittenden, who had lost her husband, Frank. From the other side of the village came Mrs Goodman and her two boys, who had managed to survive the conflict with good fortune.

People were coming.

Harriet read the sign again, then flung her arms around Timothy, as her eyes grew watery. She couldn't stop the tears from flowing, even if she had wanted to. She was crying bitter tears for the past, for her boys and for the lost men of the village; she was crying hopeful, joyous tears for the generosity of her friends and neighbours; and she was crying for the love of her new family.

Timothy held on to her, gently stroking her back.

'Oh, this simply won't do, Timothy,' she said at last, taking in a long inhalation. She dabbed her eyes, secured a smile in place, just in time to welcome her first visitors. 'Mrs Morris! How lovely of you to come along to offer your support.'

In less than an hour, the village hall was filled with the flutter and bustle of activity. On one side of the room, Lina was serving a steady stream of villagers with refreshments, and in the centre was Harriet, taking in parcels of unwanted garments from kindly well-wishers. Mr Wynn, having offered his services to Timothy, who had disappeared soon after his consultation, was sitting with his arms folded, enjoying the spectacle of it all over a bottomless cup of tea.

Later, Harriet's sister, Naomi arrived, clutching a bag in both hands. Her face was drawn and sullen, as she passed the bag over to Harriet. 'It's not much—just his old shirts and trousers. Frank didn't want them.'

'Oh, Naomi. It's more than enough,' Harriet said. 'Thank you.'

Naomi offered a brief stiff smile. 'It's all that I could bear to part with; I just can't bring myself to do it in the way that I know it needs doing: fully and completely, once and for all, for the good of everyone.'

'I've not brought all of Malcolm's things, either,' Harriet confided. 'For the same reason: I just couldn't. How is one supposed to discard such things as a pair of pyjamas—so intimate, so private and so...them?'

'I know. I have kept Jim's pyjamas, too. And his toothbrush,' Naomi agreed. 'And what of Edward's belongings?'

'No, not yet,' Harriet replied. 'In time...'

'Oh?' Naomi said, staring at Harriet in anticipation of an explanation.

The explanation, that she felt that she had Malcolm's permission to dispense with his things because of the interpretation of a medium through a ridiculously high-pitched conduit by the name of Kaifa, was rather too farcical to attempt; even to her own sister. Instead, she said, 'Cup of tea?'

'Yes, please.'

'Good. And you must come and meet Malcolm's widow, Lina. *Lovely* girl.'

They walked side by side across the hall, and Naomi whispered, 'Yes, I heard about that. She isn't *really* his widow, though, is she..? Come, now, Harriet.'

'No, of course not,' Harriet replied quietly.

'Lina, this is my sister, Mrs Dengate… Naomi. Is she allowed?' she questioned her sister. 'Seems to be the way…'

Naomi nodded, and the pair shook hands and greeted one another with smiles and informal 'how do you do's.'

'*Naomi* would like a cup of tea, please,' Harriet said, turning to her sister and adding, 'Lina is a marvellous waitress. We found her working in the British Tavern, opposite what was once the majestic Cloth Hall in Ypres centre.'

'Right at home, then,' Naomi said, taking a cup from Lina.

'Yes. Well, actually,' Lina said, 'Before the war I was a teacher.'

Harriet was struck with mortification. 'What? A *teacher*? Why ever didn't you say so before, my dear? A teacher?'

Lina shrugged. 'Yes.'

'You're a qualified teacher and you're serving tea in a village hall, for goodness' sake!' Harriet exclaimed.

'I don't mind, really,' Lina said. 'You've been so good to Poppy and me; I will do anything.'

'Even so,' Harriet said.

Lina frowned and said, 'Did you say *Mrs* Dengate? I thought your parents' name was Dengate, Harriet? Have I got this wrong?'

'Oh, there's a story,' Naomi said with a laugh. 'My maiden name was Dengate, and then I married James Dengate from Ewhurst.'

'And, to complicate matters further,' Harriet added, 'Naomi's husband, James has a sister named Hannah Dengate, who in turn married my brother, Herbert Dengate.'

Lina burst into laughter. 'This is an English joke, yes?'

Naomi and Harriet shook their heads.

'Unfortunately not, no,' Harriet answered.

'And are you related to your husband?' Lina said with a disapproving turning up of her nose.

'Apparently we share the same great-great-great-grandparents, so only very distantly,' Naomi said.

'How exciting,' Lina said.

'Is it?' Naomi said. 'I rather find it all rather—'

'*Mrs McDougall's Benevolence and Investigation Society*?' a loud female voice called across the hall.

Without turning, Harriet knew that the ear-piercing shrill belonged to her sister-in-law, Hannah.

'Speak of the devil,' Naomi murmured.

Harriet and Naomi rolled their eyes in unison, before spinning around in a synchronised, mirrored movement with bleak smiles on their faces.

'Hello, Hannah,' they greeted together.

'What does it even mean?' Hannah asked, marching over to them. '*Benevolence? Investigation*?'

Naomi stepped in and gestured vaguely to the goings-on in the hall and said, 'Benevolence, it means charitableness, goodwill—'

'I know what it means, Naomi, but...*Investigation Society*?' Hannah stammered. 'What are you investigating? How many cups of tea the village can consume in one afternoon?'

Harriet crossed her arms and bit her lip, as she formulated her answer. 'No,' she eventually said. 'I shall be helping men and women in their quest for answers as to what became of their sons, lost to the Great War. Where mystery, elusiveness or ambiguity prevents clarity, I shall be there to assist in any way that I possibly can.'

An insulting, scoffing sound erupted from Hannah's lips. 'And what qualifies *you* in such endeavours?'

'Nothing whatsoever aside from my sheer, dogged determination,' Harriet responded curtly.

'Well, it sounds all very Sherlock Holmes, if you ask me,' Hannah commented.

'I take that as a gracious compliment, Hannah. Thank you,' Harriet said. 'Now, if you'll excuse me, the Reverend Percival has just arrived, doubtless to level his own criticism in my direction.'

Harriet exhaled sharply, trying her best to maintain what she hoped was a pleasant, amiable appearance, as she approached the Reverend Percival. 'Good morning.'

The Reverend Percival bowed his head. 'Mrs McDougall. What an accomplishment! Many, many congratulations.'

181

'Oh, thank you,' Harriet answered, slightly taken aback. She surveyed the room, judging there to have been twenty to thirty people milling about. It was a greater number than that for which she had hoped, yet something didn't feel quite right, as she looked at the assembled group.

'What prompted such a charitable effort, might I ask?'

'Nobody else was doing anything,' she said, pointedly. 'Our men who survived—and God alone knows how they did—the greatest, most barbaric conflict that the world has ever seen, have been largely abandoned by the state and by individuals and organisations that should know better and owe them a darned sight more.'

The Reverend Percival frowned and touched his chin. 'It's a *very* difficult and complicated situation,' he weighed. 'Politically, economically, I mean, taking the Paris Peace Conference as...'

He kept talking, but Harriet had stopped listening. She was watching Fraser rummaging among a pile of clothing in the centre of the hall. He was scrutinising a blue striped Oxford shirt and Harriet realised at once what the problem was: barring Timothy, not a single former serviceman, who *really* needed assistance, had walked through the door. Not one. What she had organised here was nothing more than a jumble sale, overseen by a pompous rodent-like solicitor, who would charge a small fortune—even after the agreed discount—for the privilege of his advice; advice which, thus far, had been given to just one man. The likes of the soldier from Seaforth Highlanders, whom she had met at Charing Cross, were nowhere to be seen here. What the devil was his name, now? She cursed herself for having forgotten him, just as he had said she would.

'...It's really far more complicated than a member of the fairer sex could be expected—,' the Reverend Percival continued to bluster.

'Oh, Reverend Percival,' Harriet interjected with a laugh, 'I do think you are rather confusing *ignorance* of the current political and economic state with *indifference*; quite where the Austria-Hungary border sits, the reparations imposed upon Germany or the organisation of the League of Nations are all of *no* interest to me. Poor men—in every sense of the word—damaged in the mind, walking our streets in their *service uniforms*, unable to feed or clothe themselves and with nowhere to live... Now, *that* concerns me greatly.'

'It's very noble of you, Mrs McDougall, very,' he squirmed. 'Now, I really must get back to the vicarage. I presume we shall be seeing you at church this Sunday?'

'Perhaps,' she answered.

'Good day to you,' he said, scurrying from the hall at high speed.

Deep anger and frustration pulsed through Harriet's veins. She folded her arms in an attempt to stifle the quivering in her hands. Yes, she felt fury towards the Reverend Percival, but a larger portion was self-directed at this foolish little enterprise that had, if the truth be told, helped nobody. She thought of the pompous sign outside, which Timothy had kindly made for her. *Mrs McDougall's Benevolence and Investigation Society.*

What utter drivel.

'Mrs McDougall! Come quickly!'

Harriet anxiously hurried from her bedroom towards the sound of Lina's urgent voice. She found her in her bedroom, gazing out through the telescope into the garden.

'Whatever's the matter?' Harriet asked.

'Dragonflies! Hundreds of them! Look!' Lina said, stepping back from the telescope.

'I thought something dreadful had happened,' Harriet said, regaining her breath, as she trod carefully around the collection of wooden zoo animals, which Poppy had set up on the floor. She sidled up to the telescope, placing her right eye on the viewing ring. 'Good golly, you're right. Well, I've never seen such a—' Her words faltered as her eye then settled elsewhere on something most disagreeable. She stared for a moment longer, then hurried to speak so as not to arouse Lina's suspicions. '—I think they might be...now, what variety are they?' She tried to laugh, but it sounded as false as it actually was. 'Malcolm would have known, of course.'

'I don't know dragonflies in my own language, never mind in English,' Lina confessed.

'Perhaps the Southern Hawker?' Harriet suggested, gently tilting the telescope away from the cluster of dragonflies and towards the garden shed. Beside it, unequivocally in a passionate embrace with lips locked firmly together, were Fraser and Louise Ditch. Harriet shifted the telescope upwards and turned to Lina.

'Interesting sight,' Lina said, and Harriet couldn't tell whether she was alluding to her son's disreputable proclivities behind the garden shed or to the abundance of dragonflies.

Harriet flushed crimson with embarrassment and turned away abruptly. 'You've done a terrific job in decorating this room.'

'Thank you.'

With her back to Lina, Harriet studied the white-washed walls, as though it were the first time that she had ever noticed their existence. Timothy had painted them and Lina had added some beautifully decorative blue poppies. The room had been utterly transformed.

'Right, I must get the dinner on. Have you seen Timothy at all?'

'No, I haven't,' Lina answered. 'Do you need help with dinner?'

'I think I can manage, thank you. Herrings in tomato sauce and King Edward potatoes. Stewed pears for pudding.'

'Lovely.'

Harriet headed downstairs, her thoughts knotted over that which she had just witnessed. Was she being a starchy old Victorian to find such a thing objectionable? Louise Ditch was betrothed, for heaven's sake. She entered the kitchen and cautiously approached the back door, inclining her head to try and see the shed, but from where she was standing it was impossible. Not that she needed to see *that* again. What she needed was to stop it in its tracks, she thought, flinging the door open noisily: 'Fraser!' she bellowed. 'Fraser McDougall! Could you come here, please!'

She waited a moment and then hollered again.

Moments later, her son thundered across the lawn. 'What, Ma? What is it? I'm fully expecting the house to be on fire or someone keeled over, for the terrific racket you're making that all of Sedlescombe can hear.'

'Whatever's the matter?' Harriet protested, when he neared her.

'What do you want me for?'

'I need some help with the dinner,' she feigned. 'Peeling potatoes.'

'Well, can't someone else do it? Lina or Timothy? They need to earn their keep, for goodness' sake,' he ranted.

'Well, I don't know where Timothy's got to and Lina's busy,' Harriet explained. 'If you think I'm going to needlessly slave away over your dinner alone, you can think on.'

'Well, *I'm* busy,' he objected.

'Doing what, pray tell?'

Fraser took a breath, glanced over his shoulder and said, 'It doesn't matter. Nothing does, does it?' He ambled into the kitchen, picked up the potato peeler and huffed.

A heavy, yet unacknowledged atmosphere lingered around them in the dining room, as they ate. Harriet, at the head of the table, glanced furtively between Lina and Fraser, as she slid a piece of herring onto her fork and put it into her mouth. The shock from earlier had dissipated somewhat, though she hadn't a clue about what she might do with this information.

'Poppy!' Lina chastised, quickly pulling a knife from her grip, which she had taken from the adjacent place setting, and setting it down beside the unused fork.

Harriet watched their interaction, wondering what might be keeping Timothy. It was most unlike him to be late, and she began to worry about what Mr Wynn might have told him. Her worry translated into several somewhat outlandish theories about what might have come of him. Harriet supposed that, after all she had been through, it was only to be expected that her mind would lurch from one terrible scenario to another. She looked at Poppy, earnestly hoping that the little girl would never get to experience even half of the horrors that she herself had lived through so far in her life.

'It went very well, today,' Lina said, breaking the uncomfortable and monotonous sound of cutlery against crockery.

'It's good of you to say so,' Harriet said. 'In truth, though, it wasn't quite what I had hoped it would be.'

Lina looked surprised. 'Oh, what was wrong?'

'I don't suppose anything was *wrong*...' Harriet began. 'It just didn't serve the purpose I thought it would have.' She explained in some detail about the former servicemen, whom she had seen on the streets of London and loitering around the Admiralty Pier in Dover.

'Yes, but you can't help everyone, Mrs McDougall,' Lina said.

'No, quite; but today I helped *no-one*.'

'I got a free Oxford shirt,' Fraser chipped in.

'Thank you for that,' Harriet reproved. 'That's exactly what I mean.'

'You need to tell more people about it,' Lina said, putting down her knife and fork. 'Where did you advertise this?'

'In the Post Office window here and in Westfield,' Harriet answered.

'And how do you think the homeless servicemen in Dover might hear of this?'

'It's an obvious point, Ma,' Fraser said. 'How many homeless servicemen are there in Sedlescombe? Last time I looked about, the total ran to around zero.'

Lina shrugged. 'Let's go to the big towns and tell them.'

185

'One town at a time,' Fraser added. 'Shouldn't take too long, and I'm sure they'd all fit in the village hall. They could all come and live here to save them travelling.'

She glowered at Fraser.

'There could be a *Mrs McDougall's Benevolence Society* in every town!' Lina said excitedly.

'You forgot the *Investigation* part,' Fraser reminded her.

'Oh, yes, sorry,' Lina said with a little giggle.

'Danny!' Harriet suddenly exclaimed. 'See, I didn't forget him.'

'Who's Danny?' Fraser asked.

She went to explain that he was the Scottish soldier, whom she had encountered at Charing Cross, when she heard the front door being opened, and a clot of anxiety, which Harriet had been subconsciously holding, released. 'Timothy!?' she called, placing her cutlery down. 'We're in here!'

Timothy appeared in the doorway. 'Hello.'

'Where have you been?' Harriet said, trying not to sound as agitated by his absence as she felt. 'I've been worried. And your dinner will probably be shrivelled and inedible.'

'Sorry,' he murmured. 'After speaking with Mr Wynn, I went to see Nell.'

'Right,' Harriet said.

'Well, at least, I tried to see her. She wouldn't let me in and wouldn't let me see Anna, either.'

'Oh, how terrible of her,' Harriet said. 'Was that what Mr Wynn advised, then? Trying to talk with her?'

Timothy drew in a long breath. 'He said I had two options: take her to court, which would be protracted and costly, and would unlikely go in my favour; or persuade her to let me see Anna from time to time.'

'And she didn't agree?'

Timothy shook his head. 'I'm very sorry, but I'm not a bit hungry. I'm going to go for a lie-down, actually.'

'Alright,' Harriet said softly. 'You do that. Cup of tea?'

'No, thank you,' he said, slowly padding up the stairs, the perfect image of a broken man.

Harriet suddenly had lost her appetite, too. What was to be done with the poor fellow?

'He is very troubled,' Lina observed.

'Yes,' Harriet agreed, standing up and excusing herself from the table.

She lingered for a moment at the bottom of the stairs, wondering whether to go to Timothy, but reasoned that he might be needing to have some time alone. She walked slowly into the kitchen, not entirely convinced by her decision, rested her hands on the sink and stared out into the garden. Dusk had descended, bringing a stunning range of pastel colours to the seam between sky and land above the trees.

She opened the back door and stood, breathing in the slight chill of the twilight air. Leaning against the hedge was Timothy's wonderfully-crafted sign, ready to be resurrected next week outside the village hall. She was heartened by Lina's comments. Perhaps there was a use and purpose for Mrs McDougall's Benevolence and Investigation Society, she thought, as a warmth settled inside her heart.

From over the hedge came a flying creature of some sort. It landed on the sign and she recognised its kind again at once: a Ghost Swift moth. What else would it have been?

Harriet flinched at something touching her shoulder. She flicked her head around to see Lina.

'He told you about it, too?' Lina said.

'Pardon?' Harriet questioned.

'The red star: Malcolm told you about it, too?'

'What do you mean?'

Lina, with one hand placed on Harriet's shoulder, aligned their eyes and pointed up into the dark, blue sky. 'There—the red star—see it?'

She *did* see it. Much brighter than all of the surrounding stars and clearly reddish in colour. She saw it but didn't understand: 'What did Malcolm tell you about it? I thought that the red star referred to some horrifying gas concoction...'

'Gas? No, it's Antares in the constellation of Scorpius. At least that's what your son, Edward told him,' Lina explained. 'But you know how Malcolm is: more romantic and less astrological. For Malcolm it was the heart of the night sky, and he said, when he went back to the trenches, that every night he would look for the red star, and if I did the same, then we were connected, both of us sharing that heart at the same time. And it helped, you know. It was there for me most nights.'

Harriet pulled Lina in tightly to her side and watched as the Ghost Swift moth took flight into the darkness of the woods beyond her garden.

Historical Information

This story is a work of fiction. However, elements of it are based on truth. Harriet Agnes McDougall was a real person, being distantly related to me (my first cousin, four times removed, to be precise). She was born Harriet Agnes Dengate in 1853 to James and Harriet Dengate (née Catt) and was baptised on the 8th May 1853 in the parish church of Sedlescombe, East Sussex. She married John McDougall in 1887, and the couple had three children: John Fraser (known as Fraser) in 1888, Malcolm in 1889 and Edward Cecil in 1891. The descriptions of Harriet's wider family, including the complicated inter-marriages between her Dengate siblings is factual.

The three McDougall boys each went through Blackheath Proprietary School, followed by university. Fraser and Edward followed in their father's and grandfather's footsteps, attending Goldsmith's College in London to study Civil Engineering. Malcolm, however, chose to study Chemistry at the Bromley School of Art.

The three brothers each joined a different regiment in the British Army. Malcolm initially signed up as a private for the Royal West Kents but was later transferred to the Royal Engineers Special Brigade, specifically to 'P' Company of the 4th Battalion. This was a gas cylinder company responsible for releasing poisonous gasses from the trenches against the German lines and was appallingly nicknamed 'The Suicide Company'.

Malcolm's younger brother, Edward had joined the London Regiment of the Queen's Westminster Rifles. From April 1916, the Battalion was transferred for a brief period to Macroom, County Cork, following the Easter Rising in Ireland, before being sent to France and then on to Salonika in Greece in December 1916. Nine days after arriving in Salonika, on the 3rd January 1917, Edward died.

Six months later, on the 3rd July 1917, Malcolm had been working in the trenches in the area close to Hill Top Farm, when he retired to Hill Top Farm Trench, a short way behind the front line. The trench suffered a direct shell hit, seriously wounding Malcolm and two others. Malcolm was taken by stretcher to the Essex Farm Advanced Dressing Station, where he died from his wounds the following day. He was buried in Essex Farm Cemetery, alongside his two comrades, James Bruce Kelso and J.W. Bennett, who were also killed that day. The Essex Farm Advanced Dressing Station still stands in its original location and form and is where the Canadian war poet, John McCrae wrote the famous poem, 'In Flanders Fields.'

Harriet and John McDougall were living at Linton House, Sedlescombe when they received the two telegrams, six months apart, telling them the dreadful news that their two younger sons had died. Little information is known about how these tragedies affected this particular couple's lives, but for Harriet more tragedy was to follow, when her husband, John died on the 26th July 1919. He died at Linton House from heart failure and was buried four days later in St John's Church, Sedlescombe. Fraser returned home shortly afterwards.

The descriptions of post-war Ypres are broadly accurate: the city was almost completely razed to the ground, with nearly 400-square miles destroyed. Returning citizens were given money to assist in the building of pre-fabricated homes in the Plaine d'Amour area to the north of the former city, while the future of Ypres was being decided. The then chairman of the Imperial War Graves Commission, Winston Churchill, favoured purchasing the entire city and leaving it in its wartime state as a permanent memorial to the dead. In the end, though, the citizens of Ypres understandably chose to have their city rebuilt to exactly that which it had been before the war. Among the new buildings to emerge immediately after the Armistice was Ypres' first hotel, Hotel Splendid and the brightly coloured British Tavern, situated opposite the ruins of the Cloth Hall.

In Britain, there was a sharp rise in the practice of Spiritualism and communicating with the dead. Arthur Conan Doyle was one of its leading proponents, asserting that he was able to communicate with his dead son, Kingsley.

Harriet Agnes McDougall continued to reside at Linton House for some years. She died on the 2nd March 1933 in Hastings at the age of 80 and was buried with her husband in St John's Church, in the family's home village of Sedlescombe. Sadly, no memorial to them exists in the churchyard.

There is more information on the lives of the McDougall and Dengate families on the blog page of my website and a short video on my YouTube channel.

Further Reading:

Among the books, which I found useful in the research and writing of this book, were the following:

Arthur, M., *Forgotten Voices* (Ebury Press, 2003)

Cave, N., *Polygon Wood* (Pen & Sword Books, 2007)

Corremans, L. & Reyntjens, A., *Traces of the Great War* (Great War Books, date unknown)

Ebeneezer, L., *Faced with Mametz* (Gwasg Carreg Gwalch, 2017)

Ewing, J., *The History of the Ninth (Scottish) Division* (Naval & Military Press, date unknown)

Foulkes, C.H., *Gas!* (Naval & Military Press, date unknown)

Garfield, J., *The Fallen* (The History Press, 2014)

Gordon-Smith, J., *Photographing the Fallen* (Pen & Sword Books, 2017)

Gray, A., *South Eastern Railway* (Middleton Press, 1990)

Harrison, G., *To Fight Alongside Friends* (Harper Collins, 2014)

Lodge, O., *Raymond* (Forgotten Books, 2015)

Longworth, P., *The Ending Vigil* (Pen & Sword Books, 2003)

Lucy, B., *Twenty Centuries in Sedlescombe* (Asselton House, 1998)

Richter. D., *Chemical Soldiers* (Pen & Sword Books, 2014)

Robsertshaw, A., *24HR Trench* (The History Press, 2012)

Van Emden, R., *Sapper Martin* (Bloomsbury, 2010)

Van Emden, R., *Tommy's War* (Bloomsbury, 2014)

Wynn, S., *Dover in the Great War* (Pen & Sword Books, 2017)

Acknowledgements

I am indebted to several people, who have helped to bring this book to fruition.

My first thanks go to Patrick Dengate for, once again, translating my vague ideas, notions and requests for the cover into something wonderful; the look and feel of the image is precisely what I had in mind. Incidentally, Patrick is Harriet McDougall's second cousin, four-times removed, tracing back via a common ancestor (whom I also share) in James and Mary Dengate of Wittersham, Kent, England.

I would like to thank John Boeren, a specialist in Dutch genealogy, for his assistance with translations. Take a look at his website for any Dutch genealogy requirements: www.antecedentia.com

Thanks to the Memorial Museum Passchendaele for their assistance in locating the precise place in which Malcolm McDougall was injured and the trenches in which he worked, and to Edward De Santis who provided information about the Pioneers.

My final thanks must go to Robert Bristow for his unwavering support for me and Mrs McDougall.

Further Information

Website & Newsletter: www.nathandylangoodwin.com
Twitter: @NathanDGoodwin
Facebook: www.facebook.com/NathanDylanGoodwin
Pinterest: www.pinterest.com/NathanDylanGoodwin
Blog: theforensicgenealogist.blogspot.co.uk
LinkedIn: www.linkedin.com/in/NathanDylanGoodwin

Hiding the Past
(The Forensic Genealogist #1)

Peter Coldrick had no past; that was the conclusion drawn by years of personal and professional research. Then he employed the services of one Morton Farrier, Forensic Genealogist – a stubborn, determined man who uses whatever means necessary to uncover the past. With the Coldrick Case, Morton faces his toughest and most dangerous assignment yet, where all of his investigative and genealogical skills are put to the test. However, others are also interested in the Coldrick family, people who will stop at nothing, including murder, to hide the past. As Morton begins to unearth his client's mysterious past, he is forced to confront his own family's dark history, a history which he knows little about.

'Flicking between the present and stories and extracts from the past, the pace never lets up in an excellent addition to this unique genre of literature'
Your Family Tree

'At times amusing and shocking, this is a fast-moving modern crime mystery with genealogical twists. The blend of well fleshed-out characters, complete with flaws and foibles, will keep you guessing until the end'
Family Tree

'Once I started reading *Hiding the Past* I had great difficulty putting it down - not only did I want to know what happened next, I actually cared'
Lost Cousins

The Lost Ancestor
(The Forensic Genealogist #2)

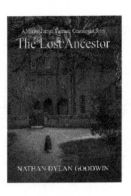

From acclaimed author, Nathan Dylan Goodwin comes this exciting new genealogical crime mystery, featuring the redoubtable forensic genealogist, Morton Farrier. When Morton is called upon by Ray Mercer to investigate the 1911 disappearance of his great aunt, a housemaid working in a large Edwardian country house, he has no idea of the perilous journey into the past that he is about to make. Morton must use his not inconsiderable genealogical skills to solve the mystery of Mary Mercer's disappearance, in the face of the dangers posed by those others who are determined to end his investigation at any cost.

'If you enjoy a novel with a keen eye for historical detail, solid writing, believable settings and a sturdy protagonist, *The Lost Ancestor* is a safe bet. Here British author Nathan Dylan Goodwin spins a riveting genealogical crime mystery with a pulsing, realistic storyline'
Your Family Tree

'Finely paced and full of realistic genealogical terms and tricks, this is an enjoyable whodunit with engaging research twists that keep you guessing until the end. If you enjoy genealogical fiction and Ruth Rendell mysteries, you'll find this a pleasing page-turner'
Family Tree

The Orange Lilies
(The Forensic Genealogist #3)

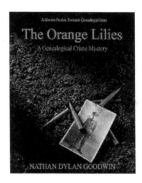

Morton Farrier has spent his entire career as a forensic genealogist solving other people's family history secrets, all the while knowing so little of his very own family's mysterious past. However, this poignant Christmastime novella sees Morton's skills put to use much closer to home, as he must confront his own past, present and future through events both present-day and one hundred years ago. It seems that not every soldier saw a truce on the Western Front that 1914 Christmas...

'The Orange Lilies sees Morton for once investigating his own tree (and about time too!). Moving smoothly between Christmas 1914 and Christmas 2014, the author weaves an intriguing tale with more than a few twists - several times I thought I'd figured it all out, but each time there was a surprise waiting in the next chapter... Thoroughly recommended - and I can't wait for the next novel'
Lost Cousins

'Morton confronts a long-standing mystery in his own family—one that leads him just a little closer to the truth about his personal origins. This Christmas-time tale flashes back to Christmas 1914, to a turning point in his relatives' lives. Don't miss it!'
Lisa Louise Cooke

The America Ground
(The Forensic Genealogist #4)

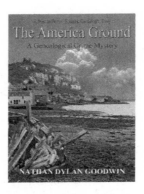

Morton Farrier, the esteemed English forensic genealogist, had cleared a space in his busy schedule to track down his own elusive father finally. But he is then presented with a case that challenges his research skills in his quest to find the killer of a woman murdered more than one hundred and eighty years ago. Thoughts of his own family history are quickly and violently pushed to one side as Morton rushes to complete his investigation before other sinister elements succeed in derailing the case.

'As in the earlier novels, each chapter slips smoothly from past to present, revealing murderous events as the likeable Morton uncovers evidence in the present, while trying to solve the mystery of his own paternity. Packed once more with glorious detail of records familiar to family historians, *The America Ground* is a delightfully pacey read'
Family Tree

'Like most genealogical mysteries this book has several threads, cleverly woven together by the author - and there are plenty of surprises for the reader as the story approaches its conclusion. A jolly good read!'
Lost Cousins

The Spyglass File
(The Forensic Genealogist #5)

Morton Farrier was no longer at the top of his game. His forensic genealogy career was faltering and he was refusing to accept any new cases, preferring instead to concentrate on locating his own elusive biological father. Yet, when a particular case presents itself, that of finding the family of a woman abandoned in the midst of the Battle of Britain, Morton is compelled to help her to unravel her past. Using all of his genealogical skills, he soon discovers that the case is connected to The Spyglass File—a secretive document which throws up links which threaten to disturb the wrongdoings of others, who would rather its contents, as well as their actions, remain hidden forever.

'If you like a good mystery, and the detective work of genealogy, this is another mystery novel from Nathan which will have you whizzing through the pages with time slipping by unnoticed'
Your Family History

'The first page was so overwhelming that I had to stop for breath...Well, the rest of the book certainly lived up to that impressive start, with twists and turns that kept me guessing right to the end... As the story neared its conclusion I found myself conflicted, for much as I wanted to know how Morton's assignment panned out, I was enjoying it so much that I really didn't want this book to end!'
Lost Cousins

The Missing Man
(The Forensic Genealogist #6)

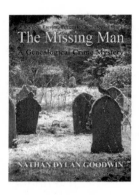

It was to be the most important case of Morton Farrier's career in forensic genealogy so far. A case that had eluded him for many years: finding his own father. Harley 'Jack' Jacklin disappeared just six days after a fatal fire at his Cape Cod home on Christmas Eve in 1976, leaving no trace behind. Now his son, Morton must travel to the East Coast of America to unravel the family's dark secrets in order to discover what really happened to him.

'One of the hallmarks of genealogical mystery novels is the way that they weave together multiple threads and this book is no exception, cleverly skipping across the generations - and there's also a pleasing symmetry that helps to endear us to one of the key characters...If you've read the other books in this series you won't need me to tell you to rush out and buy this one'
Lost Cousins

'Nathan Dylan Goodwin has delivered another page-turning mystery laden with forensic genealogical clues that will keep any family historian glued to the book until the mystery is solved'
Eastman's Online Genealogy Newsletter

The Wicked Trade
(The Forensic Genealogist #7)

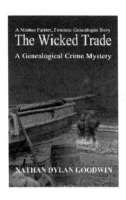

When Morton Farrier is presented with a case revolving around a mysterious letter written by disreputable criminal, Ann Fothergill in 1827, he quickly finds himself delving into a shadowy Georgian underworld of smuggling and murder on the Kent and Sussex border. Morton must use his skills as a forensic genealogist to untangle Ann's association with the notorious Aldington Gang and also with the brutal killing of Quartermaster Richard Morgan. As his research continues, Morton suspects that his client's family might have more troubling and dangerous expectations of his findings.

'Once again the author has carefully built the story around real places, real people, and historical facts - and whilst the tale itself is fictional, it's so well written that you'd be forgiven for thinking it was true'
Lost Cousins

'I can thoroughly recommend this book, which is a superior example of its genre. It is an ideal purchase for anyone with an interest in reading thrillers and in family history studies. I look forward to the next instalment of Morton Farrier's quest!'
Waltham Forest FHS

Made in the USA
San Bernardino, CA
15 February 2019